Praise for the Hamptons

"The dazzling houses showcased in the Hamptons Home & Garden mysteries aren't without skeletons in their closets. Fortunately, interior designer Meg Barrett has the golden touch when it comes to solving murders. Cozy mystery fans will adore the characters, stunning setting, and mouthwatering recipes in Kathleen Bridge's delightful series."

—Ellery Adams, *New York Times* bestselling author

"A delightful sneak peek into life in the Hamptons, with intricate plotting and a likeable, down-to-earth protagonist. A promising start to a promising series."

—*Suspense Magazine* on *Better Homes and Corpses*

"*Ghostal Living* is a marvelously entertaining tale of revenge, murder, quirky characters—and disappearing books! With a clever protagonist, wonderful details of life in the Hamptons, and plot twists on top of plot twists, Kathleen Bridge will have mystery readers clamoring for more."

—Kate Carlisle, *New York Times* bestselling author

"An excellent read."

—*RT Book Reviews* on *Hearse and Gardens*

"The descriptions of furniture and other antiques, as well as juicy tidbits on the Hamptons, make for entertaining reading for those who enjoy both antiques and lifestyles of the rich and famous."

—*Booklist* on *Better Homes and Corpses*

Books by Kathleen Bridge

Hamptons Home & Garden Mysteries

Better Homes and Corpses
Hearse and Gardens
Ghostal Living
Manor of Dying
A Design to Die For
A Fatal Feast
The Perfect Staging for Murder

By the Sea Mysteries

Death by the Sea
A Killing by the Sea
Murder by the Sea
Evil by the Sea
Buried by the Sea

The Perfect Staging for Murder

A Hamptons Home & Garden Mystery

Kathleen Bridge

BEYOND THE PAGE
PUBLISHING

The Perfect Staging for Murder
Kathleen Bridge
Beyond the Page Books
are published by
Beyond the Page Publishing
www.beyondthepagepub.com

Copyright © 2023 by Kathleen Bridge
Cover design by Dar Albert, Wicked Smart Designs

ISBN: 978-1-960511-08-9

I dedicate this to my mom — Judith Mae Anderson Drawe. My first reader, occasional editor and best friend. Love you, Mommy. This one's for you.

Acknowledgments

I want to thank my agent, Dawn Dowdle at Blue Ridge Literary Agency, for being there for me since day one! This is book twelve. Who would have thought! I couldn't have done it without you! And to Bill Harris, my editor at Beyond the Page Publishing, for his stellar editing and sage advice. To Lon Otremba for his amazing culinary recipes and cooking tips. I'd also like to thank all the cozy mystery readers, reviewers, and bloggers who have supported my work through the years. I am beyond grateful.

Chapter 1

Patrick and I stood shoulder to shoulder in the narrow stairwell. Bolts of white lightning shot through the windows of the lantern room, filtered down, then cast shadows of Hitchcockian proportion against the damp brick walls. Thunder soon followed. It vibrated the metal steps and sent shock waves up my spine.

I held my breath.

Looking up, all I could see was a woman's shapely calves encased in seamed stockings, atop thick-heeled green suede shoes.

Then came the gunshot.

The sound pierced my hearing aids.

Even though I knew it was coming, I startled and let out a small gasp.

Patrick squeezed my hand and held a finger to his lips.

I stayed still.

From above, I heard echoing down the stairwell. "It's okay, Lara. He had it coming. Now give me the gun."

"Don't be ridiculous, Jack. Stella goes back in my bag."

"You've named your gun?"

"Doesn't everyone?"

"Indubitably. Are you sure you're alright, darling?"

"I'm fine, Jack. Don't worry. I'm not going to swoon and fall into your arms if that's what you're thinkin'. He had it coming. But it's you, tough guy, who looks a little green around the gills. Maybe you need a boost from that flask inside your breast pocket. The one you think I don't know about. Wouldn't mind a nip myself."

"Take it easy, tiger."

"You know, I'm not a tiger, Jack. I'm just a little pussy cat. Me-ow."

"Yeah. A cat that just killed a canary. Too bad we're on borrowed time, darling. We'd better make tracks before the coppers show up. Or worse yet, one of Big Al's goons."

"You're right, husband. Maybe we should keep to our plan and leave for San Francisco tomorrow."

"Not unless you're in a hurry, my love. Let's stick around awhile. This excitement has put us behind in our drinking."

Patrick dropped my hand, then bounded up the steps two at a time.

Before he reached the top, I heard Brett Golden shout, "Cut! That's a wrap."

Chapter 2

When I reached the top of the staircase, Patrick had his hands on Brett's, our new director's, shoulders. Rain sluiced down the Montauk Point Lighthouse's huge windows, making me feel like we were in Godzilla's car wash. Outside, theatrical zigzags of lightning stabbed the rough Atlantic at the easternmost tip of Long Island.

Production had waited until the perfect storm to film the final scene in the third installment of the late 1930s streaming mystery series *Mr. & Mrs. Winslow*. The series featured a wisecracking, madly-in-love husband-and-wife detecting team: private eye Jack Winslow, and Lara, Jack's former gal Friday at the Eastside Detective Agency. The story went that after Jack inherited a fortune from his great-uncle, the couple moved from their dive on the Lower East Side of Manhattan to a mansion on Long Island, only to find themselves solving murders committed by the area's high-society elite.

I took a second to peruse the volatile scene in front of me. The lighthouse's lantern room galley was tight quarters. With the addition of Patrick and me, there was barely enough room to hold the director, one camera woman, a boom technician, and the three actors — one of whom had risen from the dead and was dressed like a mob boss from a Cagney film.

The actor who played Big Al was only two steps away from Patrick. He could have easily stepped in to intervene. But he didn't. Instead, he grinned from ear to ear, one corner of his mouth trickling fake blood from the squib he'd just chomped on.

The rest of the cast and crew were looking anywhere but in Patrick and Brett's direction.

Based on my limited experience with our illustrious new director, I'd guessed the actor playing Al, along with everyone else, was hoping that Patrick would punch Brett Golden in the kisser. Or at least give him a good shiner.

If I was honest, I wished the same thing.

Our director was a piece of work. Since coming onto the set, Brett had alienated not just the crew but the entire cast.

The production's lead actors, the stunning Academy Award–winning Zoe Stockton, who played Lara Winslow, and the gorgeous Dillion King, who played Jack Winslow, scurried toward the tower's only exit. As Zoe passed, she said through pouty, matte red lips, "Exit, stage left. Enjoy the fireworks, Meg. See you at Friday's wrap party."

After they and the rest of the crew disappeared down the stairwell leading to the lighthouse's gift shop, I glanced at Patrick. His chiseled jaw was clenched, and his cheeks were flushed. I'd rarely seen him this angry. What had Brett done to make my mild-mannered Patrick so primal?

Rumor had it that Brett was going to be fired. It couldn't happen too soon. Patrick had made it this far as the screenwriter for the miniseries, he just needed to hold on a little longer.

I sidled up to Patrick, my back inches from the gigantic revolving light that flashed every five seconds to warn mariners off the shoals of Montauk Point. Gently, I placed my hand on his arm. "Why don't we settle this later?" I whispered. "We have time before the wrap party to discuss everything. It's been a long night."

Instead of listening to what I thought were my words of wisdom, Patrick elbowed my hand away, dropped his hands from Brett's shoulders, then balled them into fists. All six-foot-one of him took a step closer to Brett.

All five-foot-six of Brett took a step back, his spine meeting the railing that encircled the tower's domed windows. Unless he wanted to end up in Davey Jones's locker, jumping from the hundred-and-ten-foot tower wasn't a survivable option.

In a deep growl, Patrick said, "Sorry, Meg. There won't be a wrap party unless we, I mean *he*, reshoots the final scene."

Brett laughed. "Ms. Barrett, get a handle on your maniac boyfriend or I'll call in the *real* coppers."

Patrick didn't seem worried. Many times, when our director veered too far from the script, Patrick would call *Mr. & Mrs. Winslow*'s producer, Jeremy Prentice, and complain. Jeremy was always on Team Patrick. I'm sure, much to Brett's dismay. I was also on Team Patrick, backing up the award-winning fiction author, screenwriter, and my current (and hopefully forever) main squeeze.

I was curious how Brett had known that Patrick and I were an item? Felicity, our set designer, had been sworn to secrecy. And Elle, my best friend and partner in crimes of a vintage nature, would never betray Patrick and me. Most of my time on *Mr. & Mrs. Winslow* was spent behind the scenes. Even so, since Brett Golden came on board,

I'd witnessed him raging at one person or another. Our original director had fallen ill and had a long road of recovery ahead of him. We weren't sure he'd ever be back.

Elle's and my role on the set of *Mr. & Mrs. Winslow* was as part-time assistants to the set and costume designers. We were in charge of finding the perfect furniture, décor, costumes, and jewelry for the late-1930s miniseries. My remaining time was spent decorating small cottages in Montauk for my one-woman interior design company, Cottages by the Sea, along with upcycling my thrift finds in Elle's Sag Harbor carriage house at the back of her antiques and collectibles shop, Mabel and Elle's Curiosities.

From the first day of filming, Patrick and Brett had been at each other's throats.

Recently, so he could avoid Brett, Patrick preferred hiding out in his writing cave in the attic of his oceanfront cottage — only a mile down the beach from mine. Sometimes, he would bring his laptop to my place to watch the show's dailies in front of a roaring fire. It was early April. Even if we got lucky with sunny days in the sixties, the temps usually plummeted at sunset, calling for an evening fire.

I wasn't complaining.

Cozy fire, plus a snuggly boyfriend, equals a happy Meg.

"Might as well call the police," Patrick shouted at Brett. "And call a good lawyer while you're at it."

"Why don't we table this until we've cooled off a little?" I asked in a low, squeaky voice.

"Stay out of it," Patrick snapped, a boom of thunder punctuating his ire.

I waited for an apology. None came. I would've turned to go, but I was still curious about what set Patrick off.

I soon got my answer.

Patrick stuck his perfect nose into Brett's smushed, bulldog face. "You stole those last two lines from Dashiell Hammett's *The Thin Man* book. How many times has our producer told you that even if this series is loosely based on Hammett's characters Nick and Nora Charles, we can't take the chance of his estate coming after us? Reshoot the scene. My reputation is at stake. I'm not about to get sued for plagiarism. This isn't the first time you've tried to rewrite my words. But it will be the last."

Go, Patrick! I cheered inwardly, even though my eyes were still watery from his command that I should *stay out of it*. I'd thought we were a team, just like Jack and Lara Winslow.

The only other time I'd been the brunt of Patrick's anger had been the first time I'd been invited into his cottage. While he'd been outside showering his greyhound Charlie after our blustery walk on the beach, I'd gone snooping. I'd wanted insight into the man I'd seen from my deck, strolling the beach, looking forlorn and melancholy, sometimes adding sad verses from classic poetry to the sand with a piece of driftwood.

That day, Patrick had snuck up on me while I was holding a framed photo of his smiling wife and young daughter, both tragically killed years ago by a drunk driver. I'd startled and dropped the photo onto his stone hearth. Patrick had snatched it up and returned it to the mantel. Only this time he'd placed the smiling faces toward the wall, then had stomped out the door.

That had been months ago. We'd come a long way since then.

At least, I'd thought we had.

"Hammett croaked in the early sixties," Brett said, running his hands through his thinning, rust-and-gray shoulder-length hair. "I'm sure his work is in public domain by now."

"Wrong again," Patrick hissed. "Works published between 1923 and 1963 don't expire for ninety-five years in the U.S. And it's not uncommon for the family to petition for an extension."

"Chill out, Mr. Seaton. I'm the director." Brett took a step toward the exit. "I can do whatever the hell I want. Even rewrite the entire script." Brett trained his bulging eyes on me, then turned back to Patrick. "You seem to be distracted, Patty. Maybe your personal life is taking you away from your work. Although, I do see how that could happen. As Jack Winslow would say, she's a real looker. In a blonde, blue-eyed, Scandinavian, Ingrid Bergman kind of way. Too bad about the hearing thing." He pointed to my ears. "If not for that, I could have found a part for you, Ms. Barrett."

Now it was my turn to get angry. Not about the *hearing thing*, I'd worn hearing aids since I was a teen and had grown a thick skin when it came to asinine comments like Brett's. What bothered me was the lecherous way Brett had flicked his tongue over his thin chapped lips, then winked at me. Of course, he'd done it on purpose to get a rise out of Patrick. And by the look on Patrick's face, it had worked.

Pushing it, Brett added, "A word of advice, lovebirds. It's not good to mix work with pleasure. Look at me. I regret the day I told my fiancée she could have a role in the next episode of *Mr. & Mrs. Winslow*. By the way, Mr. Seaton, you need to write a new part worthy of her. Maybe Lara Winslow's sister. Older sister. But not too old, or I'll be the bearer of her wrath."

"I'll do no such thing," Patrick said in a strangely calm voice. "Let's go, Meg. Time to share these latest developments with our esteemed producer."

"Oh, I'm sure you won't say a word, or I'll tell Meggie here a little tale that I'm sure you don't want me to share. You're in for a big surprise, Patty, my boy. A blast from the past, so to speak. And you won't be backstabbing me to Jeremy, you brownnoser, or I'll tell Ms. Barrett about yours and my fiancée's past hijinks, which I've only recently learned about from my PI. You better listen up or I'll personally introduce Meg to my betrothed at the wrap party."

"Ha!" Patrick said, a tad unconvincingly. "You're delusional. I'm not your boy. Far from it. I have no clue what you're talking about, and I won't be blackmailed by the likes of you." Patrick turned toward the staircase, then roughly grabbed my hand.

As we walked away, Patrick whispered in my ear, "He's not worth it. He'll soon be gone. Don't let him see you sweat."

It seemed Patrick was the one sweating. Beads of perspiration had formed on his tanned forehead.

"Don't say that I didn't warn you," Brett said.

Patrick stopped short at the top of the stairwell. I went stumbling forward. He caught me by the waist and pulled me to him. He looked deep into my eyes like he wanted to tell me something important, then changed his mind. "You go first."

Did I really want to know what was going on with him and Brett's fiancée? *Carpe diem* had been Patrick's and my go-to philosophy since we'd gotten more serious.

I wanted to keep it that way.

"Ha, you never told her, did you?" Brett called after us, adding an irritating cackle. "See you at the party. It should be a wild one!"

As I led the way down the dark, narrow stairway, it felt like I was descending into an abyss of misfortune.

Turned out, I was spot-on.
Only it wasn't my misfortune.
But someone else's.

Chapter 3

"Meg, what do you think?" I glanced over at Elle, who held up her hand to shield her expressive large brown eyes from the morning sun. She was mummified in a white mohair coat, scarf, and pillbox hat. You might have thought it was January, not April. Based on my best friend's vintage ensemble, you might have also guessed that it was the twentieth century, not the twenty-first.

"This is what I think," I said. "I think you're overdressed. It's supposed to be sixty today." I looked ahead at an imposing boxlike glass mega-mansion set on a bluff overlooking Lake Montauk. Through the tinted glass windows, I spied people standing in groups of three or four, chatting, all holding full glasses of wine and small plates of food.

It was only ten. In my opinion, a little early for wine. Then I remembered that technically, Montauk was considered part of the glitzy Hamptons. If Manhattan was the city that never slept, then the Hamptons were the hamlets and villages that never stopped wining, dining, and schmoozing. I'd always thought my Montauk was the exception. Seemed I was wrong.

"Shame on you, Megan Barrett," Elle said, adding a tsk-tsk. "I told you how important this showing is. You must dress appropriately when you get an exclusive invite to a Hamptons broker's open house."

I glanced up at the glass fortress. Everyone was dressed the same as me—jeans, sweaters, and boots. Elle was the one that looked out of place, a five-foot-two polar bear or an extra in a scene from *Dr. Zhivago*. "Here," she said. "Put this vintage Dior scarf around your neck." She didn't wait for my approval before she reached inside her coat, removed the scarf, then expertly wrapped it around my neck. I had to hand it to her, it matched my turquoise cashmere sweater perfectly. A Christmas gift from Patrick.

"That's better. Now you'll be able to pass out your Cottages by the Sea business cards and maybe garner some new interior design business. While you're doing that, I'll make connections to get a pulse on what my future Montauk dream home will cost my husband and me."

I'd been thrilled last fall when Elle had shared that she and her new husband, Detective Arthur Shoner of the East Hampton Town PD, planned to move to Montauk. For now, they were both sharing the upstairs living quarters of her antiques and collectibles shop. The plan was to expand the shop to fill the entire house. Elle's shop assistant, Maurice, along with his partner, were going to move into the carriage house and help run the shop.

"Let's hurry," Elle said. "I was told that some of the stars from the reality TV show *Hamptons Premier Listings* might be here. And maybe even a few *Hamptons Housewives*. Can you imagine?"

I gave her a dirty look that she was very familiar with. "Here we go again. I don't see what's so exciting about hobnobbing with the Hamptons elite, especially real estate agents."

"Ha! This said by the same woman who last summer chased you-know-who down East Hampton's Main Street."

"Well, we all have our celebrity crushes. He was mine. You know, the one person you would get a free pass for if you were in a committed relationship."

Elle grinned. "See, you're no different than me."

I quickly changed the subject. "This huge modern house might be in your budget, but it doesn't have character like your Victorian captain's house in Sag Harbor. Although, your hubby would love it. What happened? Did you cave and let him dictate his modern design preference for your future domicile?"

"Of course not. Meg! How can you even ask that question? The only home Arthur and I will be buying is an old vintage dwelling with tons of character and tons of fixer-uppering to be done. I had it written into our prenup. I'll give Arthur a few token modern touches in the kitchen and an open floor plan."

Elle put her arm through mine, and we started toward the circular drive staged with exotic cars. I'd bet half of them were on loan from an East Hampton luxury car dealer.

"Token?" I asked. "Boy, you're generous. Didn't know you had a prenup." My thoughts went to last night's prizefight between Brett and Patrick and the dirt Brett had obviously dug up about a scandal between Patrick and Brett's new fiancée.

Elle pulled me to a stop just as I put my right foot on one of the white marble steps leading to the glass monstrosity. "I was kidding," she said with a wide grin. "No prenup. No need for one. We're madly in love. Still in the honeymoon stage."

I'd never seen Elle happier. Or Arthur. I'd thought Patrick and I were equally as happy. And even though Patrick had apologized for his gruff behavior last night, it still stung like the dickens. In his defense, I did have a penchant for butting in where I didn't belong, including being involved in more than a few Hamptons murder investigations. A few, meaning six. My father was a retired homicide cop on the Detroit PD. Curiosity ran in my veins. Or so I told myself. Perhaps it was time to step back. Let Patrick do Patrick and Meg do Meg.

Who was I kidding? I was invested in our relationship.

"Arthur's never home, anyway," Elle moaned, adding a pout as we continued up the steps to the mammoth wraparound porch with three-sided water views. "And now that we're going into the busy Hamptons season, I'll see even less of him. Seems that I'll be flying solo trying to find our perfect cozy nest. Hello? Meg! You listening? That was when you were supposed to say, *You won't be solo, buddy of mine. You've got me.*"

"Nest. Got it," I said.

"Hey, what's wrong? I know that face. Are you upset that Cole picked up Tripod?"

"It has nothing to do with Cole," I said. "Although, I do miss his dog, the big galoot. And so does my cranky feline, Jo."

Elle searched my face. "I could never understand how Cole was able to move to the other side of the world and leave his precious pup behind."

"His new wife is *supposedly* allergic."

"Supposedly? Me-e-o-ow, Ms. Barrett."

"I'm not being catty. But that's the reason he left Tripod with me. Until he sorted out things in the Down Under, Cole knew how well I'd take care of his three-legged companion. Remember, Tripod saved my life. I owe him one. Cole, not so much."

"Of course. How could I forget. Then why did Cole come back so soon? Thought he told you it could be a year. Or even a permanent arrangement. Don't tell me he's getting a divorce?"

"No. And I wouldn't care if he did. That bridge disintegrated to rubble long ago. Apparently, his better half was willing to get monthly allergy shots."

"He probably gave her an ultimatum. It was either her or the dog. Cole can be quite intense."

"That's an understatement," I said. By the time that he'd met his future wife, Cole and I had already severed our relationship. At least that's what he'd told me. There hadn't been any words of commitment between us. Plus, at the time, he'd lived in North Carolina and I in Montauk. Not very conducive to a healthy partnership.

"Well, your Jo has Patrick's greyhound Charlie to pal around with," Elle said, pulling out a lipstick from her handbag and applying it without a mirror.

"I really think my wacko cat wanted more than a friendship with Tripod. I've never seen her so mushy as when they were together."

Elle laughed. *"Mushy?* Probably because he shared his dog food with her."

"Tripod's better off in Australia," I mused unconvincingly. "Cole has a couple acres compared to my small yard. Though, I have to say, even with his handicap, Tripod could get down my steps to the beach easily enough."

"Then if you're not acting weird because of Cole and Tripod, that means something happened between you and Patrick. Let's hear it. Come on, we're missing out on all the yummy delicacies. For all we know, TV's Culinary Contessa herself might be inside. These Hamptons broker's open houses spare no expense. Last one I went to, I had caviar and crème fraîche on buttered toast points and Perrier-Jouët Belle Epoque champagne. Plus, you know you'll feel better if you get it off your chest. Spill."

Elle was right. I just wasn't sure why I felt so deflated. It wasn't my usual MO. I really did miss Tripod, but the bigger issue was Patrick's behavior last night. I knew Elle wouldn't let it go, so I gave her a quick encapsulation of last night's scene at the Montauk Point Lighthouse.

"You must forgive Patrick," Elle said. "Our new director is off-the-charts obnoxious. Did you know that Brett tried to corner me in the hallway at Windy Willows? I flashed him my wedding ring and told him to back off or he'd hear from my lawyer."

Windy Willows was the name of the oceanfront estate that production had rented to film the miniseries *Mr. & Mrs. Winslow*. Judging by the shabby condition Windy Willows was in prior to filming, it seemed the owners had been going through hard times. It had been left up to our set designer, Felicity, Elle, and me to transform the interior of the old manse into the late 1930s time period for the miniseries. Not that I was complaining about the work we had to do. As an interior designer and vintage-aholic, the job had definitely been in my wheelhouse.

But there was a hitch when it came to Windy Willows. I had a somewhat creepy connection to the estate and carried around the worry that any day I might run into two of my least favorite people. In a proverbial nutshell, once upon a time, my fiancé Michael had an affair with his ex-wife Paige. Subsequently, Michael became my ex-fiancé and Paige's husband for the *second* time. Paige's last name was Whitney. Her father was the CEO of Whitney Publications, whose umbrella included *American Home and Garden* magazine, of which I'd been editor in chief. To top that off, coincidence of all coincidences, when production was forced to move from Shelter Island to Bridgehampton, they chose to rent the Whitneys' summer estate, Windy Willows.

I'd recently let go of my resentments regarding Michael, thanks in part to Patrick. But if you looked up the word *sociopath* in the dictionary, I'm sure you'd find Paige Whitney's name. Enough said.

Elle interrupted my thoughts in a soothing, best friend voice, "I'm sure Patrick was just taking out his anger with Brett on you. You know he loves you, baby."

She gave my arm a love tap, and I grinned. "You're right, oh wise one," I said. "He apologized a zillion times. And I accepted. But when I asked him about Brett's warning having to do with his fiancée, he was tight-lipped. Either that or Patrick had no clue what Brett was talking about."

"Let's go with that thought for now. How about this? Tomorrow, before the wrap party, we're meeting with Felicity to go over what's needed for episode four. I'm sure she'll know the inside scoop about this mysterious fiancée. Forewarned is forearmed."

I frowned. "If you say so. And of course, you won't be solo when you look for your new abode. It will need my stamp of approval, forget about Arthur's."

She high-fived me. That's my girl," Elle said, reaching for the mansion's door handle.

"Before going inside, you might want to wipe the lipstick off your pearly whites," I said.

She took out a vintage floral hankie from her handbag and swiped it across her top front teeth. "Thanks for the heads-up," she said, reaching again for the door handle to one of the huge double doors.

Before she could open it, it was flung open by none other than *Hamptons Premiere Listings* star Finn Larsen. Watching the reality TV show was one of my guilty pleasures. Not that I would ever divulge that bit of news to Elle or Patrick.

"Oh, m-m-my," Elle stuttered. "It's you!"

Her body sagged, and I had to grab her elbow.

Was it too late to turn and run?

Chapter 4

After we'd walked into the grand hallway and Elle literally rubbed pumiced elbows with one of the Hamptons Housewives, the one with the long black hair extensions, body that a beanpole would be jealous of, and the lips of a puffer fish after it got stung by another puffer fish, I'd guided Elle to a chair and brought her a glass of Perrier. Even after she'd chugged it, her cheeks remained neon pink under a constellation of freckles. She wore the same crazed look as when she'd found a piece of signed Deco jewelry at a garage sale for a dollar.

Elle was one of the most down-to-earth women I knew, not to mention the most kindhearted and philanthropic. But when she was around celebs, she became an awestruck teenager.

As soon as word spread that Elle was in the market for a new home, the brokers circled like sharks in a feeding frenzy.

Within seconds, we were forced onto a tour that made me rethink my love of all home goods and furniture in shades of white and cream. I yearned for a colorful throw pillow, even if it happened to be in my least favorite shade — puce.

"What do you think?" Sheryl, the stunning six-foot-tall broker who was hosting the open house asked as we stepped into the His Suite on the mansion's upper level. It was the antithesis of the Hers Suite, where there had been so many white furry pillows that I was sure someone had scalped a herd of alpacas.

This masculine suite was more to my liking.

"Didn't our stager do a fabulous job on this Wobbly-Sobbly design," Sheryl announced. "You two probably don't even know what I'm talking about. Just know that right now, it's an interior design style that is very in vogue. Our stagers are really in touch with the latest cutting-edge trends. That's part of the reason that we at Hamptons Home Realty have such a quick market turnaround. Home buyers aren't just buying a home — they're buying a lifestyle."

I'd read the same spiel on the brochures we were given when we walked in the front door. Little was mentioned about Montauk's acres and acres of parks, protected preserves, and walking trails. Or Montauk's quaint downtown and fishing harbor. This house and this

15

real estate company belonged in East, Bridge, South, or West Hampton, not in Montauk.

Elle's eyes lit up. "Oh, Meg, this reminds me of what you did in Claire's cottage, Little Grey."

Sheryl stuck out her already ample chest in pride and crowed, "I haven't shown one male client this suite without them falling in love with it."

"I could crawl under the duvet right now. It feels like we're in a spa," Elle cooed.

Elle was right, the room had a similar design influence as what I'd done in my next-door neighbor's cottage. Claire loved the thought of bringing nature inside. I said, "Sheryl, I think you mean Wabi-sabi, not Wobbly-Sobbly. The principles of Wabi-sabi were based on Buddhism — making peace with transient nature. Design using warm and earthy hues, white-washed terracotta brick walls, layered textural linens and rugs, worn wood edges on furniture, subtle wall art, baskets, bifold screens, dried and green plants. The main tenet of Wabi-sabi is finding artistry in imperfection. Imperfection from an artisan's hand forming a clay pot or vase, the crack in Grandma's vase that shows its age."

"Well, whatever you call it, our *Manhattan* stagers did a fabulous job," Sheryl said, looking down her perfect nose at me. I could tell by the scowl on Sheryl's face she didn't like to be upstaged or corrected. I had gotten carried away. But that was one of the things I loved about different styles of furniture and home décor, there was always a story or history behind them. "Sorry. You were saying?" I said to Sheryl's pursed lips.

There was one difference between this room in comparison to what I'd done in Claire's. I could tell everything was store-bought and straight off a boxed store shelf. Even the cracks running down the vases were engineered to look timeworn. I wasn't complaining, I'm all for the look. But the whole tenet behind Wabi-sabi was real imperfection, not faux. In Claire's, I used repurposed items that were flawed, irregular, handmade, or plucked from the outdoors. I'd even found an antique Japanese bowl that perhaps a hundred years ago someone had applied kintsugi to, the art of fractured beauty, by patching the bowl with glue mixed with 24k gold powder. The goal was to accentuate the repair instead of disguising it.

"Meg's an interior designer," Elle boasted. "I'm sure you've heard of her. Give her your card, Meg." Elle was my biggest fan, just as I was hers.

"Sorry, I didn't bring any," I said, patting my jeans pockets. All I usually brought with me were my keys, phone, and a tube of lipstick that could be used as blush on my pale complexion.

"I'm sure I have one in here someplace." Elle dug into her vintage Hermès Kelly bag. Knowing Elle's great-aunt's connection to the movie business, I wouldn't be surprised if Grace Kelly, who the handbag was named after, used it in one of her movies. Most of Elle's clothing and jewelry collections were handed down to her from her great-aunt Mabel, who back in the day was an assistant to the famous costume designer Edith Head (think *To Catch a Thief*, *Sabrina* and *Roman Holiday*).

"Voilà!" Elle shouted. "Here." She handed my Cottages by the Sea card to Sheryl.

Sheryl took it from Elle's hand like it had cooties. "Our last stop is the His Suite master closet. We have to get moving, I have clients waiting for the next tour."

And I have a life to get back to, I thought as we followed her inside the His Suite closet, which was about the size of my cottage.

Sheryl threw her arms out wide and said, "If you're in the business, then I'm sure you recognize Samantha Z's closet aesthetic. Her closets are renowned in the Hamptons."

"She only does closets?" Elle asked.

The homeowner's broker didn't answer. She was too busy caressing a mahogany center island that looked like it'd been swiped from the men's department at Bergdorf Goodman. Each cubby held a folded dress shirt in a plastic sleeve. I couldn't tell if the dress shirts belonged to the homeowner or were just part of the staging. "Why on earth would anyone who lives in Montauk need dress shirts?" I blurted out. "Montauk's all about laidback living. Or at least it used to be."

"Oh, darling-g-g," the broker drawled, her incisors glistening under the masculine staghorn chandelier. "Half of the men who spend the season in the Hamptons drive or fly via helicopter to the city on weekdays. Leaving their wives, girlfriends, and kiddies behind."

A sexist comment if ever I heard one. Then again, she was a

female broker. Working for a living. It couldn't be easy in the Hamptons. For every listing there were probably fifty different companies vying for a piece of the pie. Then I noticed the huge rock on her ring finger and thought maybe real estate was just her hobby.

Now, who was being sexist?

"Arthur would love this closet," Elle cheered. "I'll rephrase that: until he took up stinky sportfishing, he would have. When I met him, he wore a new suit every day. Now he throws on a sports jacket that half the time doesn't match his pants. Hey, Meg, I'd bet you would do a fabulous job decorating closets."

"Hmmm, I'll think it over," I fibbed.

I glanced at the wall in front of me, where at least three dozen identical white T-shirts with attached price tags hung from a brass (or gold-plated) bar. We hadn't been shown the laundry room. Maybe there wasn't one, and whoever lived here was meant to toss his soiled once-worn T-shirts into the trash, then reach for another. A new twist on the term *disposable income.* Which was what you'd need lots of to live in this house.

Near the end of the tour, we'd finally learned what the place was listed for—six million. As we started to walk to the staircase, Sheryl grabbed Elle's arm and whispered into her ear. I read her lips when she said, "If you're interested in putting in an all-cash offer, I'm sure the owners would throw in the furniture, décor, and art, for just under half a million."

"I'll think about it," Elle said, adding one of her pixie grins that made her look like she was in her twenties, not her early thirties, like me.

I knew Elle was lying about the décor, because not one item in the place had any history, age, or one-of-a-kind specialness to it. However, I was sure that half a million dollars was a fair price because of all the designer name-dropping that Sheryl had done— Versace, Ralph Lauren, Kelly Wearstler, and Jonathan Adler, just to name a few.

Elle and I shared the same design aesthetic. We'd met at *American Home and Garden* magazine in Manhattan. After Elle left her position as an assistant in the Americana division of Sotheby's, I'd hired her to be our antiques and collectibles editor. I'd loved my job at the magazine. Everything had been going swimmingly until I walked in on my cheating fiancé entwinned in the arms of his ex-wife. Shortly after, I fled Manhattan for cathartic Montauk and opened Cottages by the Sea. After Elle's great-aunt Mabel willed her a hefty bank account, a load of stocks and bonds, a historic captains house in Sag Harbor, along with a successful antiques and collectibles business, Elle soon followed me to the Hamptons.

Elle didn't squander her wealth. She was one of the top donors to local Hamptons charities. I was also a donor, only I donated my time. I basically lived hand-to-mouth, or should I say client to client. Which was the reason I'd jumped at the chance to work part-time with the set and costume designers on *Mr. & Mrs. Winslow*. Elle worked for fun and the joy of loaning out her exquisite vintage clothing and jewelry collection to the miniseries.

After the tour, I deposited Elle back in the main living room, where she was quickly surrounded by her adoring minions. I went in search of food. Elle was with her people. I wanted to be with mine.

While looking for the kitchen, I was accosted by an R2D2-style robot whose metallic arm was extended toward me and holding an iPad. In the corner of the screen was the head of a woman wearing heavy Chanel double-CC earrings. She was explaining some details about the mansion's square footage. I'd thought I'd seen everything. Seeing brokers using AI robots to FaceTime prospective clients on the other side of world made me wonder what the future held for my offspring. If I ever had any.

I waved at the iPad and couldn't help myself from saying, "Hey, R2-D2, how's it hangin'?" The robot immediately pivoted toward the wall to avoid my image.

I tried not to take it personally.

It took me ten minutes to find the mansion's *second* nitty-gritty service kitchen. No one would call me a chef. I couldn't cook a lick. But I would consider myself a seasoned gourmet taste tester. My father was a fabulous home chef, and lucky for me, so was Patrick.

Patrick had most likely learned his skills from his deceased wife. Catherine had been a restaurateur and award-winning chef. Not that he'd told me this himself.

Anything having to do with his wife and child seemed to be off-limits for discussion. Taboo. Forbidden.

Was I jealous of a ghost?

Not one bit.
Liar, liar, pants on fire.

Chapter 5

Just as I popped a rosemary and olive oil crostini, topped with truffle and wild mushroom pâté, into my mouth, a familiar face entered the kitchen. "Alice," I mumbled, crostini crumbs falling onto my sweater. "Shouldn't you be out there with the rest of the brokers?"

Alice's upper lip twitched, and she attempted a weak smile that didn't reach her squinty hazel eyes. "Oh, Meg. I'm not one of them. I never will be. It took me two years to get my junior broker's license. Coming here was a bad idea. Look at them out there. They're out of my league. I might as well be from another galaxy. I'll never fit in." She pointed an unpolished fingernail at the kitchen's exit. Like myself, Alice wore jeans, a sweater, and boots. Only Alice's jeans were stained, her nubby sweater had enough pills to stock a pharmacy, and her boots were caked with mud.

I went to her and put my arm around her shoulders. "Alice, my mother always told me to never argue for my limitations. Now skedaddle, you're as important as any one of those movers and shakers."

She cringed. "Mover and shakers, why'd you have to say that!"

"Just wait until they hear about all your exclusive clients."

"Clients that might leave Sand and Sun Realty and go with a bigger company now that Aunt Barb isn't at the helm."

Barb, my friend and the person who'd sold me my property, had recently moved to Florida with her hubby. Barb had been the impetus to spreading the word about my interior design business, and Elle and I had promised to help her niece if she needed it.

Glancing over at Alice's hunched shoulders and quivering chin — it looked like she needed it.

"Come with me," I said, putting my hand on her back and pushing her through the kitchen's double swinging doors.

We parted the crowd and went to where Elle was chatting with Finn Larsen. *Perfect,* I thought.

"Ms. Warner-Shoner, you won't believe this!" I said loud enough to quiet the crowd. Which was my sole intention. "Alice from Sand and Sun Realty just confided that she has an exclusive, not-yet-on-the-market estate that will be perfect for you." Then I leaned over and whispered into Elle's ear, "Play along."

Finn couldn't move his eyebrows or tanned forehead because of all the Botox and fillers, but he managed to shout, "Shazam!" Then he pumped the air with his fist. A trademark move he'd patented on *Hamptons Premier Listings*. He turned to Alice, whose mouth was wide open, and said with a Norwegian accent, "I'd love to hear about this off-market property. We can go, what do you Americans say, *halfsies* on the commission."

I waited for Alice to speak. She didn't.

Smiling, I said, "Oh, Mr. Larsen. Don't you know that Sand and Sun Realty has been in the Hamptons forever. Their extensive client list includes families that have been in Montauk since the 1920s. They've never shared their properties on multiple listing sites or social media. *Or* with another broker. Sand and Sun is more of a boutique real estate agency. And, well, you know about the boom lately in Montauk. There's no reason for them to advertise. I know if it wasn't for Sand and Sun Realty, I wouldn't have found my charming oceanfront cottage. And my neighbor Claire wouldn't have found Little Grey."

"Little Grey?" Finn asked, his blue eyes meeting mine.

"You don't know about Little Grey? It was built by John Greenleaf Thorpe, the same architect who built Grey Gardens in East Hampton."

Finn reached in his pocket and pulled out a card. Ignoring me, he handed it to Alice. Alice took it but it slipped through her fingers. When she bent to retrieve it, the glass of red wine she'd been holding splashed onto the whitewashed wood floor.

There was a collective "Oh-h-h" as Sheryl rushed over.

"You idiot," she said to Alice. "Who are you? I don't remember inviting you."

So much for my attempt to champion Alice. I didn't feel duplicitous because everything I'd said about Sand and Sun was true. What I did feel bad about was how excited Alice looked when Finn handed her his card.

As Sheryl frantically patted wads of paper toweling on the area where the wine had seeped between the chevron floorboards, I glanced at her spikey red-soled stilettos and thought they would do more damage to the floor than the wine. (To rest my point from earlier, even though Sheryl wore designer shoes, she also had on jeans and a sweater.)

Finn said, clicking his tongue, "Tsk, tsk. I don't allow red wine at *my* open houses. And only white food and sauces. A lesson free of charge, dear Sheryl, from a pro."

Sheryl looked up, her cheeks the color of her wine-soaked towel.

Finn added a smug expression to his handsome face, then turned to the room of brokers, who were all nodding in agreement—even as they held their cabernets and merlots.

"Meg. Alice. Let's go," Elle said. "We won't be needing anyone here to find me my perfect Montauk estate. I'm going with Sand and Sun Realty."

Finally, my down-to-earth bestie had returned from planet Hollywood.

I took Alice's elbow and guided her toward the front door. She was still holding Finn's business card. I snatched it out of her hand and threw it in Finn's direction. "Keep your card. Alice Moss won't be needing it."

Before we were thrown out, we rushed out the front door and down the steps. When we were safely by Elle's car—actually, it was her husband's Lexus, her turquoise vintage pickup apparently wasn't couth enough for a Hamptons open house—Alice blurted out, "I told you I'm bad luck. And I told you that Aunt Barb made a big mistake trusting me with her company. I should call her. Or, Meg, maybe you could do it for me."

Elle grabbed Alice's shoulders and forced her to make eye contact. "Meg will do no such thing. I was planning on coming to you as my broker. I just went to that open house to get an idea of what things were selling for in Montauk."

"And to hang out with celebs from a couple reality television shows," I chided.

"Oh, Elle. You don't have to hire me," Alice said with a whimper. "Sand and Sun doesn't have any big listings that would fit what you're looking for. I attended Aunt Barb and Uncle Jack's going-away party at your gorgeous Victorian captain's house in Sag Harbor. I'm sure Sand and Sun's listings would be too small-fry for what you're looking for."

What Alice said wasn't entirely true. The commission, even on a small cottage in Montauk, would be enough to get Alice through a long, hard winter. What was true was that Elle was looking for something bigger than a cozy cottage like mine. Something with water views, lots of land, and hopefully an outbuilding for our vintage works in progress that we would have to move out from her carriage house so that Maurice and his partner could move in.

Not about to give up, I said, "Alice, you have access to multiple listings, all you have to do is accompany Elle and Arthur as their broker. Then you will split the commission with the seller's broker. What Mr. Larsen was hoping you would do with him."

"Oh, I don't kn-n-now," she stammered. "You saw what happened. No one will take me seriously."

"Meg and I take you seriously," Elle said, grabbing Alice's hand. "Nothing more to discuss. And if there's anything else we can help you with, let us know."

Alice managed a weak smile. "I did get a call this morning that a potential seller was ready to sign a contract. The old Everett Halstead property. It's too small for you, Elle. But I think, because of its location, it should be an easy sell. If only for the land. The house looks like it hasn't been decorated since the thirties. It will definitely have to be staged. And I'm sad to say, I know nothing about home décor."

I looked at Elle. Elle looked at me.

"Is that so," I said, raising an eyebrow, knowing both of us were thinking that the 1930s was the same time period for the set of *Mr. & Mrs. Winslow*.

Elle's eyes sparked with excitement. "Do you know if Mr. Halstead would consider selling the contents of the house?"

"Oh, his granddaughter wants to get rid of everything. She's the one who called me. She said that she's planning on calling a junk removal company."

Elle and I slapped each other a high five. Neither one of us was beneath being called junk removers.

"Worry about nothing, little grasshopper," I said. "Elle and I will take care of everything. Even staging the cottage."

Elle piped up, "And Meg has a construction team at her disposal. Duke and Duke Jr.—they are truly diamonds in the rough."

Alice smiled and it transformed her face. She even had a matching pair of adorable dimples. "Maybe you're right," she said. "With your help, I won't let Aunt Barb down." She stuck out her chin, brushed away her dishwater blonde bangs, which made her look like an Afghan hound in need of a grooming, and said confidently, "Let's do this! Woman power!"

Elle put her arm around Alice's shoulders. "Come with us. You can leave your car here. It's still early, let's go see the Halstead property and get an idea of what we're dealing with."

"Don't say I didn't warn you," Alice said with a grin as we walked toward Elle's car.

Alice got into the backseat. I stepped toward the front of the car. I'd called shotgun, wanting to get an unencumbered view when we pulled into the Halstead property.

Suddenly, a silver Rolls-Royce with a uniformed chauffeur at the wheel came whizzing by. Flattening myself against the car, I let out a few choice words, holding my middle finger in check — after all, this was the Hamptons, and I did have my interior design business to think of.

I watched the chauffeur park and get out of the Rolls. He went around to the rear passenger door, took off his cap, and opened the door. Out came a woman with long, glossy, bright auburn hair. Then, surprise, surprise. None other than our director, Brett Golden, stepped out. They both went up the steps. There was something familiar about the woman's profile, lanky figure, and red hair.

Brett ran ahead of her, opened the door and held it open. Which was amazing because *Mr. & Mrs. Winslow*'s director didn't have a chivalrous bone in his body. Before I could get a better look at the woman, the pair disappeared inside.

Was she Brett's new fiancée? The one who had some kind of relationship with Patrick? But more important, I asked myself, what the heck were they doing at a broker's open house in Montauk? *My* cozy little hamlet.

Even though I'm not Catholic, I made the sign of the cross. Before getting into Elle's car, I glanced up to the heavens and whispered, "Let our obnoxious director get fired *real* soon."

Chapter 6

The exterior of the Halstead cottage was charming. It had a wide balustered front porch and two chippy white rocking chairs. But what lurked inside was something from a Stephen King novel.

The owner's granddaughter, Delia Halstead, served us murky tap water in cartoon jelly jars. I received a sixties Huckleberry Hound and Elle was presented with a faded Bugs Bunny and Yosemite Sam. Poor Yosemite was missing his trademark red handlebar mustache. The jelly jars were vintage, just not from the thirties—nor was anything else that I saw in the shabby front room.

Elle and I would have to give realtor Alice a quick tutorial on the art nouveau, deco, and prewar periods of design. Not that the mid-century items wouldn't sell. They would. They just couldn't be used on the set of *Mr. & Mrs. Winslow*. Like me, Elle was trying not to let her disappointment show.

"I thought we'd be further along in getting this thing on the market," Delia said in an accusatory tone. I saw Alice sink back into the sofa. Which wasn't hard to do, seeing that dingy gray stuffing oozed from both sides of the back cushion.

Glancing around the room, I tried to imagine it after it was cleaned out. It had good bones, and based on all the ashes in the grate, the fireplace must be in working order. But I was afraid to see what the rest of the place held. This three-bedroom cottage would be the perfect showcase for our fixer-uppers. "That's why Elle and I are here," I said. "We're going to help Alice stage the cottage."

Taking a step toward the sofa, Delia directed her gaze at Alice. "And don't even think that I, I mean Grandfather, is going to pay for any staging. Your commission will be enough to cover it. I'm thinking we should ask a million five. Not a penny less. And we need to do it soon. Grandfather should have been in a nursing home years ago. Scratch that. Decades ago."

Delia wasn't attractive, per se. I guessed she was around the same age as Elle and me. Her mousey brown hair matched the color of her eyes. Her complexion was so pale it almost looked translucent, making me want to pinch her cheeks to see if any blood would surface. But her tall stature, deep commanding voice, and strong nose seemed to make up for her other lackluster features.

"Alice won't charge you for the staging on one condition," Elle said. "If the new owners want to buy anything, Meg and I will get the proceeds."

Go, Elle!

My mind went back to the broker's open house we'd just attended. The half million dollars they wanted for the interior furnishings and art was far more than what we'd net. But there was still room for a nice profit.

From the folds of the sofa, Alice mumbled something my hearing aids couldn't pick up. Then she added, "I haven't met Mr. Halstead yet. Shouldn't he be here to sign the contract and discuss the staging and price?"

Delia waved her hand like she was irritated with the thought. "He's on board with anything I decide. Just leave me the papers and I'll get him to sign." Then she took a furtive look out the grimy side window to where a metal outbuilding stood. It looked big enough to house a small airplane. Delia cleared her throat, then glanced down at her gold watch (a Cartier or a good fake). "I don't have time for this. I need to get back to Manhattan for dinner."

"I'm sure that's not legal. Alice should be here when your grand-father signs," I said. "Is your name on the land title?" I wasn't about to let Delia intimidate Alice. It was the reason we were here.

She didn't answer, just took a step toward the front door.

Elle placed her glass on a pile of vintage *Popular Mechanics* covered in a blanket of dust, then stood. "Alice, I wouldn't leave any paperwork until you meet the property owner."

Delia turned to face us, then put both hands on her narrow hips. "Who exactly are you two? Alice told me she works alone. She also said she would lower her commission from six to four percent if I chose Sand and Sun. Maybe I should continue my search for a different company. There's about a million to choose from in the Hamptons."

I laughed. "Good luck finding any brokers who would do it for four percent."

"Alice doesn't have the paperwork with her," Elle said. "She'll have to come back."

Alice got to her feet but kept a submissive pose. I stood and winked at her, giving her a thumbs-up.

Alice straightened her spine, and in a confident tone, the first I'd ever heard from her, she said, "I'll honor our agreement about the commission. But I insist that your grandfather is present when we sign." Then Alice headed toward the door, nearly knocking Delia over as she brushed past her.

Elle and I followed.

From behind, Delia said, "He keeps disappearing. God knows where. We've barely exchanged but a few words since I came to town. I'll be back on Saturday. I'll try to tie him down. Alice, keep glued to your cell phone." She laughed nervously. "That's *if* I can tie him down . . . Not literally, of course."

Always ready to defend the underdog, I asked, "But he did agree to sell, right?"

"Of course! What are you insinuating? I suppose you should know that my grandfather hasn't been right in the head since he worked at Camp Hero during the sixties." Delia raised her right pointer finger and made the "cuckoo" gesture by circling the air by her ear. Realizing how crass she sounded, she said, "Selling his home is traumatic. The man is in his eighties or nineties, for God's sake."

I wasn't a fan of the way Delia talked about her grandfather. He wasn't around to defend himself. And why hadn't she known his age?

"Camp Hero?" Elle asked.

"My father thinks that the rumors about Camp Hero are true when it comes to my grandfather. He just wasn't the same after he retired from the military. All kinds of things supposedly went on. Mind control. Experimental drugs like LSD. Grandfather would never talk about it. My family thinks he was one of the army's guinea pigs, just like in the TV series *Stranger Things*."

Elle and I glanced at each other in surprise.

A couple decades ago, Camp Hero, which stood on the shores of the Atlantic a few miles east of my cottage, had been turned into a New York State Park. During WWII, Camp Hero functioned as a U.S. Army base, and then during the Cold War it became the Montauk Air Force Base.

"Now," Delia said, looking down at a chipped fingernail, "if you don't mind. I have an appointment to keep before I head back to the city."

We filed outside, the rusty hinged screen door slamming behind us loud and clear.

Delia sure was a piece of work.

As we walked to the car, Elle said to Alice, "I'm proud of the way you handled that. Barb will also be proud when we tell her."

"I couldn't have done it without Batman and Robin."

"More like Thelma and Louise," I said. Elle laughed, but Alice looked confused.

Another thing we had to introduce her to — must-see movies.

Once we reached the car, I glanced back at the cottage. Delia was standing behind the screen door watching us. As I reached for the car's door handle, I caught movement out of the corner of my eye. A bent, wizened figure with a mostly bald head, sporting a tuft of white hair like a vintage troll doll's, was peering at us from the side of the metal outbuilding. "Look!" I said, pointing. "That must be Mr. Halstead."

"Where?" Elle asked. "I don't see anyone."

And just like that, he disappeared. I knew I hadn't been hallucinating.

Not wanting to upset Alice, I laughed and said, "My bad. It was just a swaying hydrangea bush."

I had a premonition that getting Everett Halstead to sign the broker agreement might be like taming a feral cat.

As we drove away, the term *no good deed goes unpunished* came to mind.

Chapter 7

Friday morning had dawned dark and gloomy—a mirror of Patrick's mood the previous evening; scratch that, the previous *two* evenings. He'd barely said two words at dinner, and even complimented me on the meal, which *he'd* made. I'd been wise enough to realize that Patrick's angst had something to do with Brett's Dashiell Hammett plagiarism or Brett's mysterious fiancée. Either way, it made for a less than rousing game of Scrabble, which I'd won (first time ever!). With the embers giving off their last spark, I'd said in a cheery tone, "Remember, tomorrow's the wrap party. I'll meet you there. Elle and I are going early to talk to Felicity about what's needed for the next episode. Great script, by the way."

Instead of responding, Patrick placed Jo on the floor, stood, then roused Charlie from her cozy bed in front of the hearth. He herded Charlie out my cottage's French doors. Having been left behind like an afterthought, I'd followed them out to my deck.

At the top of landing, Patrick had turned to face me. I'd stepped toward him, ready to fly into his arms, but he'd held out his hand like a crossing guard warding off oncoming traffic. "I'm not going to the wrap party. But you have fun." *Was he kidding?* A brisk wind had whipped rogue locks of sandy brown hair in front of his angry, deep green eyes. I'd waited for an explanation. None came. Under the dim porch light, I'd noticed Patrick's downturned lips, the same lips that hadn't bothered to kiss me as he'd turned and followed Charlie down the thirty-six steps to the beach.

Per our usual evening routine, we'd say our goodbyes on the sand. Lips locked. Hearts racing. The tide nipping at our heels. That hadn't been the case last night. I'd felt so distraught that I'd scurried to the deck railing, and with a desperate, whiny voice, yelled down, "But, you have to go. You're the screenwriter."

Either my words had been drowned out by the turbulent surf or ignored by a turbulent boyfriend. I'd realized as man and dog disappeared into the black moonless night that there was still so much I didn't know about Patrick James Seaton.

Based on Wednesday's scene at the lighthouse, there was one thing I did know—Patrick wasn't afraid of confronting our irritating director when it came to *Mr. & Mrs. Winslow*. Which, in my mind, narrowed down the reason he'd been so distracted—Patrick didn't want to go to the party because he wanted to avoid Brett's fiancée.

Later, around midnight, all snuggled in bed, I'd said to my fat, belligerent Maine coon, "Whaddya think, Josephine Eater Barrett? Will I be able to talk Patrick into going to the party tomorrow?" Jo's answer had been to swipe a meaty paw in my direction, then turn to face the wall. Fumes of noxious fur followed in her wake. "Thanks for the support, buddy."

Hours had passed before I'd been able to fall asleep. When I finally did, my dreams were interspersed with scenes akin to an old Bogie and Bacall film that featured Patrick in the arms of a mysterious redheaded woman.

"I think we have everything sorted out," Elle said, interrupting my gloomy thoughts about the previous evening.

Elle, Felicity, and I were seated at the ginormous mahogany table in the formal dining room at Windy Willows. The location of tonight's wrap party—the one that Patrick *wouldn't* be attending.

After I'd pulled through the gates, I'd noticed that a huge white party tent had been set up in the center of the estate's topiary garden. Jeremy, our producer, had been standing next to the tent, looking up at the schizophrenic sky with a scowl on his face. The weather was, at best, on the iffy side. Cold and blustery, with a plethora of thunderclouds.

"Felicity," Elle continued, "thanks for the storyboards, they're fabulous. Now that we see your vision, Meg and I can scour the Hamptons and beyond for some great period pieces. Right, Meg?"

I turned to *Mr. & Mrs. Winslow*'s set director. "Yeah, sure. Go, team!" Then I glanced down at the gorgeous watercolor renderings littering the table. Felicity's attention to detail made it easy to see what would be needed for the next episode, scheduled to take place on Block Island, Rhode Island. I knew from my trips to the island, only a boat ride from Montauk, that the rocky terrain, dual lighthouses, and quiet beauty would make the perfect setting for bootlegging, pirating, romance, and, of course . . . murder.

Felicity peered back at me from behind round black-rimmed glasses. "Something's wrong. Usually, you're more excited about finding the perfect décor for our next episode. Does it have anything to do with you-know-who?" She turned to Elle. "Is that why you were grilling me about Brett's new fiancée last night?"

Elle averted my gaze and shrugged her shoulders.

Now it all made sense. I'd called Elle last night after Patrick had left and told her that he wouldn't be coming to the wrap party. Instead of hounding me to call him or telling me to walk down to his cottage and talk him into coming, Elle had remained quiet. Not her usual MO. Elle must have learned something about Brett's fiancée from Felicity.

I took a deep breath. "Don't worry, guys. I can handle it. Whatever happened was in the past. Sock it to me."

Elle glanced at Felicity. "Should it be you or me who tells her?"

"Definitely you."

Even though my heart was racing, I said, "It can't be that bad."

Suddenly, the French doors from the entryway were thrown open and a familiar-looking woman with luxurious, long red hair, straight from a L'Oréal *Because I'm worth it* commercial, entered the dining room. As she got closer, I noticed the trademark mole above her upper lip. Unable to help myself, I stuttered, "Oh m-m-y God-d, you're Julie David!" At least I thought it was Julie David. I hadn't seen a recent photo of her in the tabloids and was surprised at all the wrinkles lining her usually luminous skin.

"Last time I checked," Julie said. She added a quick smile that morphed into a quick frown. "Have you seen Brett? I need to talk to him. He has a lot of explaining to do. The big phony."

I remained mute, stunned that the once-famous actress was in the same room with us.

"No. We haven't seen him," Felicity answered for all of us.

Julie continued across the dining room with quick measured steps, then exited out the doors leading into the kitchen hallway. From the back, Julie looked years younger than the front. It was then that I realized Julie David had been the woman in the Rolls-Royce with Brett at the Montauk broker's open house.

I turned to Elle, hoping she would tell me that the actress who'd just breezed by, trailing the scent of perfume, fame, fortune, and scandal, had nothing to do with Brett *or* Patrick. My hopes were dashed when Elle nibbled her lower lip and Felicity examined a piece of lint on her sweater. I froze. So, it was true. Julie David must be engaged to Brett. Not only that, she'd supposedly had some kind of past with Patrick.

To confirm things, a booming voice, loud enough to cause my hearing aids to buzz, said, "Where'd my fiancée go?" I didn't need to turn to see who it was, because I recognized Brett's nasal twang. "Hello-o," he said in a condescending tone as he walked over to Felicity and put his forefinger to her temple. "Anyone in there? Where is Ms. David?"

Felicity pointed to the doors leading to the hallway.

Brett narrowed his gaze and asked, "Did she seem mad?"

"We only saw her for a second," Felicity answered.

He laughed. "I think it's that time of month. I'm sure you ladies know all about that."

I doubted that Julie David would be getting cramps anytime soon. Not even hot flashes. The age difference between her and Patrick had to be thirty-five years. Which made it strange to think they'd had a December/May fling.

There were a few things I remembered from the Page Six headlines. Julie David had clocked more time in rehabs than she had on her movie sets. Which said a lot, seeing that she'd been acting since a teen. Plus, she'd had more marriages than you could count on one hand, making her super-duper wealthy. I wasn't surprised that someone as famous, or should I say *in*famous, as Julie David might have met Patrick. What was incredible was that Julie would have anything to do with Brett Golden—especially marry him.

I recalled that the *Daily News* had dubbed Julie the Black Widow, because soon after she married them, each of her husband's had died.

Bad luck? Or had Ms. David helped them along?

As if reading my mind, Brett clapped his hands to get my attention. "Where's *your* Romeo, Ms. Barrett. I hope he plans to heed my warning." He gazed out the bowed window, where five cars were parked. Not one of them was Patrick's navy Range Rover. "When Mr. Seaton decides to show up, please tell him to find me before he talks to Julie. There's something we need to clear up."

I opened my mouth to tell Brett that I wasn't Patrick's keeper, but he was already at the door. He pushed it open and called out in a creepy adolescent voice that was loud enough for my hearing aids to pick up, "Jules, darlin', don't be mad. Come on, baby girl, it was only a teensy-weensy white lie. A fib, for God's sake! Ask my son, he'll tell you what happened. Even my daughter knows it's only a temporary situation."

After his voice trailed off, I got up and sat next to Felicity. "Please tell me. What do you know about Patrick and Julie David?" Elle and Felicity exchanged glances. Felicity picked up her phone from the table, tapped the screen a few times, then held it to my face.

I felt my heart beating against my rib cage. "But. But . . . this was dated around the same time as Patrick's wife and daughter's accident."

Before I had a chance to make sure I had my dates right, Brett's son burst into the room. "Where's Dad? I mean Mr. Golden." Matt was his father's personal assistant. A better description would be that he was Brett's whipping boy and gofer.

"Hey, Matt. Wait up." Olivia, Matt's sister and Brett's daughter, came barreling into the dining room. Olivia was also the head makeup artist for *Mr. & Mrs. Winslow*. The third episode had been a family affair, a way for our cheapskate producer to keep costs down. And now, Brett wanted to add thespian has-been and fiancée Julie David to the mix.

"We need to address this together," Olivia said to Matt's back. Her pink cheeks were puffed out and she was out of breath. "You know I'm the only one he'll listen to. He'll just get angry with you. Let me tell him your plans. I'll soften the blow. Maybe we should wait until after the party?" Olivia shared a few of her father's better features. Her short curly hair changed colors almost daily, which probably went hand in hand with being a makeup artist. Today, her chestnut brown hair was streaked with pink highlights.

Matt paused for only a second. His cheeks were flushed. Through gritted teeth he said, "This is something that I must do on my own. I don't need your help."

"He'll never let you do it," Olivia said, desperation in her voice. "Especially if I'm not there to run interference."

Then we watched her follow Matt out of the dining room and into the hallway.

Once, in *Mr. & Mrs. Winslow*'s craft services tent, Elle and I had been in line with Olivia and Matt. Olivia's plate had been piled high with some kind of mystery stew. Her father had walked in, then chastised Olivia about her weight gain since coming on set. Asking if he should start calling her by her childhood nickname, Chubby Teletubby. I'd tried to defend Olivia by pointing out the abundance of carb-rich meals provided by the budget caterer that our producer hired. Their idea of a salad was wilted iceberg lettuce topped with a couple shakes of faux bacon bits. Even her brother Matt had tried to stick up for her, pointing out that Olivia had lost fifty pounds in the past year. Brett's face had turned a purply red, then he'd taken his focus off his daughter and started chastising his son, pointing out his ineptitude as a personal assistant. I'd just been happy our screenwriter hadn't been there. Patrick didn't need any more fuel to add to an already blazing fire where Brett was concerned.

Our producer, Jeremy Prentice, was the next one to stick his head into the open doorway of the dining room. Jeremy came toward us with a bounce in his step, his pure white ponytail swinging from side to side. Instead of making a hip fashion statement, I had a hunch he was too cheap to get a haircut. He paused at the dining room table and said, "Hope everyone's ready for our big wrap party. I've invested tons of money and didn't even have to hire a party planner. They rip you off. Especially out here in the Hamptons. Ladies, do me a favor. Please don't take more than two shrimp cocktails, there was a problem with the seafood supplier. I have to go pick up the stuff from that rip-off gourmet market in East Hampton."

Felicity and I exchanged glances, knowing his version of a lot of money wasn't the same as a normal producer's. Lucky for Felicity, Jeremy never cut corners when it came to the set design, staging, and his actors.

"The tent's pitched," he said, seemingly proud of himself. "I just hope the weather holds out." As usual, Jeremy Prentice was dressed like he didn't have a penny to his name, instead of half a billion. Elle had told me that she'd once seen him shopping in the men's department at the Salvation Army outlet. He didn't have children and had never been married. He had dated supermodels and young actresses, snaring them based on his street cred in the film industry. But Patrick had told me that Jeremy's dates quickly vanished after he asked them to split the check.

"What were you ladies talking about? You look pretty glum. Let me guess. Brett Golden. Did he tell you that he wants the infamous

Julie David to join our cast?"

"No," Elle answered, even though I'd told her and Felicity about what I learned at the lighthouse.

"Brett told me I should give her a million an episode." Jeremy scowled at the thought. "I think Mr. Golden's gonna be angry when I tell him his fiancée isn't in our budget. Plus, she's way too old to play Lara's sister. That would be ludicrous. Even if having the Black Widow in our cast would boost our ratings *and* she acquiesced to taking the part of a dowager great-aunt, I would still have second thoughts. Also, based of all her past misdeeds on movie and television sets, I'm sure the insurance I'd have to take out on her would be astronomical. If she and Brett are a package deal, they both go. Hell, even if she's not part of the deal. Golden's days are numbered."

My heart quickened at the news. Maybe Patrick's past with Julie David wouldn't even come up tonight. Suddenly, I felt relieved that Patrick planned to stay away.

Nodding his head toward me, Jeremy said, "Got a text yesterday from Patrick. Something about plagiarism. Know anything about it?"

So, it seemed our producer also knew about Patrick's and my relationship. I nibbled my bottom lip and mumbled, "You'll have to talk to Patrick."

"I've been trying to. He's not answering any of my voicemails. Is he here?"

"Nope," I said, grabbing Elle's empty legal pad. Glancing down, I scanned the blank page like it had something important written on it.

Jeremy looked over at Felicity with a mischievous sparkle in his dark hooded eyes. "I was looking for our assistant director. Have you seen Ms. Meyers? I want to hear her answer to a question I asked this morning. I bet you can guess what it was."

Felicity shook her head. "Sorry. She's about the only one we haven't seen."

"If we see her," I said, "we'll tell her you're looking for her."

"Thanks, kiddo."

I waited until Jeremy left the room before grabbing Felicity's phone. On the screen was a headline in *Variety*: "Author Drops Actress on the Doorstep of the Betty Ford Clinic." Under the headline were two photos. One showed Patrick in front of the facility, supporting a half-comatose Julie David. The other was Patrick leaning in to give her a kiss. It wasn't clear what part of her face he was going for. Because of their age difference, I tried to imagine it was her forehead, not her lips.

I handed the phone back to Felicity. "Is that it? A paparazzi photo that could have been doctored for the tabloids?"

"Well, you're not going to want to hear this," Felicity said. "Ms. David told me that she wanted to talk to our screenwriter. She said she had something important to tell him."

"I've never seen her around here," I said. "When did she tell you this? How did you find out Julie was Brett's fiancée?"

"Today's the first time I've seen her at Windy Willows. But I ran into her and Brett earlier in the week," Felicity said with a frown. "I bumped into them on the street in East Hampton. It was pretty awkward. If Julie hadn't introduced herself as his fiancée, I wouldn't have known. It was quite a scene. She had an obnoxious entourage of paparazzi following behind them. April must be slim pickings for celeb photos. The vultures seemed quite thrilled to see the Black Widow." Felicity removed a legal pad and felt-tip pen from her portfolio case. Without looking up, she said, "That's when she asked me to give Patrick the message. Brett wasn't too pleased."

Neither was I, if truth be told.

I refused to panic. However, I was beginning to wonder why, when things were going smoothly in my love life, something like this happened? I knew how much Patrick loved his wife and child. There had to be a logical reason for the photo showing him and Julie together. I stood. "I need to talk to Patrick."

Elle looked at me. "You're sure that's a good idea?"

"No, I'm not sure, but I'm going to do it anyway."

Chapter 8

I chose the library to make my call. Three walls in the room were filled with floor-to-ceiling books, most of which Elle and I had scored at antiques shows and thrift shops. In front of a large bowed window was a huge mahogany desk topped with an antique world globe and 1920s leather desk set. Steeling myself for what Patrick might tell me, I sat on one of two leather sofas flanking a gas-lit fireplace, the mantel of which was adorned with a fictional Winslow coat of arms.

I took out my phone and glanced down. My hand started to shake. No text or call from Patrick.

As if my fingers took on a life of their own, I sent a short-and-sweet, hopefully not-to-cloying text to Patrick. *Missing you. XO, M.* Then I put my phone back in my pocket. Patrick was a big boy and had every right not to come to the wrap party. I just wished he trusted me enough to tell me what was going on.

Closing my eyes, I repeated a few mantras I used when meditating on my beach. In between the mantras came a tinny, ringing sound. My eyes flew open. *Patrick!* He must be calling me. Then I realized what I heard was the chiming of the grandfather clock in the corner of the library. It was four o'clock — three hours until the wrap party.

No need to wallow, I told myself. I'd stay at the party for an hour, enough time to make an appearance and leave in time to meet Patrick for a walk on the beach. If I found more dirt on Patrick and Julie David at the party, so be it.

Giving myself a few more minutes to absorb the whole situation, I glanced around the library, surprised that the room was still staged from one of the scenes in *Mr. & Mrs. Winslow.*

On the Persian carpet, next to a brass horsehead walking stick, lay the remains of a blue and white Chinese ginger jar. Last week, Patrick and I had watched one of the takes in the scene where Jack's great-uncle, who has a fondness for horse racing, gets into a tight spot with his bookie and tries to defend himself by turning the tip of his walking stick into a dagger. Our heroine Lara steps in to save the day by clocking the bookie on the head with the ginger jar. Instead of ceramic, the jar was constructed of Styrofoam. Once it connected with the noggin of the actor playing the bookie, it broke apart like pieces in a jigsaw puzzle. Special effects would later add the soundtrack of broken glass and no one would be the wiser. It had been great fun until Patrick heard the actress Zoe, aka Lara, add in some corny dialog that hadn't been written in his script. Then Patrick and Brett got into it.

Again.

After that, I'd decided to stay away from the set when they were filming. The exception had been Wednesday night at the lighthouse. Big mistake. Now that I'd truly learned my lesson, I'd wait like the rest of the world to view the finished episode.

I got up from the sofa, picked up the walking stick and twisted the brass horsehead handle in order to retract the blade. Then I leaned it against the mantel. Knowing it was from the 1930s and might come in handy on set, I'd purchased it at the Bridgehampton Antiques Show. The walking stick had also come in handy last August when I'd been chased by a potential murderer. But that was another story, for another time. One to keep on the back burner. Just like anything having to do with Patrick and his possible illicit relationship with Brett's elderly fiancée.

I threw the foam ginger jar pieces in the trash bin under the desk and put the library back in its original condition. Now the room was ready for filming episode four. Glancing out the window, I saw Jeremy pulling out the long drive in his early-model Prius, no doubt going to pick up his shrimp. I wondered if he'd found Nikki Meyers, and if he did, had she accepted his offer to take over as director? *Please*, I thought, *let it be so.*

Glancing over at the library's other door that opened to the hallway, I thought about sneaking out to see what our motley cast of characters were up to, Julie David included. Then I changed my mind.

For once, I would let things go. What made my choice easier was the fact that Patrick was involved in one way or another. And, truthfully, did I want to pass on any intel to him concerning Brett and Julie? If Patrick and Julie had a past, he certainly wasn't admitting it. Patrick should know that this far along in our relationship, I would never judge him.

A wave of disappointment tsunamied over me. Then an idea came. I would take a trip to Sarabeth's on the Bay in Watermill and talk to Patrick's former sister-in-law. See if she knew anything about Julie and Patrick. Since meeting Patrick's deceased wife's sister last August, we'd become fast friends. Not besties, because as chef and owner of a top Hamptons restaurant, Sarabeth had little time for socializing. But she understood all about Patrick's ability to shut off his emotions.

After taking one last look at my phone—alas, nothing from Patrick— I stepped toward the French doors to the dining room. I put my hand on the brass handle at the same time that Nikki Meyers, our assistant director, whizzed by. I watched her stop and say something to Elle and Felicity. From the angle I was standing at, or spying from, I couldn't read her lips. But I could read her worried expression. Then she disappeared from my view.

On the first day of filming episode three, we'd all been surprised when the legendary Nikki Meyers had walked onto the set as our assistant director. Nikki had a stellar reputation in the movie business, owned a lucrative production company, was on the board of directors for the Academy Awards, and had even written, directed, and produced mine and the rest of world's favorite romantic comedy, *What Happiness Means*. No one had an answer for why Nikki signed up to work *under* Brett Golden. And even more surprising was the way Nikki acted when she was around Brett. He never seemed to get under her skin like he did with the rest of the cast and crew. When Brett and Nikki were on set together, Nikki was constantly smiling and agreeable to whatever outrageous ideas Brett came up with. And believe me, there'd been some doozies.

From the few chats I'd had with Nikki, I could tell she was very down-to-earth and accessible. She was attractive in an old school Doris Day/Sandra Dee way, with short blonde hair and blue eyes. I'd guessed she was in her late thirties, early forties.

Nikki hadn't minded when I turned into a fangirl and gushed about the many times I'd watched her rom-coms, dreaming of having the same happy endings in my relationships as shown on the big screen. Once, Nikki told me that she'd become an incurable romantic on the heels of a disastrous relationship, followed by meeting her husband—the love of her life. I could tell by the fact she wasn't wearing a wedding ring that he must have passed away. Perhaps her movies had given me and other women false hopes in the relationship department, but that never stopped me from running to the theater to catch her latest film. I wouldn't exactly characterize my past relationships with Michael and Cole as disastrous. Well, maybe mine and Michael's. But those relationships led me to Patrick.

There still was a chance for that Hallmark/rom-com movie ending.

After turning to take one last look at the library, I opened a French door and stepped into the dining room. Time to focus on all the fun things we needed to procure for the next episode. Elle and I had planned a trip to Block Island as soon as the ferry started running. Checking out the locale for our next episode would be the perfect elixir to keep my mind off what-if scenarios and onto the interior design of an old nineteenth-century boardinghouse.

Hopefully by then, our director, Brett Golden, would be long gone.

A girl could only wish.

Chapter 9

After sitting back at the dining room table, I leaned over and asked Elle and Felicity, "What's wrong with Nikki? She looked worried. Not her usual happy face. Without her voice of reason and suggestions, of which Brett almost always agrees to, we might be in big trouble."

Elle shrugged her shoulders. "Got me. She was looking for —"

I cut her off. "Let me guess, Brett? Jeremy? 'Cause if it's Jeremy, I just saw him leave."

"Guess again. No, Nikki wanted to see Matt."

Felicity took off her glasses and started rubbing the bridge of her pert nose. She wore her short blue-black hair cut at an angle with one side longer than the other. It suited her small face, the style reminding me of a flapper's from the twenties. When not filming, Felicity would fly back to California to be with her husband. Elle and I would often include Felicity in our escapades, dragging her from one vintage shop to another, so she wouldn't feel lonely without her hubby.

"You don't think Nikki Myers is having an affair with Brett's son, do you?" Felicity asked. "Nikki's a lot older than Matt. I've seen them whispering together. Nikki's always hanging around him when he brings out his guitar. And, I notice he only sings love songs. Once I saw Nikki take Matt's hand in hers."

"She's probably just trying to instill confidence in him," I said. "I heard one of the camera crew call him Doormat Matt because of the way he allows his father to treat him. When Matt sings and plays his guitar for the cast, it's the only time he seems confident. I think he's very talented, but that's surely not his father's opinion."

"I agree," Elle said. "I love when Matt plays his guitar. I can picture him performing at the myriad coffee bars we have in the Hamptons. If Matt stopped hiding behind his oversized Clark Kent glasses, stood up straight, and didn't gnaw on his bleeding cuticles, he'd be a doppelganger for a young Paul Newman. He must have gotten his good looks from his mother, because he looks nothing like his father."

Felicity leaned in and whispered, "Let's hope what Jeremy says is true. We'll get Nikki as our director and Brett and his fiancée will get kicked to the curb."

I glanced at the door to the foyer. "From your lips to God's ears. So, let me get this straight. Since we've been here, we've had Julie David come through, then Brett looking for Julie, then Matt looking for Brett, then Olivia looking for Matt, then Jeremy looking for Nikki, and finally Nikki looking for Matt."

Elle laughed. "For a recap: Our director is looking for his famous actress fiancée; director's son is looking for director; head makeup artist is looking for brother; our producer is looking for assistant director; then assistant director is looking for Brett's personal assistant-slash-son."

"It's like a wedding conga line," I said, helping Felicity put her watercolor sketches back into her portfolio. "I wouldn't be surprised if the pair of black Scotties who trade off playing Jack and Lara's dog Whiskey come prancing by next."

"We should start charging admission," Elle said. "I have a feeling that this wrap party might have more fireworks than the Fourth of July. Meg, Patrick's smart to stay away. But if Brett is fired tonight, Patrick might want to see the expression on his face."

"Don't worry. I'll be sure to relay every detail. I can even video it."

"Maybe we should go see what all the fuss is about?" Felicity said, placing her portfolio case on an empty chair. "Something weird might be going on."

"If we let them work everything out," I said, "perhaps things will resolve themselves. Keep our noses clean." Both women looked stunned. "I'm serious. I'd rather talk about episode four. I've lots of great ideas."

Elle laughed. "Did something happen to you in the library? An alien abduction? That first sentence doesn't sound anything like nosy you. Oh, I get it. Something happened when you called Patrick."

"Nothing to report. I sent him a text. He didn't respond."

"Just as well," Elle said. "Meg, with your past, you're right, the last thing you should do is investigate anything having to do with Brett Golden and she who shall remain nameless."

"You can name her. Julie David," I said, adding an unconvincing laugh.

"Maybe we should warn our director that Julie is only marrying him for his money," Elle said. "The age difference between them is humongous. That has to be the reason." Suddenly, Elle's cheeks flushed. She must have realized that the age gap between Patrick and Julie was even more *humongous*. To cover, Elle quickly added, "Though, I do feel sorry for aging actresses. Men just don't age the same. And it's okay for a fifty-something male to have a twenty-something girlfriend."

"Not quite true," I said. "The other day, I caught a soap opera that my great-grandmother used to watch. The same actresses, from decades ago, hadn't aged a bit. Thanks, I'm sure, to Botox, fillers, face-lifts, and turtlenecks."

"Maybe Julie David can't afford all that?" Elle said.

Felicity glanced toward the doorway to the kitchen hallway before saying in a low voice, "Well, if Julie is marrying Brett Golden for his money, she'll be in for a big shock. Did you know our director has been sleeping here? Up on the third floor? The servants' floor."

I was stunned. "I thought the owners, the Whitneys, took over the third floor when they were in the Hamptons."

"I guess while they're away, no one will be the wiser," Felicity said. "I overheard our penny-pinching producer say that he would take Brett's lodging out of his salary. Not only is Brett staying here, but so are his kids, Matt and Olivia. Knowing that we've already had to switch our main set from Shelter Island to Bridgehampton, there's something else I'm worried about. There are rumors that the owners of Windy Willows are trying to sell. We have a two-year rental contract. Jeremy will have a fit if that happens."

"Oh, no! That would be terrible. Where would we go?" Elle asked, turning to me. She knew all about my past connection to Windy Willows. With pleading eyes, she moaned, "The Whitneys can't do that, can they?"

I shrugged my shoulders. "I wouldn't put anything past the Whitneys." I felt torn. Relieved at the prospect the Whitneys would be moving out, and sad thinking about all the work and time it would take to find a new estate for filming. Brushing aside my worries because I had other things to obsess about—like Patrick—I said, "I am surprised Brett and his offspring are staying here. Now that I know that, if I had to guess who was marrying whom for their money, it would be Brett marrying Julie."

"He'd better be careful or he'll find himself on a cold metal gurney in the morgue," Felicity said. "Just like the rest of her husbands. Brett's narcissistic enough not to care about marrying the Black Widow."

So, Felicity also knew about the rumors.

"The black widow?" Elle repeated.

I explained to her about Julie David's past. "She's been dubbed the Black Widow for a good reason. However, even if Brett is a jerk, I'd rather not see him dead. And if he's so broke, then why was he looking at a six-million-dollar cottage in Montauk?" I filled Felicity in on yesterday's broker's open house, then swallowed hard at the thought that Julie and Brett might become Patrick's and my neighbors.

"Could the reason Ms. David seemed upset have something to do with Brett and his offspring squatting here?" Elle asked.

"Got me," Felicity said. "Our director has major money problems. I overheard him complaining to a camera guy that his ex-wife got the Palm Springs house and the Paris apartment, and while he's been in New York, his lease ran out on his Beverly Hills condo."

I laughed. "If his ex spent any time married to him, she deserved both places."

"I wonder if Jeremy will feel remorse about turning Brett and his kids out onto the street? Even the gold-paved streets of the Hamptons."

Elle added a snort. "Have you met our producer? He won't even bat an eyelash."

"Let's hope," I said, making prayer hands, "that per our producer, Brett will soon to be fired."

There was a moment of silence, during which I'm sure we were all wishing for the same thing.

We spent the next two hours making a list of what was needed for the opening scene of episode four. Elle planned on meeting with our costume designer tomorrow to brainstorm which gown our lead actress would be wearing from Elle's extensive vintage wardrobe and jewelry collection.

"Meg, how does Block Island fit into episode four?" Elle asked, flipping shut her notepad. "I know you read Patrick's script."

"The twist at the end was fabulous."

"I agree," Felicity said.

I gave Elle a recap and promised to get a copy of the script from

Patrick. Then I asked Felicity, "What did our director think of Patrick's script? Or shouldn't I ask."

"He hasn't read it yet," she answered. "Even though he's had it for months. I know Nikki Meyers read it. She loved it."

Finally, things were looking up. "Let's hope she takes over as director."

Felicity raised her hand to silence me, then ratcheted her head in the direction of the library. "Did you hear that?"

It took me a minute to realize that the low guttural screams, akin to an animal with its leg caught in a trap, weren't the malfunction of my hearing aids. Felicity and Elle froze in their seats, mouths agape.

I sprung up, grabbed the heavy silver candelabra from the center of the dining room table, then crept toward the screams.

At the glass doors to the library, I ground to a halt. Before me was what appeared to be a murder scene from a future episode of *Mr. & Mrs. Winslow.*

Only this scene wasn't staged.

And I had a feeling that the body lying on the rug wasn't an actor playing dead . . .

Chapter 10

Olivia blocked my view of the top half of the body. But I recognized her father's bottom half. I also recognized the brass horsehead at the top of the walking stick that earlier I'd leaned next to the library's fireplace. From the upright position of the walking stick, I'd speculated that its retractable blade must be sticking somewhere in Brett Golden's body.

Calmly, I laid the candelabra on the carpet, then turned to the two wax figures at the dining room table. "You better stay here. I'll handle it."

Neither Elle nor Felicity protested.

I opened one side of the French doors and stepped into the library. Olivia turned and looked up at me, confusion in her dark watery eyes. Tears flowed down her full cheeks, making sooty rivulets in her expertly applied makeup, then disappeared into her open mouth, which emitted howls so deep in her throat that I expected Brett to rise from the dead and tell his daughter to shut up. As he had many times before.

But he remained still.

As I stepped closer, I could see why.

I let out a few of my own howls, causing Olivia to pause hers and look at me in surprise. Her silence only lasted a second.

I'd been right about the blade's tip.

It was in the middle of Brett's abdomen, under his rib cage. And not only that, but he had a bloody gash on his left temple.

Did someone hit him with the handle of the walking stick, then finish him off with the blade?

Chapter 11

I crouched next to Olivia and tapped her on the shoulder. She cringed and pulled away. "Olivia, have you called 911?"

She shook her head no and continued to wail. Judging by all the raw emotion, I'd put her in the bottom slot as her father's killer. But I'd been wrong before. Olivia spent her days hanging around a slew of professional actors. Maybe she'd learned a thing or two?

I checked for a pulse, but unfortunately I couldn't find one. Someone coughed, causing me to startle. I turned to see Elle and Felicity standing behind me.

Felicity avoided looking down at Brett's body. Not that I could blame her.

Elle, on the other hand, looked down and said, "I'll call 911. Then Arthur." Her face was uncharacteristically impassive.

Who was this new Elle? She was usually on the squeamish side and always the first to run and hide at the first sign of trouble. Perhaps marrying a cop had rubbed off on her. Maybe *I* was rubbing off on her. Then, surprising me even more, Elle crouched next to me and shot a few photos of the scene. Something I'd done at our other crime scenes.

She put her phone away, then said, "Olivia, have you touched your father's body? Or the weapon?"

Olivia shook her head no.

"I checked for a pulse," I said.

Elle nodded her head at me then stood. "Felicity, you should wait by the gate. Make sure no one comes in or leaves Windy Willows."

Still avoiding looking down, Felicity said, "Sure. I'll gladly go. But what about . . ." She nodded her head in Olivia's direction.

Pushing down the rising acid in my throat, I said, "I'll take care of Olivia. We'll be in the, uh . . . kitchen."

I'd first thought about bringing Olivia into the dining room, then realized she'd be able to see what was going on through the glass doors to the library—not to mention the parade of first responders and law enforcement that would soon be passing through.

Elle put her phone away and said, "I'll join you in the kitchen after Arthur arrives. Once again, Bridgehampton is in Southampton

PD's jurisdiction. But I'm sure they'll need help from Arthur and East Hampton."

While Felicity and Olivia were looking in the other direction, I read Elle's lips as she looked down at me and mouthed, "Murder magnet."

Hopefully that charming moniker would end with Brett Golden. Either that or I would have to start wearing a body cam to prove my innocence in similar types of situations.

After grabbing Olivia under her armpits, I managed to pull her up, then steer her out of the library exit that opened to the hallway, then into the kitchen.

The kitchen was staged for *Mrs. & Mrs. Winslow.* Designed in a style similar to the downstairs kitchen and servants' dining room from another streaming series, *Downton Abbey.* Much to the homeowner's delight, production had replaced the Whitneys' 1970s appliances with top-of-the-line models disguised to look like they'd been in the mansion since the 1920s.

Olivia sat with a plop onto a wooden chair, then grabbed the edge of the long farm table like she was on a sinking *Titanic.* Just in case I needed to read Olivia's lips, I took a seat at the short end of the table. Plus, it wouldn't hurt to assess her facial expressions and body language. I'm not a pro, but I've learned a few things from my cop father. Everyone has a tell, he'd told me. My tell was the surfacing of the Barrett blotches—crimson puffy welts that traveled up from my belly button to the top of my head. But in all fairness, my Barrett blotches also emerged during times of embarrassment and excitement.

"Are you sure it's okay to leave him alone?" Olivia asked, tucking her short, curly, pink-tipped hair behind her ears. "I need to see my brother."

Olivia was quite beautiful. Her eyes were large like her father's, but they were a clear luminous green, instead of a dull brown. She had high cheekbones and full lips that looked natural, not enhanced with fillers. The only thing I would change about her appearance were the layers of face and eye makeup that she used.

Our head makeup artist from the first two episodes of *Mr. & Mrs. Winslow* had once given me a brief history on the "Mask of Death" period in cosmetics that dated all the way back to the Marie

Antoinette and Queen Elizabeth I eras, when arsenic, nightshade from the belladonna plant, and lead would be used to make the face paler. They even put poisonous belladonna drops in their eyes to make their pupils larger. On top of that, he'd said that during that same time frame, some women and even men would use a combination of lead and mercury to make their lips and cheeks a rosy red. The arsenic, nightshade, mercury and lead would eat away their skin, and the belladonna drops would cause blindness. To compensate, they would add more poisonous layers to cover the damage. But what had surprised me even more was when he'd revealed that lead was still being used in makeup and beauty creams all the way to the mid-1930s. I sure hoped Botox wouldn't go down in the history books as a twenty-first-century beauty no-no.

However, I didn't think it was vanity that caused Olivia to wear so many layers of makeup. When she applied Zoe's, our lead actress's, makeup, it never looked heavy-handed. She really did have a gift. Perhaps the reason Olivia was so made up had something to do with her father's digs about her weight—causing her to compensate by hiding behind a mask.

During my heavy Goth eyeliner stage in high school, I'd hoped to distract my peers from focusing on my hearing aids and instead focus on my eyes. Eventually, my father had pulled me aside and given me the same pep talk that I knew my mother would have given if she'd been alive.

"I should stay with him," Olivia repeated. "At least until the ambulance arrives."

"Elle's with your father," I said. "She won't leave until the first responders arrive."

"Who would do such a thing?" There was doubt in her eyes, and for a moment I thought she was accusing me. "I've done the makeup on horror movie sets, but I've never seen a real dead body. Could it have been an accident? Some cruel prank my father's playing?" Knowing the answer, she started crying again.

I got up from the table, went to the farm sink, opened the bottom cupboard, and got out a roll of paper towels. Glancing out the window over the sink, I found the answer to the whereabouts of two people on my mental suspect list—assistant director Nikki Meyers, and Brett's son and Olivia's brother, Matt. Matt's guitar was by his side, per usual, and the pair looked to be in a deep conversation.

The sky had gotten even darker from when I'd first arrived. I'd thought about going out there to tell them about Brett—just so I could gauge the looks on their faces. But time was ticking, and before the cops got a hold of her, I needed to focus on Olivia.

Or did I?

Why was it my job to play detective? Because of Patrick. That was why. If he didn't have a rock-solid alibi and someone squealed about the fight at the lighthouse between Patrick and our director, Patrick could be pulled in for questioning.

No. I wouldn't go there!

I broke off a couple sections of paper toweling, turned, and handed them to Olivia. Then I sat back down at the table.

Olivia wiped her eyes, then blew her nose. Sniffling, she said, "Do you think this means Matt and I will be let go from *Mr. & Mrs. Winslow*?"

"Sorry, I have no idea." What I wanted to say was, *Reality check, your father was just brutally murdered.* But I wasn't one to judge someone else's grief. I'd been known to laugh at funerals and weep at weddings.

"I'll have to live with my mother," she whined "Wherever that might be. We don't get along. Do you think when the press gets ahold of this, it might help my career, instead of killing it?" At the word *killing*, she broke into sobs. "I must call Mother."

"That sounds like a good idea."

"I don't know where my phone is." She sniffled. "Might be outside under the tent."

"Want to use mine?" I didn't want to hear about Olivia's future career or living woes. I wanted to know where she was before she found her father, and if she knew the whereabouts of everyone else before the murder. And more important, if Olivia knew why her father had been in the library in the first place.

"Maybe you should wait for your brother before you call your mother. Where is he, by the way?" *I knew exactly where he was.*

"Oh, Matt's not my biological brother, not even half." The tears stopped, and she looked off in the distance before saying, "He was adopted by my father and father's first wife. After the divorce, Matt's mother took up with some rich sheikh and moved to Dubai. Matt never hears from her. Wow. That's redundant—rich sheikh," she said with a giggle. Then tears welled and her expression turned serious. "At least that's what my father told him. Matt has a different version of the story. He remembers his parents constantly fighting . . . He thinks his father bought off his mother in the divorce so he could have sole custody of Matt—like he was chattel."

"That's awful. I couldn't help but overhear you earlier, wanting to run interference between Matt and your father. It's hard to be in the middle, but it shows you've got Matt's back. I know your father could be a little intense. I'm sure it's not easy. Especially with all three of you working and living together."

I must have hit a nerve. Olivia shifted uncomfortably in her chair, then her green eyes flashed with anger. "I stick up for Matt. Matt sticks up for me. It's what siblings do. Matt wants to be a singer-songwriter. Father won't hear of it. You should hear some of his songs."

"I have heard him. His songwriting is wonderful, and his voice, so mellow and soothing. Not to mention his guitar playing. With all that talent, why couldn't he just walk away? He's an adult. Can't he make his own choices?" I knew the answer to my questions, just from watching the dysfunctional dynamics between Matt and his father. Sometimes, Brett would throw a few jabs Olivia's way, too. But it was obvious that Olivia and Brett had had a closer relationship than Brett and Matt. Was it because Olivia was his blood daughter and carried the Golden genes? Even though it wasn't the right time to think bad of the dead—I wouldn't put it past Brett Golden.

"My father wouldn't let him leave. Like you said, my father's pretty intense." She gulped, "Was intense. What will become of us? I need to see my brother. I want to be the one to tell him." Olivia put her hands on the table, planning to get up. I shot over to her and put my hand on her shoulder, then gently pushed her back. "You're too distraught. How about this. Why don't I go look for Matt and your phone? I won't tell Matt anything. You can give him the news. In the meantime, you can use my phone to call your mother." Before she could protest, I handed her my phone.

She grabbed it, tapped in a number, then put the phone to her ear. After a few seconds, she said, "It's going to voicemail, as usual— Hey, Lisa, it's your daughter. You remember me, right? Anyway, something bad happened to your second husband, my father. Call me on this number when you can." She ended the call and handed me back the phone.

"Told you," she said, frowning. "Doubt she'll call back. On the other hand, she'll probably cheer when she hears the news of my father's demise. No love lost there. Though she has her reasons. Like we all do." Oliva slapped her hand to her mouth, realizing what she'd just said.

"What reasons?" I asked, sitting back down at the table.

Olivia reached for a clean section of paper toweling, dabbed her eyes and cheeks, then handed me back the rainbow-hued, soggy towel. She gulped. "You know how he was—hard to love."

I wasn't surprised by her admission. Suddenly, I felt sorry for her. Her father had been a jerk, and it was obvious Olivia and her mother, who she called by her first name, weren't that close.

She must have seen something in my gaze.

"It doesn't mean I didn't love him. If that's what you're thinking." She waited a beat, then added a little too vehemently, "Of course I did!"

I patted her hand. She pulled it away.

"I'm sure that you loved him. Do you mind me asking one more thing?" Before she said no, I kept going. "How did you manage to end up in the library? Do you have any idea why your father was there?"

At first, I didn't think she heard me. Finally, she said, "I have no idea why he was there. It's where they kept the real brandy. He pretended not to drink in front of *her*. He told me she gave him an ultimatum. Father wasn't big on ultimatums. He probably went to the library to cool off after their whopper of an argument."

"By her, do you mean his fiancée?"

"Fiancée, that's a joke. She belongs in a crypt, not with him."

"What were they fighting about?"

"I don't know how it started, but I know how it ended. Matt and I were in my makeup studio, cleaning up. They were next door in the billiard room. You know the one with all the trophies and that creepy deer or elk head with the sad eyes that hangs over the fireplace."

"Uh-huh."

"We heard them arguing through the walls. We tiptoed into the hallway and listened. Suddenly, the crypt keeper's engagement ring that was bought with my father's hard-earned money came flying out the door. It landed next to me on the hallway floor." She hesitated before saying, "I let it lay there. Then we heard my father threaten that he would go to the tabloids and tell them that the infamous Julie David was drinking and drugging again. Which I'm sure she was."

"How did Ms. David respond?"

Olivia looked toward the copper pot rack above the stove. "I don't know. We left in case they came out into the hallway and saw us. Matt wanted to go in and break it up. For some reason that I can't fathom, he likes the old witch. He's very vulnerable when it comes to people. Good thing I'm here to have his back." She looked around to make sure no one heard her, then whispered, "We went outside and shared a cigarette to celebrate that the old bitty might be out of the picture. Cruella de Vil is always looking at me with those large violet cow eyes of hers. As if she feels sorry for me. Don't need her pity. I have an awesome life—I mean I did." She sniffled, then continued, "After the ciggy, I came inside to console my father. I wanted to tell him that Matt and I support him, and that he'll be better off without the Black Widow. You see," she said, smiling, "I'm the only one who can calm my father down. Me and that big snifter of brandy. That's when I— you know—found him."

"That must have been a shock. I'm so sorry. Matt didn't come with you?"

"No."

"Do you have any idea who might have done this?"

"Isn't it obvious?" she answered, her cheeks pink with anger. "Julie David."

And here I thought from my limited interaction with Olivia that she was sweet as sugar—strychnine might be a better analogy when it came to her father's fiancée.

I decided to cut Olivia a break. If someone had done to my father what they'd done to hers, there would be no holding me back. "How long were you outside? Did you and Matt see any—"

"You're making me sad. I can't believe he's gone. Why are you interrogating me? I hope you don't think I had anything to do with Father's death. That would be heartless." She leaned toward me and scanned my face.

"Whoa, take it easy, Olivia. I just want to help. Maybe there's something you can remember, while it's fresh, to help us—I mean the police—catch his—"

Before I could finish my sentence, Elle came into the kitchen. "They're pulling in the gates now." She looked from me to Olivia. "How's it going?" Although Elle sounded confident and in charge, I could tell she'd been crying. I should have known my kindhearted friend would have a hard time keeping her emotions in check.

"We're waiting for Olivia's mother to call back," I said in an over-the-top, upbeat voice. "Olivia misplaced her phone. I'm leaving mine and going to look for hers in the tent. Maybe you can console Olivia, while I—"

"Look for Matt," Olivia finished.

"And look for Matt," I repeated.

"And don't tell him anything. I will."

"Promise," I said, holding out my pinky finger.

She gave me a dismissive look.

You're welcome, I thought.

"Meg, before you go," Elle said. "Can I talk to you for a minute?"

"Sure," I answered, then followed her into the hallway, then into the dining room.

I waited while she reached into her large tote bag and brought out a burnt piece of paper. "I found this smoldering in the library's fireplace. I even burned my fingers trying to get it out. I think it might be important. I'm going to give it to Arthur when he arrives. You want to look at it?"

Of course I wanted to look at it, but I heard a howl coming from the kitchen. Olivia. "I'll have to look at it later. Stay with Olivia while I go find her phone."

We went back into the kitchen. Elle went to Olivia's side and placed a hand on her shoulder. Like she had with me, Olivia recoiled from Elle's touch.

"Elle's going to stay with you," I said. "You're in good hands. Elle's husband is the lead homicide detective on the East Hampton Town Police."

"He is?" Instead of it being good news, Olivia looked like she had a sudden case of heartburn.

"You can tell Elle anything that might help the police catch you father's killer. She'll be very professional and discreet."

Olivia didn't answer, just shrugged her shoulders. She looked down at my phone resting on her lap. So, she *did* want to hear from her mother.

I left them and went through an archway that opened to the butler's pantry and grabbed someone's oversized black raincoat hanging from a hook. After I put it on, I went back into the kitchen. Elle was sitting next to Olivia. I hoped Olivia would confide in Elle. Later we could compare notes. Judging by the scowl on Olivia's face when I walked back into the kitchen, I didn't think Elle would get too far.

I waved goodbye, opened the door, and stepped outside. I was hoping that Matt and Nikki would still be sitting on the bench. They weren't. Only Matt's guitar. I think it was the first time I'd ever seen him without it. Looking up at the stormy sky, I grabbed the guitar, then placed it under the bench to keep it from getting wet, and took off for the party tent.

Here we go again, I thought, hurrying my pace.

Where, I had no clue.

All I knew was that someone had lost their life by unnatural means, and once again, I was in the thick of it.

Chapter 12

It started to drizzle, and thunder rumbled, reminding me of the time in the lighthouse with Patrick and Brett. Could that have been only two days ago?

Lightning stabbed the gray sky and I stopped in my tracks. My mind went back to the horrific scene inside the library. How could someone do something so brutal to another human being? Having had my own share of stumbling upon dead bodies, I should have known the answer. You never get used to it. Suddenly, I realized that the murder weapon with the concealed blade at its tip could have only been used by someone who knew about its secret.

I took a deep breath of humid salty air and followed the gravel path that led to the topiary garden. As I was winding my way in and out, I saw movement behind a tall yew tree. I crept closer and through an opening in the branches I strained to listen and at the same time read Nikki's lips. I was pretty sure she said something to the effect, "Don't send the documents here. Send them to my Bel Air address. Fax a copy to Montauk Manor, Suite four . . ." When I realized she'd hung up her phone, I ducked out of sight.

I hurried past a large koi pond littered with pale pink water lilies, then continued to the middle of the garden, where Jeremy had placed the party tent.

I'd considered telling our assistant director about Brett's murder, then decided she would find out soon enough.

I was on a mission.

Instead of tables and chairs, Jeremy had brought in rustic-looking picnic tables that he'd topped with a few dollar store votives. You'd think he'd go all out to celebrate the hard work and dedication of *Mr. & Mrs. Winslow*'s cast and crew.

During postproduction of episode two, when our former director was still at the helm, he'd hosted our wrap party at the Michelin-star restaurant Pondfare in Montauk. Thinking of that evening reminded me of how happy Patrick had been. Which in turn reminded me of how unhappy he'd been with our new director.

Our murdered director.

Patrick!

I needed to tell Patrick about Brett. What if he'd changed his mind and planned on coming to Windy Willows? My phone was back with Elle. If I found Olivia's phone, I could use it to call him.

I searched the area under the tables for the phone. Nada. I was about to give up, go back, and call Patrick from my cell, when I spied Julie David exiting the summerhouse on the far side of the cutting garden. Julie turned to someone who was still inside, waved, then started in my direction.

I made a quick decision to return to the main house. By now, the cavalry had arrived. Seeing Julie confirmed that she'd been on the grounds at the time of the murder. That was all I needed to keep her in my crosshairs—or should I say, Southampton's crosshairs. Before I'd talked to Olivia, I couldn't figure out what motive Julie would have to kill her fiancé *before* the wedding. Now that I heard Brett threatened to expose her with faked or factual allegations about her sobriety, I needed to keep her at the top of the list.

Thought you weren't going to make a list, Megan Barrett.

I charged out of the front of the tent, tripped on a stake that wasn't attached to a rope, and fell onto the cold wet gravel, landing in a push-up position. Once on my knees, I realized that I'd taken a serendipitous fall. Two feet in front of me was Olivia's phone. Luckily, like me, the phone had also fallen facedown. I grabbed it. Next to it was an unusual-looking cigarette butt. I knew it was French because my ex-fiancé Michael smoked the same brand. Another reason I was happy we'd parted ways. I recalled Olivia saying she and her brother smoked a *ciggy* when they were in the tent. I stood, pocketed the cell phone, thought about pocketing the cigarette butt for DNA—old habits die hard—reconsidered, then did a quick scan to make sure that all my body parts were intact. They were.

After picking gravel from my bloody knees and wishing I hadn't worn a dress for the party when jeans would have been fine, I stood and glanced around.

To the south, I saw Julie approaching the tent. I limped toward a huge fountain with a statue of Adonis in the center, hid behind it, and waited until she passed. I could tell she'd been crying, making me wonder if Julie already knew that Brett was dead. And if she did, who'd told her?

That was all I needed to change my mind about going back to the mansion. First, I'd check out the summerhouse. The gorgeous glass structure was a mega version of my folly/studio. I knew the summerhouse had been featured in a scene of episode three, where Jack and Lara trick a trio of murdering smugglers into swapping a valise of cash (cut-up paper) for bootlegged crates of hooch. Patrick had told me about the scene. Not because he'd fought with Brett, but because Nikki Meyers had been the one directing the scene. It had gone off without a hitch.

As I got closer to the summerhouse, I saw who I assumed was Julie's chauffeur coming down the steps. The cap in his right hand was a dead giveaway. Cementing his identity was the Rolls I'd seen parked outside the library's window. The same car that dropped Brett and Julie at the broker's open house on Thursday. Brett didn't have a Rolls. He had a domestic rental that production paid for, one he never stopped complaining about.

"Hey," I called out.

The goliath, muscled chauffeur glanced my way. Then, ignoring me, he sauntered away in the opposite direction of the main house.

I followed.

He hurried his pace.

I hurried mine, increasing my speed as much as possible with my sore knees. "Yo, buddy," I called out. "I just want to ask you a question."

I knew he heard me, but he didn't turn to look back. Instead, he broke into a run.

I charged after him, adrenaline wiping away any pain.

At the estate's privet hedges, he stooped through an opening and disappeared from view.

Cautiously, if you could call chasing after a potential killer cautious, I did the same.

Whack! Instead of a human chest, it felt like I'd hit a brick wall.

He bared perfect white teeth and snarled, "I don't know who you are, crazy lady. But you're one second away from getting a bloody nose."

Before I could reassure him that I wasn't a lunatic, he spun me around and pushed me back through the opening in the hedge. I went hurtling through to the other side and fell to my knees for the second time in a space of minutes.

By the time I stood, I knew he was long gone. I wasn't hurt from the fall, more from the "crazy lady" comment, of which he was probably right. I did, however, get a good look at him and would have no problem picking him out in a lineup.

Feeling like I'd just learned a valuable lesson—*mind my own beeswax*—I plodded toward Windy Willows.

Halfway back, the lesson wore off when I remembered I had Olivia's phone. I took it from the raincoat's pocket and glanced down. Her screensaver showed a photo of her and her brother. Even though they weren't blood relatives, they sure looked happy together. Luckily, I didn't need her thumbprint to open the phone. After a few tries, 4321 worked as Olivia's password. Such a simple password meant she didn't have much to hide. I, conversely, had a password even the CIA couldn't decode.

There was only two percent left on the phone's battery. I quickly tapped in Patrick's number. It went to voicemail. Just hearing his voice on the recording grounded me. I said into the phone, "Don't come to Windy Willows. I'll explain later. Oh, it's Meg. I'm using Olivia's—" The phone died, then I stowed it in the pocket of the raincoat that I'd pilfered from the pantry. Just as I did, the drizzle turned into a soft rain. I pulled up the hood just in time for a no-holds-barred downpour from the heavens.

Perhaps the pounding rain was a sign from the universe that I should tell the authorities everything? Minus any mention of Patrick, of course—then let it go.

Only that wasn't possible.

Because when I reached the outside door to Windy Willows' kitchen, opened it, and stepped inside, all hell had broken loose.

Chapter 13

Julie and Olivia were wrestling on the kitchen floor. Olivia had a choke hold on Julie David's neck. Matt appeared to be trying to break it up by pulling Julie away from his sister. At least I'd thought that was his goal.

"Leave me alone," Julie whimpered. She grabbed a section of Olivia's hair at the same time that Olivia grabbed a section of hers. The only difference was that Julie was wearing a wig. A darn good one.

The wig went flying like a Cousin Itt Frisbee, did a somersault, then landed on top of the stove. Olivia released her hold on Julie, then broke into uncontrollable laughter.

Losing her wig seemed to take the hurricane-force wind out of Julie's battered sails. She scooched backward until her spine rested against the vintage Hoosier. Her sparse, short white hair sprung out in all directions. She looked like she'd seen a ghost, or even worse, her fiancé's, or should I say ex-fiancé's corpse. I hadn't a clue that Julie's trademark long, glossy auburn hair wasn't real. *Dave's Hamptons*, the local who's-who magazine, would have a field day if they saw Julie David right now.

Julie slumped forward like a rag doll that had lost its stuffing. After a few seconds, she raised her head and glanced over at Matt and Olivia. "I don't understand, Olivia. Why are you attacking me? Now look what you've done."

Olivia's large eyes got larger. "You vain old woman. You're worried about your wig when my father's dead body was just wheeled out the front door. The same body you stuck with that knife thing."

"Knife thing? What knife thing? I have no clue to what you are talking about. And I'm not worried about my wig. I'm worried about you," Julie said.

Olivia's mouth opened wide. Before she could come up with a retort, Julie said, "Olivia, I heard you, earlier. You were upset that your father refused to bankroll that special effects company he'd promised you. And rightly so. He wasn't big on keeping his promises. I know. He threatened to cut you off if you didn't let it go."

"I don't know what you're talking about," Olivia said, glancing over at me. "You're delusional. Understandable after your infamous nervous breakdowns."

Julie didn't take the bait, just said in a soft, resigned voice that my hearing aids barely picked up, "You didn't see me in the hallway. I've seen the way he treats you since I've been in the Hamptons. I only had an inkling of it when we'd all go out for dinner in LA." She glanced over at Matt. "Both of you. Forcing you to be his personal slaves. Matt, you should be out on your own. You have a beautiful voice. I know how he held you back. Same with you, Olivia. Never giving you credit for all the things you did for him. I hate to tell you, but don't expect a dime from his estate. Because he didn't have one. Found out he hired a private investigator. So, I hired my own."

Matt was speechless. Maybe because he thought what she'd said was true.

"You're a psychopath!" Olivia screeched. "I didn't kill him. And who cares about money? Only you — the Black Widow. Have you been drinking? Drugging? I know *you* killed our father! And I know all about your little spat earlier."

"Then you know that I broke off our engagement. So what motive would I have? Matt, I know you are torn about betraying your sister. But you saw how your father was when I told him I was through. I appreciate that you came to my rescue."

Julie had just refuted Olivia's claim from earlier that she and Matt went out for a cigarette after Brett and Julie's argument. I should have picked up that cigarette butt to get it analyzed for *two* sets of DNA. Lesson learned.

"You're a liar," Olivia screeched. "You're just trying to cover for killing my father by bringing Matt into it."

"I'm not saying he killed your father. I'm saying that Matt saw how angry he was." Julie started a slow crawl toward the stove to retrieve her wig.

I couldn't watch her slither one more inch. I hurried to the stove, took the wig off the front burner, and handed it to her. Julie quickly put it on. Even though it was slightly askew, she looked all the better for it. Then Julie said in a softer tone, "The two of you are one of the reasons that I broke off my engagement. That, and your father's lies about his finances. Along with another reason that I care not to share."

Julie looked over at me and extended her arms in the air, like she was a toddler wanting to get out of her high chair. I had no choice but to help her to her feet. I wasn't choosing sides. But she made such a pathetic figure that for a moment I was on Team Julie.

"I don't believe a word you're saying. Right, Matt?"

Matt didn't answer. I turned to Olivia. "You just told me a little while ago that after the fight you and Matt witnessed in the billiard room between Ms. David and your father, that you and your brother went outside."

Olivia shot me a deadly look. Then she said, "Why are you asking questions, anyway. We did go outside. You must have heard things wrong. You were interrogating me minutes after I found my father's dead body. This is none of your business. Stay out of it."

I put my hands in the air. "Okay. Okay."

Matt stood, then helped Olivia up.

Olivia broke free of her brother's grasp and marched over to Julie. "So, you broke it off with my father, got into another argument, then cut him with the cane and left him to die in the library."

"What are you talking about? How can you cut someone with a cane? Library? I've never been in the library," Julie said. "That's preposterous. You saw him, Matt. You came into that trophy room and defended me. If anything, when I told Brett that the engagement was off, he looked like he wanted to kill *me*. Tell her, Matt." Julie turned to Olivia. "If it wasn't for your brother, Olivia, I fear Brett would have seriously hurt me."

Matt looked flustered. Without his black-rimmed glasses he looked even younger than he was. He blinked a few times, his baby blues pooling with unshed tears as he looked first at Julie, then his sister.

"You're making that up. Matt wasn't with you. He was with me," Oliva said, breaking into sobs.

Julie stretched out her arms to comfort Olivia. Olivia took a step toward her at the same time that a young female Southampton officer stepped into the kitchen.

We would never know if Olivia was moving toward Julie for an embrace — or to punch her in the mouth. I had a hunch it wasn't for a motherly hug.

"Who wanted to hurt you?" the officer asked in a sharp tone. Her commanding voice didn't match her thin frame and delicate bone structure. The name tag on her shirt uniform read *Officer Connie Temple*.

No one answered.

"Let's move it. You three are coming into the dining room to join the others." Then Officer Temple turned her clear hazel cat eyes to me and asked, "Who the heck are you?"

Before I could answer, she said, "Whoever you are, come along. You can join the party." Her long fingers closed around my wrist so tightly that I worried she'd leave marks.

"Hey, slow down. Can't you see that I'm wounded?" I added a little yelp for effect.

"Yes. And why are you in that condition? Never mind. You can tell it to Chief Boyle when he arrives."

"Can I at least take off this raincoat?" I asked her.

She paused before saying, "Put it on a chair. It might have to be tagged for evidence later." As she turned away, I swiped Olivia's phone from the coat's pocket and slipped it into the right pocket of my dress. Spotting my phone on the kitchen table, I walked backward, grabbed it, and stowed it in my left pocket.

Officer Temple and I followed the three out of possibly four (Nikki) murder suspects into the hallway. As I walked, or was dragged, I mentally changed the number of suspects to five, adding Julie's bully of a chauffeur to the mix.

Patrick hadn't crossed my mind.

Or did just saying that he hadn't meant that he had?

A few seconds later, it was like we'd walked into an Agatha Christie mystery.

Julie, Matt, and Olivia sat next to Nikki and Jeremy at the dining room table. The five of them faced Elle and Felicity. When Officer Temple reluctantly let go of my wrist, I took a seat next to Elle.

Elle's homicide detective husband was standing at the head of the long table, playing the role of Hercule Poirot, sans Poirot's mustache. But like Poirot, he was decked out in expensive hand-tailored menswear, and I could smell the spicy scent of his expensive aftershave. He was peering into suspect number four's eyes.

If anyone could get it out of Nikki Meyers, it would be Detective Arthur Shoner. He had a way of being both intimidating and caring at the same time. His only fault, which I'd witnessed in the past, was that when he'd set his sights on his person of interest, he tended to have tunnel vision. Good thing I'd been there in the past to remind him of other possibilities. Not that he appreciated my input, only concentrating on how I was always exposing his wife to dangerous situations. However, in this case, it had been Elle who'd pulled me into working on *Mr. & Mrs. Winslow*.

I'd missed what Arthur had asked but heard what our assistant director (possibly new director?) answered. "I talked to Brett a couple hours ago. Then I took a walk in the gardens." Nikki glanced sideways at Jeremy, who was sitting beside her.

Jeremy winked at her. "Please tell me you reconsidered after I texted you a counter offer. And now that *he* is gone, there won't be any reason not to take the job," he said, hope in his eyes.

Nikki gave him an incredulous look. Her blue eyes were rimmed in red. It was obvious that she'd been crying. "I already told you my answer. My answer is no. I thought I was pretty clear."

"Ms. Meyers, did you see anyone else in the garden?" Arthur asked.

Nikki glanced over at Matt. "I sat with Matt for a while. Other than that, no. How did Mr. Golden die?" she asked.

"A good question, Ms. Meyers," Olivia said matter-of-factly, winding down a tube of lipstick she'd just applied to her lush lips. "We all know you wanted to take over as director. Maybe you hastened things along by murdering my father." It appeared that Olivia was an equal opportunity accuser.

"You've got that one wrong, Olivia," Jeremy said.

"What are you talking about, Mr. Prentice?" Olivia whined. "My father was a wonderful director. He told me you were very happy with him."

Jeremy broke eye contact with her and looked at Nikki. "Sorry, kiddo. Why would Ms. Meyers kill your father to become our director? I'd already called her this morning and offered her the job."

"You did? Why would you do that?" Olivia shrieked. "He had a contract. It included the three of us. He told me himself, right, Matt?"

Matt looked nervously around the table, avoiding Arthur's gaze. "Right," he finally answered.

Her outburst didn't seem to affect Jeremy in the least. He said quietly, "He didn't have a contract. You know that, Olivia. Don't you remember our conversation from earlier in the week?"

"I'm sorry, Mr. Prentice," Olivia said. "I forgot." Olivia knew which side of the bread was buttered if she wanted to stay on set. "Once they catch my father's killer, Matt and I are more than willing to carry on in our same capacities. I'm sure you understand how upsetting this is."

"Of course I do, my dear," Jeremy said, sounding sincere.

Matt opened his mouth a few times. But nothing came out.

"Can you stop playing with that lipstick case," Officer Temple said to Olivia, adding a click of her tongue.

Olivia defiantly started tapping the case harder against the table.

Officer Temple strode to the other side of the table and snatched it out of her hands. I'm glad she did. Because I was ready to reach over and stop her myself, just to keep Olivia from maiming the nineteenth-century lacquered finish.

"Give it back," Olivia said as tears welled.

"Connie. Give her back her lipstick," Arthur demanded.

Officer Temple refused. "Evidence. DNA."

"We'll be taking DNA samples as soon as your chief arrives."

Officer Temple rolled her eyes at Arthur, then tossed the lipstick case onto the table. It bounced, and I winced, but kept my mouth shut. A scratched table was the least of our worries.

"Do you have a problem, Officer Temple?" Arthur asked.

"Of course not," she said, obviously lying because I caught eye roll number two.

As the power struggle between East Hampton Town homicide detective and Southampton PD officer played out, I got kicked in the ankle by Elle. She faced me and whispered, "What in the world happened to you? Are you okay? Blood is dripping down your legs." Then she plucked something out that was tangled in my hair.

I glanced at my reflection in the ornate gilt-framed mirror that hung above the sideboard. Now I had an inkling of why Julie's chauffeur called me "crazy lady." My shoulder-length blonde hair was littered with leaves and twigs. It looked like I'd climbed a barbed-wire fence to escape from a 1930s insane asylum. Like Olivia, trails of mascara stained my cheeks. Only mine were caused by the rain. Hers from grief. I used the back of my hand to get rid of the smudges, wanting to look more credible for when the new

Southampton chief showed up. But I only made it worse. Now I resembled a clone of Michael Keaton's Beetlejuice.

"I'm fine," I said out loud. "Tripped over something." Then I cupped my hand over my mouth and whispered, "The good news is that I found Olivia's phone."

Arthur straightened up. "Ms. Barrett, I'll take that phone."

Darn. My whisper must have sounded louder than I'd thought. When wearing hearing aids, the way my voice sounded in my head when speaking was different than how it came out of my mouth.

"Give it to me! It's mine!" Olivia shouted, reaching across the table for it.

I looked over at Arthur. He nodded his head toward Olivia. I knew from my father that until there was a search warrant, Arthur couldn't legally take the phone.

I went to hand it to Olivia, but Officer Temple reached over my head and grabbed it. "No, Detective, she can't have it. I was told to hand all evidence over to the chief. He's due any minute. In fact, until he arrives, I was told to wait. No one should be questioned. Just a reminder that this isn't your jurisdiction, Detective Shoner."

Elle's cheeks flushed pink and she opened her mouth to defend her husband. I jabbed her in the ribs as a warning not to complicate matters.

"It's my phone. Give it back," Olivia said, giving me a look that would melt ice.

"Hey," I said, "I was giving it back."

"Yeah, sure you were. Where were you when my father was brutally murdered? Someone here did it. And I know for a fact that it wasn't Matt or myself."

I didn't engage. Just because Elle, Felicity, and I had each other as alibis, that didn't mean Southampton PD wouldn't believe there was nepotism involved because of our ties to Arthur and the East Hampton Town PD.

Plus, this wasn't the first time the three of us had to vouch for each other.

Arthur stoically gave Officer Temple a deadpan look, then he retrieved his phone from the inside pocket of his suit jacket and put it to his ear. Without saying a word to Officer Temple, he walked to the library's open French doors and stepped inside.

You couldn't find a more highly decorated and revered homicide detective in the Hamptons than Detective Arthur Shoner. I had a feeling that bossy Officer Temple would be finding that out as soon as her chief arrived.

Chapter 14

As I'd thought, the new chief of the Southampton PD acted more like of a colleague and partner of Arthur's instead of the head of the investigation.

Chief Boyle wasn't too pleased with Officer Temple's attitude toward Arthur, and she was quickly delegated to the task of standing by the gates and turning away the cast, crew, and waitstaff who'd come for the wrap party. Frugal Jeremy had only hired two servers.

Except for law enforcement and crime scene investigators, no one was allowed in or out.

One by one, we were brought into the morning (mourning) room for a quick interrogation by Chief Boyle and Arthur. After our first meeting, I was surprised at how much I liked the new Southampton chief. Of course, it was possible that his down-home friendly nature could have been a Columbo-like ruse to get people to open up. But I believed he was genuine. And he must have had a lot of respect for Arthur, because he let him take the lead on asking the pertinent questions. The most pertinent of which was "Where were you during the hours of four and six?" I knew where Felicity, Elle, and I were, in the dining room—next to the library, where the murder took place. Which made me wonder why we didn't hear Brett call out in pain after he'd been stabbed.

How the crime was committed seemed obvious. It was the who and why that remained the big questions. Arthur had vouched for Elle's and my innocence. Elle and I had vouched for Felicity's. Jeremy had an alibi for Brett's window of death. He was seen on a surveillance tape at the front gate leaving Windy Willows. There was also footage of him returning after his shrimp cocktail run. That left Olivia, Julie, Matt, Nikki, and Carson.

Carson, I kid you not, turned out to be Julie's chauffeur, butler, and manservant. Unlike Carson from *Downton Abbey*, this Carson was huge, muscular, and in his late twenties or early thirties, with nary a gray hair on his head. After I'd squealed to Arthur and Chief Boyle about my earlier encounter with Julie's chauffeur, showing them my skinned knees as if they were a prize from the state fair, Chief Boyle had sent out a search team. Soon after, a Southampton officer found

Carson crouching in the bushes on a side street bordering Windy Willows.

When Carson was led into the dining room, he'd lunged in my direction. The only thing that stopped him was Julie's low, husky voice, "Carson, calm down. Come sit next to me. We've talked about this."

They had? It wasn't hard to figure out what "this" was. The butler/chauffeur had a temper, and I had the wounds to prove it. I'd never admit that I'd fallen twice—once when I tripped on the tent stake and the other when I'd been catapulted through the hedges by Carson. I figured playing the long-suffering martyr might put me in a favorable light with Chief Boyle. Besides, Carson, the incredible hulk, deserved credit for both assaults. The big bully.

During the interminable questioning period at Windy Willows, I kept checking my phone for a message or a phone call from Patrick. Nothing. My calls to him totaled nine, along with a dozen or more texts. I was starting to take it personally.

As my father would say, innocent till proven guilty, so while Julie was being interrogated by Arthur and Chief Boyle, I took out my phone and Googled her. Afraid of what might come up, I hadn't put Patrick's name in the search bar next to Julie's. Owing to her long career in show business, I scrolled through multiple pages relating to thespian Julie David. In the older articles, I found one photo from the 1970s showing a stunning young Julie coming out of a coroner's inquest following the death of husband number two. Death from a heart attack was the judge's ruling. Nothing suspicious to me, seeing that her deceased husband was in his nineties. On further research, I found out that Julie's first husband had been in his late eighties when he'd died. Her subsequent marriages were also to elderly, infirmed men—most not lasting six months. All were super wealthy, so it was easy to see how she'd gotten her nickname. Maybe Julie had a daddy complex?

Brett Golden was in his late forties or early fifties. Why had she gotten engaged to someone without a foot in the grave? Trying to break a bad run? And there was still the question of Patrick, who was much younger than Julie. It was hard to picture Patrick and Julie *sitting in a tree—k-i-s-s-i-n-g*. But then there was the photo on Felicity's phone.

When Julie came back to the dining room, she seemed even more traumatized, frail, and yes, older, than before she'd been questioned. If she wanted a new role to invigorate her acting career, perhaps she could get one starring in a remake of the old black-and-white film *Night of the Living Dead*. Then I glanced again at my reflection in the mirror and realized that we made quite a pair—I could be her understudy.

I saw Olivia turn her head and observe Carson helping Julie into her chair. There wasn't a trace of pity in Olivia's eyes. It seemed certain that when Arthur and Chief Boyle talked to Olivia, she'd squeal about the fight she and Matt had witnessed earlier between Julie and her father. But what about her anger with her father after he told her that he couldn't fund her special effects makeup enterprise?

I made a mental note to tell Arthur what Julie had said during her tussle with Olivia.

After she sat, Julie slumped back in her chair and gazed zombie-like in my direction. I got up and went over to the Southampton officer standing guard next to the door to the hallway. "Is it okay if I get Ms. David a glass of water?" I asked in a whisper.

He looked over at Julie and nodded his head that it was okay.

"Why is everyone doting on the old has-been from the silent movies?" Olivia spat. "Matt and I are the ones who lost our father. He was just another patsy for one of her murder schemes." Olivia broke into sobs and Matt pulled her to him.

Not worried about Olivia's wrath, I got up and walked to the open doorway leading into the hall. When I entered the kitchen, a forensics team dressed in white jumpsuits and booties were taking photos. I asked for a glass of water, pointing to the cupboard where I knew the glasses were. One of the crime scene investigators, wearing gloves, removed a glass from the cupboard and filled it with tap water. As she handed it to me, she said, "You want someone to patch up your knees?"

"The bleeding's stopped. I think I'll live," I said, adding a nervous giggle.

She shrugged her shoulders. "You've got your water. You better get back into the dining room with the rest of them."

Yes, the rest of them, I thought, wanting to profess my innocence. But I kept my mouth shut and went back into the dining room.

All the usual and unusual suspects were sitting at the table, including Elle, Felicity, and Jeremy. The question-and-answer period must be over. I walked over to Julie, placed my hand on her shoulder, and she jumped, almost causing me to drop the glass. Carson shot up, grabbed the glass from my hands, and took a sip. Then he placed the glass in front of his boss. "I'll get Ms. David anything she needs from now on. You stay away, crazy lady."

Julie looked apologetically at me but seemed too weak to say anything more.

It was obvious that Carson was more than Julie's chauffeur or majordomo. He was more of a bodyguard.

Which begged the question, why did Julie need a bodyguard?

Chapter 15

At the end of the day, I assumed the authorities' suspect list had been narrowed down to five: Julie, Olivia, Matt, Nikki, and Carson. Elle and Felicity had been the last ones to be interviewed by Arthur and Chief Boyle. Chief Boyle told Olivia and Matt that they weren't allowed to stay at Windy Willows. Ironically, Julie had offered to share her suite with them at the East End Yacht Club. I assumed Carson, who I'd decided should be renamed Lurch, the butler from *The Addams Family*, due to his size and the way he grunted one-word answers when questioned by anyone besides Julie, was also staying at the yacht club. Felicity and Nikki had rooms at Montauk Manor with the rest of the cast and crew, except for the show's main stars, Zoe and Dillion. They'd each rented their own beachfront homes in nearby East Hampton.

Patrick had been the only one ever invited to Jeremy's home. Jeremy owned an oceanfront estate in Bridgehampton with enough rooms to house the whole cast and crew. Patrick had told me that Jeremy had spared no expense, saying that the property and main house were something out of *Architectural Digest*. Who would have thought that our scrooge of a producer lived so lavishly? Certainly not me.

Just by hanging out with everyone at the dining room table for hours, you would think I'd get a glimpse into their personalities. I hadn't. Julie was the only one who I was starting to change my mind about. There was something about her that was vulnerable and almost endearing. And I couldn't get it out of my head how despondent she'd looked sitting on the kitchen floor without her wig. I had a sense that she'd been beaten down one too many times, and perhaps, with this last blow, she might stay down for the count.

Around eight, Arthur told Elle to go home. Then he'd called me into the foyer and asked if I'd show him where Brett's rooms were.

I'd never been on Windy Willow's third floor but that didn't stop me from pretending that I had.

I led the way up two winding *Gone with the Wind* staircases. As we walked down the long hallway, I played a game of *Let's Make a Deal*, trying to guess which door belonged to Brett. Door number one opened to Olivia's room. I knew it was hers, mostly from all the makeup scattered around the room. Door number two belonged to Matt. I knew it was his room by the crumpled pieces of paper on the floor by a small trash can. When Matt wasn't playing guitar or singing, he would be writing down song lyrics.

Based on the adjoining door I saw in Matt's room, I walked to door number three and took a stab that Brett's room would be next. Having a connecting door with Matt would allow Brett to have access to his indentured-servant son 24/7.

"Are you sure you know which room is Mr. Golden's?" Arthur asked from behind, frustration obvious in his tone.

"I thought you'd want to see where his kids are staying. Or should I say two of our suspects."

"*Our* suspects?" he said.

I opened the door, and *Bingo*, I'd been right. It was Brett's.

I took a step inside and Arthur pulled me back. "Oh, no, you don't. You can stay in the hallway. Or go home. Your choice."

He knew which choice I would pick. Even though heading home was tempting. *Home.* A warm fire, my cozy cottage, a cup of tea. I nixed the scenario of me coming back to Brett's room and replaced it with the vision of Patrick holding me in his loving arms. *Think positive, Meg. Be happy that Patrick wasn't here today. Also, be happy that Elle's hubby* is *here.*

Arthur pulled on a pair of gloves, then put hospital booties over his Gucci loafers. I watched him methodically canvass the room without touching or moving a thing. A true professional. I didn't have his willpower, which for the moment had me trying to figure out how I could get back into the room. Alone. Old habits.

"Yo, Arthur," I called from the open doorway. "What's on that receipt you just took a photo of?"

He turned toward me. "For the sake of this investigation, you better call me Detective Shoner. And you know I can't tell you what was on the jewelry receipt." I thought he'd slipped by adding the word *jewelry.* Then I noticed a mischievous glint in his eyes. He was passing me some intel. Finally trusting me and my observations. It had only taken us six shared murder investigations.

"Yes, Detective Shoner."

He took a few more photos, put his phone back in his breast

pocket, then said, "Okay, let's go. I'll have Marcus . . . Chief Boyle, send up his team. You can go home now. Unless there's anything else you want to share?"

I'd already told him about the raucous WWE match in Windy Willow's kitchen and the accusations between Olivia and Julie. And of course my run-in with Julie's Carson, but I'd forgotten to tell him about what Olivia had shared about the argument she and her brother overheard between her father and Julie David. I was sure that Olivia had already told Arthur about it earlier. But I believed my version might be more impartial — sixty degrees of separation and all that. When I got to the part about Julie throwing her engagement ring at Brett, I saw Arthur's eyes light up.

"I already know all about the argument. Ms. Golden told me. But she didn't tell me about the ring. Anything else?"

"Julie said that Matt came in and saved Julie from his father. I bet Olivia, Ms. Golden, didn't tell you that."

Arthur opened his eyes wide.

I was enjoying this newfound comradery. "Hours before the murder, when Julie passed through the dining room looking for Brett, I'd noticed her huge engagement ring. It was so big that I was surprised she could lift her hand. It had to weigh in excess of six carats. Oh, wait, did anyone find the ring? It wasn't on Julie's hand when I followed behind — I mean was dragged by Officer Temple into the dining room. And Olivia said she'd left it in the hallway after Julie threw it at Brett."

He laughed. "Slow down. Take a breath. I want to find out who did this. I especially need to know if my wife is safe around these people."

"So, you *do* think it's one of the five."

"Too early to be sure. But I know Chief Boyle does. I suppose someone could have been hiding out on the property somewhere."

"Wouldn't they be caught on camera at the gate?"

"You're forgetting about when you chased Mr. Smelts into the bushes. It could be done."

"That's his last name? Carson Smelts."

"Yes. Let's get on with it. I want to see my wife before she goes to sleep."

"Oh, don't worry, I know Elle. She'll be waiting up. Just one more question. Promise. Was that photo you just took a receipt for the engagement ring? You don't have to show me the photo. Just curious about how much Brett paid for it."

Arthur stepped out of Brett's room. He raised a thick furry eyebrow and gave me "the look." I'd thought Elle had patented "the look," but Arthur, and even Patrick, always did a great job of cloning it.

"A teensy hint? Pretty please. Fifty k? A hundred k? Am I close?"

"Not even in the ballpark," he answered. Arthur had just admitted that the receipt was for a ring.

"Higher? Lower?"

He glanced down at the Persian carpet.

"Thirty k? Ten k?"

At ten k, he immediately raised his eyes. *Ka-Ching!*

"So, Brett bought Julie a lab-grown diamond. As you well know, Detective, because I helped you shop for Elle's vintage engagement ring, if this engagement ring had been a mined diamond, or blood diamond, as some call it, it would have cost around a hundred thou. The ring might explain why Julie called Brett a big phony."

Arthur raised his other eyebrow. He sure knew how to work them. "You never mentioned that."

Seeing that Arthur seemed open to sharing, I figured I'd be totally transparent. That way I could let it go. I filled him in on the parade of people who'd passed us in the dining room prior to Brett's murder. I also told him about why each person had been looking for the other. Then, I continued to spew a quick analysis of what each person's motive could be. And miracle of miracles, he didn't stop me. "Julie David—Brett was going to tell the tabloids she was drinking and using drugs, or he lied about his finances. Carson—to protect his boss. Matt and Olivia because of the way Brett treated them like chattel *or* for his inheritance. Or Matt because his father wouldn't let him live his dream of being a musician. And Olivia because her father wouldn't bankroll her special effects company."

"Special effects company?" Arthur asked. I filled him in on what Julie had said in the kitchen. "Then there's assistant director Nikki Meyers because she wanted to be director, or maybe she was blackmailing Brett or having an affair with him? Hard to believe—that last one. Ick. Actually, to kill him in order to take over as director doesn't make sense. Because Nikki was offered the job way before Brett was killed. It's also possible that Brett made sleazy advances at Nikki and she had to fight him off. Like what he'd done to Elle."

"Say what! He'd better not have touched my wife," Arthur said, making fists and directing his dark angry eyes at me.

I wished I hadn't opened my big mouth. I had a feeling I'd blown my chance of having Arthur see me as a comrade in the crime-solving business. I took a step backward. "No. Brett didn't touch Elle. I promise you. If he did, I would have kicked him where it hurt. Trust me. So, what do you think? Whodunnit?" I asked, trying to change the subject from his wife to Brett's murder. "Did Elle manage to give you the paper she rescued from the library's fireplace. You probably don't want to hear this, but Elle has been amazing during this murder investigation."

"*This* murder investigation!"

Oops.

"Are you kidding me!" he shouted. "My wife needs to stay totally out of it. And, no, Elle didn't give me any paper. So, do you really want to hear what I think, Ms. Barrett?" Arthur said, eyes blazing. He stepped so close to me that I could smell his Tic-Tac minty breath. "I think it's way too early to do much of anything but gather evidence and interview people. Tell me again about the weapon. Is it true you bought it as a prop? That was quite a prop. Aren't they supposed to use rubber blades or something less lethal? Is there an armorer on the set? What if the dead guy had used it against Elle?"

Let the dance begin, I thought. Arthur had always been protective where Elle was concerned, but this was over-the-top. Even for him. Well, maybe not.

"Calm down," I said, waiting for steam to come out of his large ears. "Yes, I bought the walking stick. Your wife was with me when I did. And I watched the scene it was used in. No one even came close to getting hurt."

He stepped into me until we were nose to nose. I was five-foot-seven. Arthur was five-foot-six. "You're asking the wrong person about an armorer," I said. "Ask our producer, Jeremy Prentice."

"Oh, I will," he growled, then took off down the long hallway.

I followed behind him.

"Hey, wait. I have a hunch."

Halfway down the second staircase, he turned around. He knew because of my hearing loss that I would hear him better if he faced me. "I don't have time for hunches. I need to stay here for another hour. At least. I want to get home to my wife and ask her about this guy—our victim—and the paper she didn't give me. That reminds me. Where's Patrick? Isn't he the screenwriter?"

"Uh-h. Yes," I said, stopping at the top of the third-floor staircase. "But the wrap party wasn't supposed to start till seven. No doubt he was turned away at the gate." I prayed that what I said about Patrick was true. "Can you please humor me?"

"It seems all I do is humor you, Ms. Barrett."

"And how has that turned out for you in the past?" I asked, getting tired of the sparring. I knew he was doing his job, and I knew he was Elle's husband. Sometimes we just couldn't help but revert back to the first time I'd gotten involved in one of his cases. When I had to fight him every step of the way to prove he was wrong about a certain murder suspect who I knew was innocent.

"I just want you to check on something in Olivia's room," I said. "I promise I won't go inside."

He didn't answer, just moaned as he trudged back up the steps to door number one. "Olivia told me that when Julie threw the engagement ring into the hallway, she left it there. It might be nice to see if she'd been lying. You and I know what the real price of that ring was. But I bet Olivia had no clue it was a lab diamond."

"And what would that prove?" Arthur asked.

"That she's lying," I said simply.

This time, when he entered Olivia's room, he closed the door behind him. A few minutes later, he came out holding a can of Pepsi. As he walked toward me, my hearing aids picked up a loud rattling from inside the can.

"How'd you know?" I asked, looking at the can.

"Was once on a drug case. Found tons of cash stashed inside weighted soda and vegetable cans." He held the can to my right ear and rattled it. "You can buy them on eBay."

"So, I was right. Olivia did take the ring."

"Yes. Ms.—Meg, you were correct. Sorry about being so hard on you. This case just hits a little too close to home." He gave me a sheepish grin.

"I understand," I said. "Elle's as precious as a real diamond to you. And to me, for that matter."

A few minutes later, I exited the mansion. If not for the fact that we would soon be filming episode four, I would've liked to take off for at least a month. Maybe go to Detroit and see what's going on with my father and Sheila. Bring Patrick with me? Even a staycation would be nice. But I knew Jeremy would never allow a hiatus. Especially if it turned out that Nikki hadn't murdered Brett and was available to fill the slot of *Mr. & Mrs. Winslow*'s new director.

In the past, I always felt a thrill working on the set. I sure hoped that would be the case after they arrested whoever killed Brett Golden. What if they never found out whodunnit? My father liked to repeat a depressing statistic that forty percent of murders go unsolved. With that thought, combined with the murder scene, I doubted that I'd ever fall asleep tonight.

There was a definite chill in the air as I walked toward my car. Floodlights switched on as I got closer to my Wagoneer. At first, I'd felt comforted by the light, then I saw something glistening on the hood of my car. I took baby steps toward it.

Someone had left a gigantic, slimy-looking dead koi on the hood of my car as a parting gift.

I'm sure at one time the fish had been a beautiful tangerine color, now it had a gooey, milky film covering its entire body and eyes. It had to be three feet long. When it was alive it could have swallowed my arm.

Why did I think this had something to do with Julie's Carson? I couldn't imagine anyone else with enough guts to pick up the diseased-looking thing. No note was attached, but I got the message loud and clear. I'd been asking too many questions. Why didn't they put the gross thing on Arthur's Lexus or Chief Boyle's SUV? Why mine?

In Japanese culture, koi, part of the carp family, symbolized friendship, love, courage, and strength. In this case, did that mean that a dead koi symbolized the opposite?

The old Meg would have taken a tree branch and brushed the poor creature to the ground and taken off. The new, transparent Meg went inside and brought out both Arthur and a forensics tech to document the disgusting scene.

Just one more thing to share with Patrick.
Boy, did I have a lot to tell him . . .

Chapter 16

I didn't step into my cottage until ten. Jo was waiting in the dark, her golden eye glowing like a crystal ball. There was no need to find out what my immediate future held when it came to Jo. Because I knew it would entail feeding her a can of stinky sardines to make up for leaving her alone for so long.

After Jo was satiated—scratch that, she was never satiated—I stepped out to my deck that overlooked the Atlantic. The clouds were gone and the moon was out. I took in the cool, salty air, then exhaled slowly. For the moment, I soaked in the view and put what had happened at Windy Willows away on a shelf in my brain. I'd bring it down later when I felt centered enough to analyze things. It was a trick my mother had taught me when I was young. When something bad happened, she'd say, "Put it on the shelf, darling. We'll look later. Together." After she'd passed away, I'd put her death on a shelf for almost a year. Not wanting to believe she was truly gone. It was my father who'd helped me bring it down and deal with the pain. With that thought, I wondered how much weight Patrick had on his shelf.

Speaking, or thinking, of Patrick, I grabbed a flashlight, then gingerly walked down the steps to the beach. My knees throbbed with pain, but I was a woman with only one destination in mind. I was still wearing my dress and the stiff ocean breeze produced goose bumps on my bare arms and legs. At least I thought the goose bumps were from the wind. More likely, I was just nervous about telling Patrick about the wrap party that wasn't—the only thing wrapped had been Brett Golden's corpse as they bagged him for a ride to the morgue.

I walked as fast as possible, following the shoreline to Patrick's. When I got there, I craned my neck and saw that his cottage was dark. Instead of charging up his steps, I made a decision that I thought was wise at the time—to let him have a night of peace before he heard what had happened at Windy Willows.

Essentially, I chickened out.

Shivering, I looked up at the chubby-cheeked smiling moon. Taking the moon's happy countenance as a sign, I searched for a piece of driftwood on Patrick's beach. After I found one, I wracked my addled brain for the proper verse to pen in the sand. One that Patrick would see when he took Charlie out for her morning walk. By the time I came up with one, my teeth were chattering, and my skinned knees were pulsing with their own individual heartbeats from the stinging salt spray.

This Sea that bares her bosom to the moon
The winds that will be howling at all hours
And are up-gathered now like sleeping flowers
For this, for everything, we are out of tune.

Lately, *we are out of tune* seemed applicable to Patrick and me. I knew there was no need for me to list the poet—Patrick knew his Wordsworth.

As I turned to go back to my cottage, I had a change of heart. I swiped my foot across the sand, erasing the melancholy stanza, and thought of something more uplifting, but still apropos, by William James, the American father of psychology.

We are like islands in the sea,
Separate on the surface
But connected in the deep.
                    W.J.

Later, when I reached my deck, instead of going inside I went into my walled garden and slipped through the opening at the rear, then took the overgrown path to my glass folly/design studio.

Once inside, I turned on the overhead crystal chandelier that Patrick had helped me install, then switched on the space heater by the scarred drafting table that I'd rescued from a Dumpster. A little sanding and a lot of soft paste wax was all it took to make the drafting table my go-to desk when working on design plans for my Cottages by the Sea clients.

The folly's old rippled panes of glass caught the chandelier's prisms of light, then reflected down on me. They warmed me in their glow and made me appreciate that at long last I was home. I reached for an empty pad of design paper, preparing to write down everything that I'd learned from my *long, long,* did I say *long* day and night at Windy Willows. With pen in hand, I said out loud, "What the heck are you doing, Megan Elizabeth? Go to bed."

Someone rapped on the glass door. *Patrick?* I hurried to the door and opened it. "Claire! What are you doing out so late?"

She laughed. "A better question is, do you always talk to yourself? And, what are *you* doing out so late? More important, why do you look like that?"

"Oh, that."

"Yes, that."

My next-door neighbor was the same age my mother would have been if she was alive. And looking at her now in the soft lighting, I imagined that she was my mother. I ran to her, and she took me into her arms.

"There, there. It can't be that bad."

"Yes, it can," I mumbled into her comforting shoulder.

Claire waited until I was quiet before gently pushing me away so she could look at me. She swept aside my long bangs and said, "Tell Auntie Claire about it. Does it have anything to do with Patrick?"

First, I shook my head no. Then, I shook my head yes. "I don't know."

Claire reached into the pocket of her long skirt and withdrew a tissue, then handed it to me. Claire always wore long skirts. Once, she'd been an ingénue ballet dancer for the San Francisco Ballet. Just three months into her career, she'd gotten into a terrible motorcycle accident and burned her right leg. Her dancing career ended, and her poetry career began. Now, she was one of the top poet laureates in the country.

I gave her a quick recap of what had happened at Windy Willows.

"Oh, Meg, not another one."

I cut her off, "Have you seen or talked to Patrick? He's not answering my phone calls or texts."

"I talked to him early this morning. I had something important to tell him. So, I walked via the shoreline to his cottage and caught him and Charlie playing Frisbee on the beach."

"Wait. Important? You're not sick or anything?"

Claire shook her head. "No, nothing like that. But it can wait. We can talk about it tomorrow. You need a hot shower to clean those nasty-looking knees. You have antibiotic ointment? I have some, if you don't."

"You're waffling, Claire," I said in a stern tone. "I'm not a delicate flower. I can handle your news — good or bad."

"I'm moving back to California for a little while," she said. "For at least six months."

I had the urge to cry, but kept my emotions in check, then mumbled, "Why?"

"My daughter is having a baby. They've been trying for years. It's truly a miracle. She's on bed rest because of her long history of miscarriages. I'm going to move in and help."

"Of course, you have to go."

"I knew you'd understand."

"That's wonderful. When are you leaving?"

"In three weeks. I'll need you to take care of the place. I've even thought of renting it out for the season. Maybe while I'm gone, Cottages by the Sea, I mean you, can work on switching up one of the guest bedrooms into a child's room. I can't believe, at long last, I'll be a grandma."

"Of course I would do that. My pleasure. And congrats again."

Claire smiled. "Come over tomorrow. We'll choose which room. I'm going to miss you."

Maybe it was the long day, or maybe it had something to do with Patrick, but I wanted to shout, *You can't leave me.* Then I realized I was the one being the baby.

"Good thing you have Patrick," Claire said, heading toward the door.

Did I?

"I'm going home to bed, like you should," she said. "Everything will wait until the morning. As someone great once said, 'Don't be pushed by your problems. Be led by your dreams.'"

"Did you pen that?" I asked.

"No. Ralph Waldo Emerson," she said, laughing, "You should have guessed. He was this month's poet." Then Claire advanced toward the door, turned, blew me a kiss, and walked out the door.

Patrick, Claire, and I were members of the Dead Poets Society Club. Once a month, over fabulous meals and good wine, we would meet with other classical poetry lovers and talk about our chosen poet. Claire was the ringleader of our meetings. Our future meetings just wouldn't be the same without her. *What if she didn't come back?* I was used to walking over to her cottage, Little Grey, to listen to her sage advice about my love life over a cup of dark roast in her French press, along with one of her delicious scones with clotted cream. Didn't the task of fixing up a child's room mean that she definitely planned on returning to Long Island?

After Claire left my studio, I looked down at the blank notebook in front of me. She was right, I needed to take a shower and get in bed. Tomorrow I would have Patrick to talk to.

As I switched off the space heater, my phone rang. Once again, my heart pitter-pattered that it might be Patrick.

It was Elle.

"OMG, are you okay? Arthur told me about the dead fish on your car. I gave him the paper I'd rescued from the fire. He bagged it and said he'd turn it over to forensics tomorrow. Thought he'd be happy with my sleuthing. Instead, he grilled me about Brett Golden like I was in the interrogation room at the station. What did you say about Brett? He thinks I was attacked."

"Slow down, you're coming through on my hearing aids. I never said you were attacked — per se."

"Per se!"

Her response had come through loud and clear. Making my ears ring. "Sorry, buddy. It slipped out. Arthur seems more overprotective about you than usual. Anything I should know about?"

Elle hesitated, then said, "So, who do you think killed our director? Did you start one of your murder boards? I think the obvious person is Julie David. Maybe too obvious? Have you told Patrick, yet? Your father?"

Ignoring her last two inquiries, like she had mine, I told her about Claire leaving for California. Glancing again at the blank pad of paper, I said, "I'm really not in the mood tonight to go over it all."

Elle sounded disappointed. "You sound how I usually do after one of these, uh, murders."

"Long day and night."

"That's for sure," she said. "I assume we won't be going back to Windy Willows anytime soon. Even though Jeremy was pushing Arthur to give him a date when we could start setting up for episode four. Block Island will be our main location, but naturally, there will be the opening and closing scenes at Windy Willows."

"Let's worry about all that later," I said. "I don't plan on going back there tomorrow or even Sunday. Speaking of Sunday, Alice left a message on my phone that she has an appointment to sign the papers for the Halstead property. She wants us to be there. She said to bring your pickup."

"Great!" Elle said. "That will keep our minds on something besides what happened. Arthur will be pleased. Between you and me, he said that I'm not allowed back at Windy Willows until they snare whoever killed Brett. You'd be proud of me, I didn't protest and behaved like a good little wife. So, I will have to live vicariously through you."

"Oh, no," I said. "I don't want to be involved. At least not until I talk it over with Patrick. I've gotta go. Need a shower. Desperately."

"I'm sorry," she said. "How are your knees?"

"I'll live." My statement made me think about Brett Golden. Would he be missed? Or had someone who he thought loved him killed him?

I heard Elle say something to Arthur, then she said into the phone, "My surrogate father just told me I need to go to bed." She laughed, then said, "Love you. Talk to you in the morning."

"Love you back."

I flipped the switch for the chandelier, hurried to the folly's door, opened it, and stepped into the darkness. Mr. Man-in-the-Moon was hiding behind a cloud. I felt vulnerable. I thought I saw an azalea bush rustle. There wasn't a breeze. My thoughts flew to the disgusting koi that was left on the hood of my car. Turning on my phone's flashlight, I searched the foliage. Suddenly, something flew by my feet. I caught a flash of white—Peter Cottontail's tail. My shoulders relaxed.

Just to be on the safe side, instead of going through my walled garden to get to my cottage, I took the gravel driveway to the kitchen door, opened it, and flew inside, almost tripping on Her Fatness. It was then that it hit me. Why did I think the koi had been left by Julie's miffed chauffeur-bodyguard? Whoever killed Brett might be saying keep your mouth shut or you're next, Meg Barrett. I dead-bolted the door.

"Don't give me that look," I said to Jo when I turned around. "Kitchen is closed."

In case Patrick came by, I left all the downstairs lights on so he'd think I was awake, then I trudged upstairs. Jo waddled up the stairs behind me, voicing a meow for each step she climbed that led her farther and farther away from her food bowl.

I took a quick shower. I'd be lying if I said that the whole five minutes I was under the large daisy-head shower spout that a certain scene from the movie *Psycho* hadn't crossed my mind. After my shower, I brushed my teeth, slipped on a pair of flannel pj's, and put my phone on vibrate, then stuck it under my pillow. Just in case Patrick called.

Jo was already on the man side of my bed. I turned back the eiderdown comforter and got under the sheets. If ever there was a long day, this would be it. I wasn't feeling sorry for myself — after all, someone had lost their life. I believed the killer had to be someone who'd been at the estate. Brett didn't have a warm and cozy personality, and I'm sure he had enemies. As far as I knew, before being hired as director, he'd never been to the Hamptons. He sure didn't have much of a relationship with the cast and crew. Nikki Meyers and Brett's son Matt took care of all the menial director tasks. As for our leads, Zoe and Dillion, I can't see them risking their careers by murdering their director. They were in high demand in the industry. If things fell through on *Mr. & Mrs. Winslow*, they would just move on to their next project.

I reached for Jo.

Jo turned her back to me and moved farther away.

I caressed the thick silky fur near her tail.

She hissed.

"Love you, buddy."

Jo turned and faced me.

It could have been my imagination, but it was as if she'd understood what I'd just said. Maybe because she knew I meant it.

As I drifted off to sleep, her stinky sardine breath was as comforting as the soft down duvet that covered me.

Chapter 17

My first stop Saturday morning was Patrick's beach. All I found was the tide lapping at the verse I'd written the night before. *Normally*, as my pen pal in the sand, Patrick would write corresponding lines of poetry above mine. But things since the lighthouse hadn't been normal. Far from it.

I wasn't a walking encyclopedia of poetry like Patrick, but I kept a journal of my favorite verses. For obvious reasons, since being in a relationship with Patrick, I'd gravitated toward those written by Keats and the other Romantics.

Before going up to his cottage to tell him about Brett, I turned my gaze to the calm sea and sent out a prayer of healing for Brett's family. The old adage *Life is short* came to mind.

The sun crowning the blue-green Atlantic, the same color as Patrick's changeable eyes, gave me a sliver of hope that things would work out where our relationship was concerned. I turned and headed for his steps, climbed them, then immediately went to his front window and peered inside.

Everything was dark.

Charlie must have heard me. She pressed her long greyhound nose to the window and let out a few "Hello" barks. I laughed in relief. Surely, if something had happened to Patrick, Charlie's barks would have been more like Lassie's when Timmy fell down the well.

"Go rouse your lazy owner," I shouted through the window. When Patrick didn't materialize, I banged on the door in frustration, then jiggled the handle. Charlie cocked her head and looked at me like I was nuts. Maybe I was. The locked door echoed the fact that Patrick had a key to my cottage but I didn't have one to his. Something to ponder later, when things were on a more even keel.

Then worry set in. It wasn't like Patrick to go out this early and leave his faithful companion behind. *And why hadn't he answered my texts and phone calls?*

I checked the back of the cottage and saw that Patrick's Range Rover was missing. That answered why he hadn't come to the door.

Before leaving, I tapped on the glass and promised Charlie that I'd find her wayward master and bring him home. I envisioned Patrick whipping up one of his fabulous breakfasts—if I was lucky, smoked salmon eggs Benedict. Afterward I pictured us walking hand in hand along the shoreline with Charlie prancing behind us. Taking it further —my phone would ring, and Arthur would tell me that Brett's killer had been apprehended and Julie David was on a red-eye to the West Coast. Either that or she was in a locked cell. Case closed.

A girl could dream.

After leaving Patrick's, I walked the beach, contemplating my next move, ending up at my favorite spot under a cliff, where I took a time-out from thinking about the murder by sitting on my favorite boulder. Patrick had nicknamed it my mermaids throne. I watched the sky get brighter over the Atlantic, promising a gorgeous spring day. A scruffy-looking gull landed on the boulder next to mine and gave me a dead-eye stare. Kind of like my obnoxious feline's when she was hungry. As the gull's mouth opened and closed, I was glad I couldn't hear its shrieks over the sound of the pounding surf and the wind whistling in and out of my hearing aids. At the thought of shrieks, I remembered Olivia's when she'd been inconsolable and draped over her father's stabbed corpse.

The curative seaside spell was lost.

I waved goodbye to the gull, then trekked in the direction of my cottage. As I walked, I formulated a plan to take my car into town and check some of Patrick's favorite morning spots. His whole incommunicado charade was getting old, but I needed to tell him about our director before he heard it on the news.

Once I got home, Jo was waiting inside the cottage's French doors. And she didn't look happy. There was something comforting about seeing her—it was almost as if I could forget what had happened and dive into the everyday routine of Jo's and my relationship. She headbutted my shin. I'd left before feeding her—a definite no-no in her book, but when I'd left for the beach, she'd been snoring.

"You snooze, you lose," I said, pointing a finger at her.

Ignoring her menacing gaze, I went to the kitchen counter and put a K-Cup of French roast into my snazzy coffee maker, then pressed the On button. My high-tech coffee maker was a gift from my father. For some reason, my gourmet foodie father wasn't a fan of microwaved instant coffee. Go figure.

As I prepared Jo's breakfast, we discussed the merits of mixing dry cat food with wet. "Think of the money we would save," I said, placing her dish in front of her. Jo then commenced with making a theatrical show of spitting dry kibble onto my hardwood floor. Her point was clear — the idea sucked.

Instead of cleaning up the dry food scattered on the floor, I left it. I knew when I returned home the floor would be as clean as if I'd gotten down on my hands and knees and scrubbed it with a toothbrush.

I filled my Yeti cup with French roast, grabbed my handbag off the bamboo coat rack by the back door, and went in search of Patrick.

Three minutes later, I pulled onto Main Street.

Montauk was quiet. Which was expected at seven a.m. in the off-season.

The shops surrounding the village green were small and unpretentious, carrying anything one would want for a fun vacation. Sixty percent of the stores were closed until Memorial Day.

Main Street housed a few breakfast places, including my favorite, Paddy's Pancake House, which had the best eggs Benedict (except for Patrick's) and ham and cheese crepes. There was a toy shop where kids could buy hermit crabs in small mesh cages, sparklers, firecrackers, and smoke bombs for the Fourth of July; ice cream shops; four or five surf shops; clothing stores; Michelin-star and down-home restaurants; Green's Department Store, which had a full-service pharmacy; and gift shops, including the Seashell Hut, whose ninety-year-old proprietor once came to my rescue when I'd been chased down the beach by a crazed killer — another story to tell at another time.

I pulled next to Blissful Bites Bakery on Edgemere, idled the car, and lowered my driver's side window in order to inhale the scent of fresh-brewed coffee and yeasty bread escaping from the open doorway. There were only two people inside. Both women. No Patrick.

As if I was on neighborhood watch, or more realistically, an obsessed girlfriend stalking her beau, I made a few slow laps through town.

It wasn't Monday, so I doubted he would be at Paddy's, but I took a chance, anyway. Mondays were reserved for Patrick's and my standing appointment with my surrogate uncle, my father's best friend, and former Detroit PD coroner, Doc. I parked in front of the restaurant, something I could never do during the summer tourist season, and went inside. All I found were the usual plaid-shirted fishermen and women—filling their bellies with a hot breakfast and their thermoses with hot coffee. I asked Rose if she'd seen Patrick. She hadn't.

After leaving Paddy's, I headed for the harbor side of Montauk. I passed Hooked, the bait and tackle shop in front of the marina. Two men were inside, but neither was as tall as Patrick. My next stop was Mickey's Chowder Shack. Mickey's opened at six a.m. in order to cater to the hardworking Long Island fishing crews whose commercial boats were docked nearby. Mickey's was known for their prepared boxed lunches that rivaled those of a top-rated Hamptons eatery. Each boxed lunch came with Mickey's famous shrimp fritters. Mickey's allowed dogs, so I had little hope that Patrick would go inside without Charlie.

Turned out I was right. When I turned into Mickey's parking lot, Patrick's Range Rover was nowhere to be seen.

Disappointed, I headed back to town. Like a homing pigeon to its roost, I ended up at my favorite refuge—The Old Man and the Sea Books.

Earlier, I'd texted the proprietress, Georgia, an SOS. And just like she'd done many times in the past, Georgia had offered me a port in the storm. A safe place to unravel my doomsday what-if thinking.

Chapter 18

Once inside The Old Man and the Sea Books, I slunk into the wing chair next to Georgia's and filled her in on what had gone down at Windy Willows.

Georgia shook her head and gave me an incredulous look, then she said the same thing that Claire had last night, "Oh, Meg, not another one."

This time I just shrugged my shoulders and moaned, "Yes, another one. This can't keep happening." I slipped off my sneakers and put my stockinged feet up on the ottoman. "Where the heck is Patrick? I've looked everywhere. I'm ready to call Arthur so he can send out an all-points bulletin. But then again, I don't want to tip Arthur off about anything relating to Patrick until I know that Patrick was far away from Windy Willows yesterday. I should have pounded on his door last night. What was I thinking? He might think I've been keeping the news of Brett's murder from him on purpose. Am I being paranoid?"

What I didn't tell Georgia was that Arthur, aka Detective Shoner, had pulled me aside last night to tell me that the Southampton Police Department wanted to talk to Patrick about the murder. Apparently, someone tattled about the scene at the lighthouse on the final day of filming. I'd protested that he'd been nowhere near Windy Willows, so how could he possibly be a suspect. Arthur had replied, "Then he has nothing to worry about. The sooner he makes his way to Southampton PD headquarters, the better." Then he'd handed me Chief Marcus Boyle's card with the address of the Southampton PD printed on it—as if I didn't know where the station was.

Hopefully, Chief Boyle wouldn't look up my rap sheet from when I was charged with trespassing after curb shopping on Ocean Drive on trash-pickup day. I'd scored a pair of Louis XV Bergère chairs that just needed new upholstery and had thrown them in the back of my Wagoneer. To me, trespassing was a lesser crime than throwing those antique chairs away. Arthur hadn't been too happy when my sidekick Elle called him. He'd gotten the charges dropped, but that didn't stop him from bringing it up every time he came into my cottage and saw how I fixer-uppered the exquisite chairs. So much so that I eventually put them in a client's cottage so I wouldn't have to hear it anymore.

"Yes, you are being paranoid," Georgia, my sensible septuagenarian friend, answered. "It's only eight in the morning. Take a deep breath. You need tea. It'll help center you."

I took a couple quick inhales and exhales, then laughed. "That's always your answer. Tea."

A small fire burned in the fireplace, toasting my toes. If it wasn't for being worried about Patrick, I'd hunker down and spend the whole day cocooned inside. Shut out my world so I could escape to new ones, just by picking up a book.

Mr. Whiskers sauntered over and nuzzled my feet. Such a calm, sweet creature, the opposite of Jo. Still, I wouldn't trade Jo for the world.

Tabitha, the gorgeous tabby I'd inherited, *long story*, who hadn't gotten along with my feisty feline, was snoozing on Georgia's lap. For being in her late teens, Tabitha was still going strong. I'd bet her days with Jo helped her appreciate living with mellow Georgia and Mr. Whiskers. If Tabitha wasn't on Georgia's lap, you'd find her snoozing between the stacks of books. The *two* days she'd lived with Jo and me, she'd found totally creative places to secret away to avoid Jo. My cottage only had seven rooms, but it had taken me hours to find her.

"I'm sure Patrick's okay," Georgia said. "And from what you've been telling me, I think he's the one who should be contacting you. You've left him enough messages."

"True. I need a vacation. Can I move into the room above the shop? You know how I love small spaces. Claire can feed Jo, and Elle can work with Felicity on *Mr. & Mrs. Winslow*." Then I remembered that Claire was leaving and my anxiety soared.

"You're being silly," Georgia said in an upbeat tone. "You've never shied away from dealing with these kinds of things." Georgia reached for a pet brush and started brushing Tabitha. I laughed at the thought that Jo would ever let me come near her with a brush—the only way would be if it was made from tuna. "Patrick would never leave Charlie alone overnight," I said. "What if he never came home last night? The cottage was dark."

"When did you turn into such a worrywart?"

"You're talking about someone who left a high-profile job at a top home and garden magazine to escape a cheating fiancé," I said.

Georgia cradled Tabitha in her arms like a newborn, stood, and placed her gently in her basket by the fire. Turning to me, with both hands on her hips, she peered down like a stern schoolmaster. "I think that was brave. Not cowardly. No time for a pity party, Megan Barrett. And how did that move to Montauk turn out, Missy? You're a lot stronger now. You've created a new life. A good life. No more wallowing. I'm sure Patrick will be waiting at your door when you go home. Time for tea, I know just the one."

Georgia shuffled in her slippers to the sales counter—her right slipper read *So Many Books*, her left, *So Little Time*. I watched her reach under the counter and retrieve my *M* for Meg mug. At this point, instead of Meg, it might be more fitting that the *M* stood for Murder— like the title of a Sue Grafton book.

"One step at a time," Georgia said as she poured hot water into my mug from the electric kettle hidden behind a stack of hardbacks.

Another murder, another cup of Georgia's tea, I thought as Georgia plunked a tea bag containing one of her special blends into my mug. Waiting the appropriate time, she removed the tea bag, then reached under the counter for a squeeze bottle and added a shot of local honey. Her cure-all for everything from allergies to heartbreak.

Then she shuffled back and handed me the mug. "This should do the trick."

I took a moment to inhale the restorative scent. "Thanks, buddy. Let me guess. Citrus, green tea, and a hint of basil?"

"Close, but no cigar," she said, sitting back in her wingchair. "Black tea, peach, and a hint of mint." Then she laughed. "Remind me not to have you help sell my tea when the Amagansett farmer's market opens next week."

"You're right. I'm off my game. If I was ever in the game. Especially when it comes to Patrick."

"Stop, you're great together. Don't take his silence as having anything to do with you. We all have our pasts."

"You sound like Elle. I know Patrick didn't murder our director. I just need the reassurance that he has an alibi."

"If we have to," Georgia said, "we can bring Doc into it. But I'm sure there won't be a reason. You're just exhausted from yesterday and not thinking rationally. You know, if we decide to include Doc, he'll call your ex–homicide cop father and tell him everything."

Doc was not only my surrogate uncle but also my father's best friend and Georgia's boyfriend. Doc had moved to Montauk to hone his love of sport fishing. But I suspected that he'd also moved to hone his surveillance skills in order to keep an eye on me. A way for my father to keep tabs on me from Detroit.

"Maybe I should bite the bullet and call Dad."

Mr. Whiskers jumped on Georgia's lap. "I'm sure with all that your father is going through right now, that's the last thing you want to do."

"What do you mean? What is my father going through?"

"Oh, I forgot the biscotti. Be a dear and get them for me. As you can see, my lap is full," she said, adding an unnatural chuckle.

"I don't need a biscotti. I need to know what's going on with my father. Is it his health?" I choked. "Is he sick?"

"No. No. Nothing like that."

"So, what is it? Should I call him?"

"Okay, okay, I'll tell you. He's going through a rough patch with your stepmother."

"She's not my stepmother."

"Well, technically she is."

"How rough?" Sheila and my father had been married for only a short time. He'd waited two decades after my mother's death from breast cancer to marry. I'd only met Sheila a couple times. She was nice enough, but she wasn't my mother. No one could be. That bar had been set too high.

"I guess Sheila and your father had an argument," Georgia said. "Doc told me that she went to visit her daughter and grandkids for a while."

"How long is a while?" I asked, selfishly thinking that now that she was gone, my father could relax from Sheila's relentless social calendar and enjoy his retirement, which included gourmet cooking and growing organic produce. Sheila had been raised in ritzy Grosse Pointe, home of the auto barons of yore. My father and I had grown up in the city adjacent to Grosse Pointe, Detroit. Blue blood meets blue collar.

"A month," Georgia said under her breath, causing me to read her lips.

"Sheila's been gone a month! Why didn't he tell me?"

"He must have his reasons. Please don't say anything. Doc will be upset. I'm sure she'll be home soon."

"You're probably right. Maybe when this whole investigation is over, I'll take a trip home. But please tell me if you hear that Sheila's back."

"Promise. Now, drink up."

I took a sip of tea. It trickled soothingly down my throat, and with the help of the fire, warmed my bones from the damp morning's search.

Wanting to change the subject for a few minutes, I told Georgia about Alice and the Halstead property. Georgia was also a good friend of Barb's and had been as sad as me about Barb and Jack moving to Florida. Although, they would be back in the summer to help Alice at Sand and Sun Realty.

"I know all about Everett Halstead. I honestly didn't think he was still alive," Georgia said.

"I should have known you'd know about him."

"I've lived in Montauk all my seventy years," she said with a smile. "Old Everett used to work at Camp Hero when it was a military base. After his wife died in the seventies, he became a recluse. Sad really, because he had an unbelievable brain, akin to the man portrayed in the movie *A Beautiful Mind*. He was always inventing things, then trying them out on the village green. Then something went wrong after his wife died, he became paranoid to the point of wearing an aluminum mixing bowl on his head."

"A mixing bowl?"

"Yes. Among other weird attire. He said that the aluminum kept all the gamma rays that were coming off the huge radar tower at Camp Hero from filtering into his brain and controlling his mind."

"Sad," I said. "Maybe he's not competent enough to sell his property. Where will he go? I don't like his granddaughter, Delia. Do you know her?"

Georgia shook her head. "No. Like I said, I didn't even know he was still alive. Haven't seen him in town in ages."

"I wouldn't be surprised if after the papers are signed that Delia locks him up in a mental institution. We're going there with Alice tomorrow. We promised to help her stage the house in order to sell it."

"Mind if I come along?" she asked.

"Of course not. Especially if you know him. I really want Alice to be the broker, but not at the expense of someone's well-being. I know Barb would be the same way. That's why Sand and Sun has so many faithful clients, including moi."

"Great," she said. "I'll pick out some books for him to read. If I remember correctly, he was a voracious science fiction reader. I remember him coming into the bookstore when my parents were running it."

"Maybe just science books would be better," I said. "Especially if he's out of touch with reality. I saw lots of old *Popular Mechanics* in his cottage."

Georgia sighed. "If I'd known that he's been out there, living alone, in an incapacitated state, I would have checked on him."

I slapped my hand against my forehead. "Incapacitated! Oh, my God, I just realized something."

"What?"

"Maybe something serious happened to Patrick. What if the same person who killed our director did something to Patrick?"

I jumped up from the chair, went and grabbed my jacket from the hook by the door, and said, "You coming with me? I might need you as a witness. I'm getting inside the cottage to look for clues. Key or no key."

"Wait. Did you check Ditch Plains Beach? I heard the swells are huge. It could be as simple as he got up early, got breakfast from Melissa's food truck, and then went surfing."

Ditch Plains Beach was a famous Hamptons spot where on any day you could find surfers or surf watchers from all walks of life, including famous movie stars, locals, weekend Wall-Streeters, and local surf bums.

"No, it didn't cross my mind. When I went to his cottage, it was shortly after sunrise. But it's definitely a possibility. So, first we go to his cottage. If he's not home, I'm breaking in. Then we'll go to Ditch Plains."

Georgia met me at the door, grabbed her long sweater from the coat rack, and exchanged her slippers for shoes. Giving me a warm hug, she said, "Let's go find this wayward boyfriend of yours."

I opened the door, and she glanced down at my feet. "But before we go, you might want to put on your sneakers."

"Oops." I went back to the ottoman, sat, slipped on my sneakers, then joined her at the door.

"And, Georgia—"

"Yes, darlin'?"

"Thanks. I feel so much better."

"Must be the tea," she said with a grin.

Chapter 19

There was no need to break in after all, because I spied a hide-a-key rock under a hydrangea bush. Patrick had once used it when he'd left his keys at my place. Taking it as a good sign from the cosmos, I unlocked the side door and opened it. I held the door for Georgia, then followed her into Patrick's fabulous cooks' kitchen.

Charlie rushed over and gave me kisses. I gave her a few back. She even gave Georgia a few licks on the cheek. Then she barked and led us over to her empty food bowl.

Laughing, I said, "Oh, no, Charlie. Jo must be rubbing off on you. I know your daddy would never leave without feeding you. Don't squeal if I give you a little extra."

"And Charlie, don't tell Patrick we were here," Georgia added. Then she turned to me. "Let's hurry. I don't want to get caught trespassing."

"Don't be silly. He'll understand. At least I think he will." *Would he?* I thought as I walked to the fridge and took out a container of Patrick's homemade dog food. I put a few spoonfuls in Charlie's bowl. She lapped them up in seconds. Then she looked up at me for more.

Of course I gave in.

I asked Georgia to stay with Charlie while I checked the rest of the cottage. "And please be on the lookout, just in case Patrick pulls into the driveway."

"Fine. Just hurry."

Five minutes later, I walked into Patrick's great room.

"Find any clues, Nancy Drew?" Georgia asked.

"His bed was made. I guess that doesn't tell us if he came home last night. But I must give you a gold star for your suggestion that he went surfing. His wetsuit and surfing gear are missing from the cupboard in the mudroom."

"See, worrywart. Told you."

I laughed. "Where did the word *worrywart* originate, Ms. Etymology?"

"There are two schools of thought," she said in her children's story-time reading voice. "The first one is an old wives' tale that picking up a frog will give you warts. A falsehood because warts are a virus. The other possible origin came from a character in a fifties comic strip who had the name Worry Wart. Although, in this case, the comic character was the one who caused the worry, not the other way around. Kind of like you, when you get involved in one of your murders. You cause us all to worry. Especially Doc."

I knew she would know the answer. But I didn't know she would turn it around to chastise me. Well, maybe I did. "Hey, I just have a knack of showing up at the wrong place at the right time. In this case, Patrick is the one causing *me* the worry."

"You still want to go to Ditch Plains Beach? Or wait till he comes back?" Georgia went over to the stone fireplace mantel and glanced at a photo of Patrick's deceased wife and child, then quickly looked away.

"That's Catherine and Lucy."

"I thought so. Has he ever opened up to you about them?"

"Only once. But that's a start. You're right, let's get out of here." I didn't feel their ghosts in the room, but it felt like an invasion of Patrick's privacy to talk about them when he wasn't present.

I followed Georgia into the kitchen. She said, "Don't forget to put the key back in the fake rock."

"Got it," I said, taking it off the beautiful wood counter that Patrick had made in his workshop.

Before leaving, I went to the biscuit jar and gave Charlie a biscuit. Homemade, of course. As we headed to the door, I looked back to see her happily wagging her tail, her long tongue lapping up biscuit crumbs that had fallen to the floor. "You would never know that she'd once been an abused greyhound race dog," I said. "All it took was lots of lovin' from Patrick. One of the many things I admire about him."

"He is quite a catch, and Charlie is such a well-behaved pup. The opposite of your feisty feline. I'm still traumatized from the last time I kittysat."

I laughed. "Jo is a handful. But she's *my* handful."

Georgia put her hand on the doorknob, then froze. "Hey, do you hear that? It sounds like a phone is ringing. Does Patrick have a home phone?"

"No, just a cell. My phone's in your car, so it's not mine."

Georgia patted the cross-body handbag slung around her chest. "Not mine either. Stay here, I'll go look for it."

A few seconds later, Georgia came back into the kitchen with Patrick's cell phone. She handed it to me at the same time a call came through. *Julie Cell* flashed across the screen. I showed it to Georgia.

"That's strange. Do you think it's the same Julie that you told me about? The actress, Julie David?"

"That would be my guess. I can't get into his phone. I won't even try. But this explains why he hasn't answered my calls. Come on. Let's go to Ditch Plains Beach. We'll bring him his phone."

I went to the door, opened it, then held it for Georgia.

"Don't say it," she said.

"Say what?"

"Age before beauty. Even if it's true."

"I wouldn't think of it. Besides, you're gorgeous, and owing to your morning bike rides to the lighthouse and back, you're in better physical shape than me. You look fifty, not seventy, and I'd die for your thighs."

Georgia laughed. "You should come along to the lighthouse," she said, passing through the open doorway. "It's a magical trip. No one is on the road at that hour. But you'll have to get up at sunrise."

"I do get up at sunrise," I said. "But my sunrises are saved for coffee, meditation, and inspirational reading. However, I'd be game for a bike trip to the lighthouse at sunset. The sunsets off the point, where the ocean meets the sound, are spectacular."

I followed her out the door, locked it, then replaced the key in the plastic rock. Unless Charlie told him, Patrick would never know we were here.

We took the stone and crushed shell path that led to Patrick's driveway. When we reached Georgia's powder blue vintage Jag convertible, which she and her beau Motor City Doc had restored to its original beauty, we got in. Georgia fired her up, and the engine purred like Mr. Whiskers.

"What's Patrick's next thriller about?" Georgia asked, backing out of the narrow driveway. "I haven't seen his publicist, Ashley, in a while."

"I forgot to tell you the good news. Ashley's pregnant. Baby's due any day. That would explain why you haven't seen her."

"That's wonderful. So, what's the plot for Patrick's next one?"

I was embarrassed to tell her that Patrick hadn't shared anything about his next novel. "I'm not sure. He just finished tweaking the screenplay for the next episode of *Mr. & Mrs. Winslow*. And you know how explosive things have been on set." I paused after my last comment, thinking, that wouldn't be an issue now that Brett was dead. Brett wasn't just dead. He was murdered. I felt my heart hiccup, knowing that I was going to be the one to tell Patrick the news. It took everything I had not to pull Patrick's phone out of my pocket. Maybe Julie had called from jail. Instead of a lawyer, she'd chosen Patrick as her one call. *Duh.* If she'd been arrested, it was doubtful that the Southampton PD would let her use her cell phone. Soon, I would find out what was going on. And if Patrick wouldn't confide in me—then what?

I glanced at Georgia's fine-featured profile. "Georgia—"

Turning right on Route 27, and without taking her eyes off the road, she said, "I know that voice. What do you want? Whatever it is, you should ask your sidekick, Elle, to help you. I have to answer to Doc."

"It's not that bad. I just wondered if you wouldn't mind telling Patrick about Brett. After you did, I could be there to comfort him."

"Oh, no. You're no weakling. Plus, you said he got mad at you a little while ago when you had a date with a potential killer and hadn't told him ahead of time that you were meeting them."

I groaned. "Boy. You don't miss a thing."

As we got closer to Montauk's world-famous surfing beach, I felt the heat of the Barrett blotches working their way up to my cheeks. My mind was a jumble of conflicting thoughts and feelings.

And they all centered around Patrick.

Chapter 20

Georgia made a quick right onto Ditch Plains Road. When we reached the beach parking lot, I looked ahead and saw Patrick's Navy Range Rover.

"He's here! I'm such an idiot. Why didn't I think of this in the first place? I know Patrick's favorite way to escape is to go surfing. He once told me that when it's just him, the ocean, and the sky, he feels like he's inside a Nirvana bubble."

"I know that feeling," Georgia said, pulling the car into the spot next to Patrick's. "There's nothing like it. I like the analogy. Nirvana bubble."

I glanced over at Georgia's short-cropped white hair and thin muscled frame. It was hard to believe that not only did she surf, but she'd also talked meat-and-couch-potato Doc into buying his own surfboard. Doc was still learning. Georgia called him a grom, an Australian surfing term for a newbie surfer. Patrick had once called me a hodad, another Australian term, meaning someone who hangs on the beach watching the surfers. What he didn't know was that I wasn't watching other surfers—only him. And even though I thought of him as my Moondoggie, I never progressed to the level that actress Sandra Dee did in the movie *Gidget*. Perhaps, if I practiced on my bed with a surfboard, like Gidg did, I'd be more proficient at the sport.

"I'll wait in the car," Georgia said, turning off the ignition. "I want to get back to the shop, but I'll wait until I know Patrick can take you home. Leave me your car keys. I'm meeting Doc later. I'll follow him to your cottage, and we'll drop off your car."

I dug in my bag and handed her my keys. "You're the best," I said, blowing her a kiss. Then I got out of the car and headed toward the wood-planked walkway that led to the beach. Glancing over at Patrick's car, I noticed that both of his surfboards were on top on the Range Rover. He always brought two. Apparently different boards were good for different weather conditions.

When I reached the end of the walkway, yellow caution tape stretched from railing to railing. A sign hung from a post beyond the tape that read *Beach Closed*. I leaned over the tape and looked to the right. Patrick usually stowed his gear next to the lifeguard station. Nothing was there, including a lifeguard. Lifeguards on Montauk beaches didn't show up until Memorial Day Weekend. You had to surf at your own risk.

I ducked under the caution tape and looked out at the calm sea. As far as I could see, there wasn't a soul in the ocean. The swells weren't huge, but they were big enough to provide a few surfing thrills. As picture perfect as the Atlantic looked, and as bright as the sun was, I knew the water temp in April was somewhere in the low forties. Another reason to practice surfing Gidget-style on my bed — at least until the end of July.

For a moment, I got lost in a sea trance. It happened all the time. Something about the waves hitting the shore and the vast expanse in front of me had me thinking of all the wonderful times Patrick and I had shared by the ocean since we'd become exclusive.

Once, sitting on the wood bench on my deck that Patrick had made me in his workshop, he'd shared about his guilt over his wife and daughter's accident. He'd been in California working on a screenplay for one of his novels and they'd been in New York. The hurt in his eyes and the clench of his jaw had told me that no matter what I said, words wouldn't soothe him. I had taken his hand and we'd stared out at the Atlantic until long after sunset. Now I wondered if Julie David had anything to do with his remorse for being in California at the time of their death. Had he wondered if Catherine had seen the photo and article Felicity had shown me of him and Julie David? Could that be why he was avoiding seeing Julie? All these questions were pointless. Whatever had happened, he had to work it out himself. I would be there no matter what. I wasn't going anywhere.

A dog's bark broke me out of my reverie. I turned my head, just as a brisk breeze whipped my long bangs in front of my eyes. Was I hallucinating? Or was there a man and his dog walking toward me.

Almost like a warning, a stronger wind hit me head-on. It cleared my vision. I wished it hadn't. Because as the pair approached, it became obvious that the short, portly, elderly man wasn't Patrick and his collie wasn't Charlie.

Instead of going back to Georgia and telling her the bad news that Patrick was still MIA, I waited for the man to reach me, wondering if he knew why the beach was closed. I could think of a few reasons off the top of my head: an upcoming hurricane or nor'easter, a strong undertow or rip current, or a shark attack. Hurricane season wasn't here. Nor'easters were usually in the winter, and shark attacks usually happened in the summer when the water was warmer. I narrowed it down to a strong undertow or riptide.

In season, a flag would be posted on the lifeguard stand. I reasoned that Patrick must have seen the beach was closed and went with a fellow surfer for breakfast. That was why I hadn't seen his car around town.

As the pair approached, I shielded my eyes from the bright sunlight and asked, "Excuse me, do you know why the beach is closed?" I reached down and petted the Lassie look-alike on its shaggy mane.

With his long white beard, big belly, and laughing eyes, the man reminded me of Father Christmas. All that was missing was a bag of toys. Suddenly, his laughing eyes turned serious. "Oh, I heard there was a terrible surfing accident. My son told me one guy got caught in the riptide. Another ran in to save him, managed to bring him to shore, but, according to my son, one of them was in bad shape, possibly suffered cardiac arrest. I assume, if he died, it would have been in this morning's *Montauk Sun*. I read the whole paper. Didn't see anything."

I fell to my knees onto the wet sand.

"Are you okay? You want me to call someone for you?"

I shook my head at the same time that Georgia ran up to us. She looked from Santa to me. "What's going on? Where's Patrick?"

"There was a surfing accident yesterday," I choked out.

"Oh, honey," Georgia said, reaching down to help me up.

I leaned into her, sobbing.

"What happened?" she asked, removing the hair from my face so she could look me in the eyes.

"I don't know. I just know we have to get to him."

It all added up.

That was why Patrick's car was still in the parking lot.

He must have left Ditch Plains Beach by ambulance.

Chapter 21

As Georgia sped down Old Montauk Highway toward Southampton Hospital, the closest hospital in the Hamptons, an unfamiliar number came through on my phone.

I answered.

"Meg. It's Patrick."

"Oh, my God! Patrick. Where are you? I just saw your car at Ditch Plains Beach, and some guy and his dog told me that there was a surfing accident — cardiac arrest. I'm with Georgia. We went — Charlie's okay."

"Slow down. Take a breath. A dog told you all this?" I heard him attempt a weak laugh, and I nearly dropped the phone.

"Is that Patrick?" Georgia asked.

I nodded my head yes and gave her a thumbs-up. If Patrick was really hurt, would he be joking around? "Where are you?" I asked him.

"Southampton Hospital."

"So, you were involved in a surfing accident."

"Yes, the dog and the man weren't lying. They're releasing me in a few minutes. I wondered if you could pick me up. As you saw, my car is at Ditch Plains. That must be where my cell phone is too."

"I've got your phone."

"Didn't I lock it in the car?"

"I got it from your cottage. I fed Charlie. You sound a little funny. Are you sure you should be released?"

"I'll explain when you get here. I had a concussion and a slight case of hypothermia."

"Slight case," I croaked.

"They kept me overnight. I didn't think it was necessary, but they insisted. I didn't want to call you because I knew you were at the wrap party. Plus, I wanted to stay until Evan was out of the woods. Thankfully, he is."

I assumed he meant the other guy in the accident.

"I'll be there soon. Actually, Georgia and I will be there soon. Long story."

"How was the wrap party?" he asked.

"We must have a bad connection," I said. "You're breaking up."

I went to tap the End button, but before I did, I heard, or maybe just imagined, that Patrick said, *"Love you."*

Chapter 22

When I stepped into the lobby of the hospital, I saw Patrick sitting in a wheelchair. A nursing assistant was by his side and he was in the middle of autographing one of his thrillers. I hesitated before approaching them, assessing his pale face, black left eye, and hunched shoulders. He looked vulnerable in the wheelchair. I wanted to protect him and tell the silly girl that he needed to be home and tucked into bed ASAP — by me. Then I glanced at the huge grin on the girl's face and waited until Patrick handed her back the book, which I'm sure she must have grabbed off the bestseller rack in the hospital gift shop.

Patrick hated his celebrity status in the Hamptons. It was one of the reasons he lived in a small unassuming cottage in Montauk and rarely attended large events. After a new book came out, his publicist, Ashley, who had recently moved to Montauk, would coerce him into attending local Hamptons social events. Usually, he'd drag me along with him. Which was a win-win — an evening with my handsome boyfriend and an event sure to serve the best cuisine this side of the East River.

Patrick glanced up. A lock of sandy brown hair, streaked with gold, fell in front of his gorgeous blue-green eyes. When our gazes meet, it felt like he was Magneto and I was liquid iron. The relief I felt at seeing his smile translated into a torrent of tears. Tears of unadulterated joy.

As if I was in one of Nikki Meyers's romantic comedies or Florence Nightingale after ten cups of coffee, I scurried toward him, slipped on the buffed lobby floor and landed flat on my derrière. My "Ouch!" echoed off the lobby's marble walls.

Patrick's nursing assistant rushed over and helped me up. Embarrassed, I said, "Thank you." Then I took slow, measured steps toward Patrick, my head down, and my cheeks feeling like they might burst into flames.

"That was quite an entrance, Ms. Barrett," Patrick said, adding a weak smile. "Why are you crying? I'm fine. Right, Nurse Chang?"

"I'm not a nurse yet, Mr. Seaton. And you know that another night here would be better for your recovery. The doctor said so."

"I'm sure that Meg will take good care of me. Although, I might want to take home some chicken soup from the cafeteria. Ms. Barrett is culinarily challenged."

I laughed. "Hey, I resemble that remark! I make a mean grilled cheese, and I know how to open a can of tomato soup."

I felt such relief that Patrick seemed back to his old self. No doubt, his near-death experience was the reason. Now, if only I didn't have to tell him about Brett Golden's murder.

But I would have to — before someone else did. Like the police.

Chapter 23

Patrick slept the whole way from Southampton to Montauk.

After Georgia dropped us at Ditch Plains Beach, I helped Patrick onto the passenger seat of his SUV. He tried to argue that he was well enough to drive the two miles back to his cottage. Based on his pale face, drowsy look, and the huge lump on the top of his head, I nixed that idea.

As I drove the short distance to his cottage, he explained what had happened.

"When I pulled into Ditch Plains Beach, I checked my surfing app. There was a warning about a strong riptide. I decided to go check for myself. As soon as I walked onto the beach, I saw a surfer just as his board went flying into the air. He couldn't grab it and was carried away by the strong current. I was the only one on the beach. I kicked off my shoes and dove in. Captured his board on an incoming wave, then I paddled out to him. He was flailing, trying to keep his head above the water and swimming against the current." He turned to me and said, "Never swim against the current. Let it take you, relax and float, so you can conserve your energy."

I shook my head that I would. He continued, "I tried to get him up on his board. In a panic, he fought me. The board popped up. It must've clocked me on the head on its way down. Finally, I got him on the board, but by this time he'd passed out. I managed to lay on top of him and paddle to shore. Someone called 911. The next thing I remembered was looking over and seeing the paramedics giving him the paddles."

Patrick had given me a lesson on the different signals that surfers use to their fellow surfers and those watching onshore: an arm wave or hand up signals that someone is in trouble; wrists that are crossed above you head means that someone is submerged; and patting the top of your head with one hand relays that everything is okay. Then he'd gone on to tell me the most disturbing signal of all—when a surfer puts their hands together above their head in a yoga prayer pose, it signals a shark sighting. After what he'd just gone through, I made a mental note to buy a good pair of binoculars so I could watch his every move.

I shivered. "How terrifying. Were you wearing a wetsuit?"

"No. I didn't plan on going in. Remember? In hindsight, I wished I did have it on. An EMS attendant placed a thermal blanket on me. At this point, I couldn't feel my arms and legs. Then, we were both carted off in the same ambulance. The whole time inside, they were trying to revive him. His name's Evan. Suffered cardiac arrest. He's stable now. Thank God. Because he has a wife and kids." Patrick closed his eyes, as if relating the whole incident had been overly strenuous.

"Thank God you're okay. Evan's stable because of you," I said. "You're a hero."

"I'm no hero. You would've done the same thing," he said wearily, downplaying his role of saving someone from drowning and a near-fatal heart attack.

"I'm not so sure. How'd you get the black eye?"

He closed his eyes but kept talking. "Evan punched me. He was disoriented. Quite common in this kind of situation. Everything got hazy after that."

"Sounds like this wasn't your first life-saving experience," I said.

"Nope."

I turned onto Highway 27, then glanced over at him. He reached out his hand and caressed my cheek. "You get in any trouble in the last twenty-four hours?"

"You know me. What do you think?"

"Not the answer I was looking for," he said.

I passed the turnoff to my cottage and drove west toward Essex Street, the street that would take me to Patrick's. At the traffic circle surrounding the village green, I remembered that the first music concert of the season was a week away. "Are we going to go to the East End Music Fest next weekend? Like we planned?"

When Patrick didn't answer, I looked over to see that he was asleep. I made a snap decision, continued around the circle, then headed back east, toward my cottage. There was no way that I'd let him stay home alone. If we went to his place, I knew he'd get all macho on me and tell me to leave.

Two minutes later, I pulled into my drive. I parked, and gently shook Patrick's upper arm. "Time to get up, sleepyhead." His eyelashes fluttered. Then he shifted his position, turned toward the side window, and mumbled, "Catherine—"

Wow. A Freudian slip. At least, I hoped it was. What if he woke up with amnesia, like they do in soap operas and thought his wife was still alive?

Thankfully, he turned back to me and slowly opened his eyes. "Meg."

"Yes. It's Meg," I said, repeating my name loud and clear.

He sat up from his slouched position and looked ahead. "Hey, why am I here? Thought you were taking me home. I'm fine, you know. Just need a couple hours sleep." He looked at me with clear eyes. "What about Charlie?"

"Charlie's fine. I'll get her after you're snuggled in bed. My bed."

"Your bed?" He grinned, then raised a peaked brow above his good eye.

Ignoring his weak attempt at a leer, I said, "I'll walk down the beach and get Charlie. Then I'll bring her back here." I smiled. "I think she knows the way by now. I already fed her and she's good to go for a couple hours, at least. Now I know why she was so hungry. She'd gone a night without you or food."

"Oh, my neighbor fed her. I called him from the hospital last night."

I tried to hide my surprise, but it didn't work.

"I told you, I didn't want you to leave the wrap party. Actually, before what happened at Ditch Plains, I'd planned on going to Windy Willows."

"You did?"

"I did."

"Well, when I pick up Charlie, it'll be the only time today that I'm leaving you alone," I said.

"Okay, boss. I can tell by the set of your jaw that I won't win this one. And frankly, I'm too exhausted to put up much of a fight. So, I'll acquiesce to your wishes. But not to your cooking. When you pick up Charlie, there's some leftover coq au vin in the fridge. We can have that for dinner."

I laughed. "Yes, sir. But you will get one of my grilled cheeses, tomato soup, and a glass of Vernor's ginger ale for lunch. Just like my mom gave me when I was sent home from school with a cold."

"Speaking of cold, I'll welcome your hot soup. I wonder if I'll ever get the chill out of my bones."

"I'll make sure you get extra comforters. And extra hugs."

"Is that so? I look forward to it." He attempted a wink with his bruised eye, then grimaced.

"And, I'll give you a steak."

"Oh, no. Not if you're grilling it."

I laughed. "I meant for you black eye."

How could I tell him about what happened at Windy Willows? I loved this joking, lighthearted side of Patrick. "Not to burst your bubble." *Or my bubble,* I thought. "But there's something I need to tell you before we go inside."

"Let me guess. Is it about the wrap party? Sorry that I was so short with you the other night. I just didn't want to be in the same place as our incompetent director. Especially socializing, like everything's hunky-dory — paraphrasing some of your Michigan lingo. I'm sorry, I don't think I know of anyone who's gotten more under my skin than Brett Golden. Oh, wait. I pray that you're going to tell me the good news that Jeremy got rid of Brett and that Nikki Meyers is our new director."

"Well, someone got rid of him. But it wasn't Jeremy," I said, afraid to continue. Finally, unable to look him in the eyes, I gave him an encapsulated version of the sequence of events that led to Brett's demise.

When I finished and looked over, his grin had disappeared. He said, "Tell me that this is a late April Fool's joke."

"I wish it was," I answered.

"Are you okay?" he asked, glancing over at my knees, which were covered in jeans.

I'd only mentioned my boo-boos to emphasize what a brut Carson was. "I'm fine." Then I remembered that I'd left off the part about the giant disgusting koi that was left on the hood of my car. Deciding that the new, improved Meg would share everything with him, I told him about the gross-looking creature.

"What kind of message was that supposed to send?" Patrick asked. "Were you asking too many questions?"

"Just a few. When Arthur and Southampton PD showed up to Windy Willows, I turned it over to them."

"Turned it over? That was nice of you, Miss Marple."

I ignored him. "Then I told Arthur everything I knew. The koi had to be the work of Julie David's huge bodyguard. He doesn't scare me."

"Well, now that I know, he won't ever get near you again. Brett was a jerk, but he didn't deserve to die like that. And you're telling me that the only people who were at the estate at his estimated time of death was the three of you, Jeremy, Olivia, Matt, Nicki, Julie, and her chauffeur?"

"His name is Carson. But he looks nothing like Jim Carter who played the butler Carson in *Downton Abbey*. He looks more like a WWE wrestler."

"*Downton Abbey*? Oh, that PBS series, right?"

"Yes. That little ole PBS series," I said, smiling.

"No party planner or waitstaff was there setting up?"

"You know our producer. He was doing it all himself. No one arrived until after Brett was dead. Naturally, they weren't allowed in." Then I told him about what Arthur had said about the weapon used to kill him. "He was surprised something so dangerous would be used on set."

"That's not your fault. I was there when Felicity showed it to Brett. Brett loved it. Said it was like something from a James Bond movie. Plus, we were on hand when they filmed that scene. The walking stick was only waved around in the air for a few minutes. What I don't understand is if you, Elle, and Felicity were in the next room, why didn't you hear anything?"

"You got me. I know when Olivia accused Julie of using the walking stick to kill her father, Julie had no idea that there was a hidden blade in its tip. Of course, she could have been faking it. She said that Brett wanted to kill her after she broke off their engagement. Maybe he threatened her with the walking stick?"

"Unfortunately, it's too late to ask him. But we can ask her." Patrick shook his head in disbelief. "Can't wrap my head around this one. Brett Golden is dead. I need to call Julie."

Speechless, I reached into my bag and handed him his phone.

Apparently, Julie didn't answer, because I heard him say, "Hi, Julie. Just heard what happened. Call me back. It's Patrick Seaton." After he pocketed his phone, he turned to me and said, "Until she called me late Thursday night, I had no idea that she was Brett's fiancée. I hadn't heard from her in years. We met four years ago in

California. She was hired to play a part in a movie they were adapting from one of my books. I was collaborating on the screenplay. Julie had just lost a husband, and the tabloids and paparazzi were relentless in following her every move. They called her the Black Widow. It was the farthest from the truth. She couldn't handle it all and started drinking again and taking antidepressants. She was fired from the set. A few days later she called me. Said she needed help. So, I drove her to the Betty Ford Clinic. Some rag got a few shots of me dropping her off. The story went national. It was right before the uh, accident. The worse time of my life—I never knew if Catherine saw it before—. He paused. "I told you how Catherine didn't want me to go to LA."

"Yes. But you had no idea what would happen."

"I know. But I'm still working on forgiving myself for not being in New York when it *did* happen."

"Why'd Julie call you on Thursday?" I asked, blinking back tears and trying to distract him from his melancholy thoughts.

"She'd found out from Brett that I was the screenwriter on *Mr. & Mrs. Winslow.* He had a private investigator look into her past, and she wanted to warn me. Like I'd ever care. She'd seemed excited because Brett promised her a large recurring role in the series, and she wanted to talk about it. Brett told her she'd get a million an episode. It was supposed to be her big comeback. I know she didn't need the money. Her previous husbands have left her mega wealthy. She seemed excited when we'd hung up. I planned to call you Friday morning, after going surfing, I swear. But then—you know what happened."

I reached for his hand and squeezed it. He gave me a tired smile.

"Let's table this for a while," I said softly. "Wait till after your nap."

"Thanks."

"For what?"

"For being so understanding."

"Patrick, you don't have to keep anything from me. I'm here. Always. Even if it's about Catherine and Lucy. Only when you're ready."

For the first time ever, I didn't see him wince when their names were mentioned. He opened his mouth to say something, but instead bent toward me and we kissed. A long kiss. A satisfying kiss. After the kiss, he sat back against the car seat and closed his eyes.

"What's wrong?" I said in a panic.

"I have a helluva headache."

"Let's get you inside. Are you sure you shouldn't have spent another night at the hospital?"

"No need to worry. I'm fine. No need for the Barrett Blotches," he said, glancing at my neck.

What Patrick didn't know was that I was pretty sure that the warm welts on my neck appeared during our kiss.

"I had a clear MRI. No brain bleeds."

"Brain bleeds!" I repeated.

"I just have a normal headache. Probably need some caffeine. Or some tender loving care, Nurse Barrett."

I laughed. "Oh, you're going to get that, Mr. Seaton. And I'm also going to read your hospital release papers and follow the doctor's orders to a T."

He smiled. "Yes, boss."

"You've got that right, mister."

Well, that went better than I thought. I wondered what would happen when the euphoria of being alive wore off and Patrick realized there was a killer in our midst. Hopefully, it was a crime of passion, only directed at Brett. It would be a lie to say I hadn't been nose to nose with someone who'd killed more than once.

Maybe as Elle said, I *was* a murder magnet.

Chapter 24

After I'd made Patrick his *un*burnt grilled cheese, I forced him upstairs and tucked him into my bed. For all his flirting and romantic innuendos from earlier, as soon as his head hit my pillow, he murmured, "Like sleeping in a feathered nest." Then he was out for the count.

Jo hopped onto the bed, angry that Patrick hadn't acknowledged her. She began kneading his hip area to feel if he had any homemade treats in his pocket. Then she sniffed his hand, turned tail, and hopped off the bed. Before leaving the room, she gave me her famous evil eye — she only had one, but she knew how to make it work. Then she slunk downstairs as if Patrick's empty pockets were all my fault.

Before leaving the bedroom, I took a moment to study Patrick's features: the cut of his jaw, his long lashes, perfect lips, and tanned skin from surfing . . . Surfing. I never wanted him to go surfing again. Was I being unrealistic? Of course I was. I just kept picturing the scene on the beach after his rescue. Only at this moment, when he was right here in front of me, gently snoring, did I realize that he had the most solid of alibis for Brett Golden's murder.

It was too bad he'd almost had to die to have it.

I went downstairs, grabbed a sweater, then walked the mile to Patrick's cottage. I loved how empty the beach was this time of year.

By the time I reached Patrick's cottage, the sun was replaced with sooty storm clouds. Charlie was happy to see me, especially when I told her that we were going to see her daddy, who was missing her. After packing the cog au vin and Charlie's food into a market bag I found under the sink, I grabbed Charlie's leash and we left the cottage.

We made it back to my cottage minutes before the rain started — April showers, and all that.

I unpacked the food and put it in the fridge, told the cat and dog to try to get along, then I ran upstairs to check on Patrick. He was still in the same position that I'd left him, oblivious to the thunder that rattled my small cottage's windows and doorframes. Normally, if I was alone during a storm, I would take out my hearing aids and revel in the drama being played out over the Atlantic.

I tucked the duvet tighter around Patrick, then glanced over at my parents' wedding photo, which was displayed prominently on my bedside table. With all the craziness of today, I'd forgotten what Georgia had told me about Sheila leaving my father high and dry, after they'd had an argument.

My father and I weren't just father and daughter. We were best friends. I couldn't believe he wouldn't tell me about Sheila. Now that I thought about it, I never really gave Sheila a chance to get close to me. It wasn't because she'd taken my place in my father's life. It was more that she seemed the opposite of my mother. Maybe that's why my father married her. Which had me thinking about Patrick and me. *Had he chosen to have a relationship with me because I was the polar opposite of his deceased wife?* Catherine had been an award-winning chef, and from what I'd learned from Catherine's sister, she was a fabulous mother. Would I ever become a mother? I knew I'd never be chef. That didn't bother me as much as the mother part. I was an only child, maybe mothering wasn't in me. Look at the job I did with Jo—the adorable brat.

After making sure Patrick was snug as a bug in a rug, as my mother used to say, I kissed him on the forehead. Then I tiptoed toward the stairs, ignoring any anxious thoughts or insecurities about our relationship.

Because Patrick was alive!

Chapter 25

Back downstairs, a miracle happened. For the first time ever, Charlie and Jo were sleeping side by side in front of the fireplace. Jo's rear left foot was draped across Charlie's velvety gray belly. I ran for my phone and shot a photo to show Patrick when he woke up. If feline and canine can be harmonious together, so could Patrick and I. I crossed my fingers that this new, accessible Patrick wasn't just a result of his near-death experience. Hopefully, going forward, he would be more transparent with his feelings, like he'd been in the car.

Glancing toward the bay window, I saw a red blinking light on my answering machine. Not wanting to disturb Jo and Charlie, I crept over to my stunning George III writing desk. It had a drop-leaf front and numerous cubbyholes. The desk was fitted with brass casters, making it easy to move to face whichever direction I desired—the perks of having a cottage with 180-degree ocean views.

I'd bought the desk at a shop in Paris when I was on a trip to France with my then-fiancé Michael. Michael hated antiques, vintage furniture and décor. He never understood why I'd pay to have the old desk, with its chipped section of veneer, shipped back to the United States for more than I'd paid for it. It was one of the many things Michael hadn't understood about me.

Woodworking was Patrick's hobby. The first time he'd been invited into my cottage, he'd gone straight to my desk and admired its delicate cabriole legs. Then, he walked over to the built-in bookcases that flanked my cottage's stone fireplace and reached for one of my late-nineteenth-century ornate, gilt and cloth poetry books. Now that I thought about it, we weren't opposites at all. It was just that Patrick came with more baggage. I would just have to wait until he was ready to share its weight.

My hand hovered above the button that would play the phone message verbally and show it to me visibly on my Caption Call screen. Without looking at the call log, I had a guess who'd called. When Georgia had dropped Patrick and me at his car at Ditch Plains Beach, I'd asked her to phone Elle and explain what had happened to Patrick.

Now, looking down at the phone, did I want to answer and relate my morning's adventures to Elle? Or hear the latest on Brett Golden's murder? For the next hour, I'd rather stick my head in the sand. I'd had enough drama for a lifetime. I whispered to the machine, "Sorry, Elle."

While Patrick slept, I decided to go out to my design studio and work on a fun little project for a client. I went into the kitchen and left Patrick a note on the kitchen counter, telling him where I'd be, and to call me when he woke up. Then I grabbed my navy rain slicker from the coat rack by the kitchen door, slipped it on, and pocketed my phone. I exchanged sneakers for my clear rubber boots adorned with little yellow duckies, then snuck out the kitchen door without a creature or human stirring and stepped into the deluge.

On the way to the studio, I cut through my walled garden, wanting to check on my fledgling plants, hoping they were hardy enough to handle being pummeled by the pounding rain. Elle called me the herb whisperer. Growing herbs was a passion of mine. Before meeting Patrick, I'd use fresh herbs to elevate leftovers and frozen dinners. Now, I harvested them for Patrick or my father to add to their gourmet home-cooked meals.

Lucky me.

I'd never graduated to growing fruits and vegetables for a good reason. Spring through fall, the Hamptons had an abundance of organic vegetable stands and farmers' markets. As an extra perk, most of them also sold jams, jellies, chutneys, and homemade baked goods. I figured, why grow my own when all I had to do was take a quick trip by car or bike to find the freshest produce and at the same time support local farmers.

Everything seemed status quo in the garden. I looked forward to rain-free weather, when Patrick could use the walled garden's brick pizza oven to make one or *six* of his amazing pies. I envisioned a pizza party, where we could invite our eclectic group of friends. Claire! We could make it a going-away party for Claire and invite her friends and the members of the Dead Poets Society Club.

Wow, would I miss her. I couldn't imagine not seeing a light on in Little Grey's kitchen or sitting at her table while she tried out new lines of poetry on me. There hadn't been one time that her words needed editing, and it was an honor to hear them for the first time.

I ducked through the open brick archway at the back of the garden, then took the purposely overgrown path to my studio. The first time I'd discovered the little Queen Anne glass structure, it had been covered in vines and hidden behind eight-foot spikes of bamboo. In order to use the glass folly as my interior design studio, I'd replaced a dozen broken panes of glass and added a gas heater. Something about all the light pouring through the rippled panes of old bubbled glass got my design juices flowing. Even now, as I stepped inside with the rain sluicing down the peaked glass roof, I felt like I was underneath a magical waterfall.

I stopped next to a small table upcycled from the wood of an old fishing trawler and glanced at the standing corkboard I'd thumb-tacked with fabric and paint swatches for my next design project.

On the reverse side of the corkboard was a blank dry-erase board. Last night, I'd thought about using it to list all the details about the murder—like they do on TV cop shows. Julie David would have to be included. Even though she'd been a friend to Patrick in the past, he hadn't seen or heard from her in years. How was it feasible that Julie would share her suite at the yacht club with Brett's children? Could they all be in it together, playing a charade for me or someone else to witness? To my eyes, the emotions seemed raw and real. What if Julie had gotten engaged to Brett for the sole purpose of landing a comeback role on *Mr. & Mrs. Winslow*? Or, was she marrying a younger man to prove the tabloids wrong? The most bizarre scenario would be that Julie David truly loved Brett. At least until she found out his true nature and learned that he lied about giving her a starring role in the miniseries. I shuddered to think what the papers would say now that Julie's fiancé was dead. Not just dead but murdered. Elle had told me that Arthur and the Southampton PD would keep things on the down-low and that Elle, Felicity, and I should do the same.

Now that Patrick knew everything, it felt like a huge weight had been lifted. We could tackle things together. Or not tackle them at all. Leave the detecting to Arthur and Chief Boyle.

After dragging the standing corkboard next to my drafting table, I perused my choices.

I had been hired to do the interior of a tree house for Suzan and Joel Miller. Talk about fun. It wouldn't be a kids' tree house, but an adult tree house that had been designed and built by a famous Hamptons couple who'd quit their high-pressured Manhattan jobs and moved to Montauk to create upscale outdoor retreats: tree houses, micro-barns, tea houses, along with luxury *He* and *She* sheds. I was hoping that if the Millers were happy with what I did, I might get a referral to do the interior of similar small structures of theirs.

As a child, I'd always wanted a tree house or a fort. We did have one tree in our postage-stamp backyard in Detroit, but it was a Bosc pear tree. That tree bore more fruit than we could handle, which made for great eating, but not supporting a tree house. I wasn't complaining about my childhood. It was magical, thanks mostly to my mother. There hadn't been room to build a fort, but there was room for a pop-up tent. I'd read for hours in that tent. My mother helped me decorate the tent with things from her antiques shop: a worn Aubusson rug, a low Japanese table, two hippie beanbag chairs, and a large battery-operated lantern, which my mother called my Aladdin's lamp. Sometimes we'd sit for hours on our beanbag chairs, reading, eating pizza, and drinking pop (soda to non-Michiganders) until my father came back from his shift on the Detroit PD.

Wiping away a happy tear, I went over to the French antique armoire that I'd bought last August at the Bridgehampton Antiques Show. The same show where I'd bought the walking stick, aka, the murder weapon used on our director. The armoire made the perfect organizing space for old and new clients' files and office supplies.

In the drawers below the armoire's shelves, I'd stored my favorite home and garden magazines, including back issues from when I was editor in chief of *American Home and Garden*. Thinking of the Whitney connection to the magazine, I was reminded of what Felicity had told Elle and me about the Whitneys possibly selling Windy Willow's. From what I knew about Paige Whitney, I couldn't imagine her giving up the family manse. The Whitneys' finances must have really taken a hit, just like Brett Golden's. Before leaving *American Home and Garden*, I'd tried to talk Paige's father, the patriarch of Whitney Publications, into doing an online version of the magazine. He'd rudely dismissed my suggestion. A year later, three out of four of their publications had folded. The consequences seemed to be that there'd been a lack of funds in the Whitney coffers, causing them to rent out their Hamptons estate to the production company of *Mr. & Mrs. Winslow*. Even though we had a two-year rental contract, I wouldn't put it past the Whitneys to sell the estate from under Jeremy. I made a mental note to tell Patrick about it and get his opinion. He might see things more clearly. Even talk his publicist's lawyer husband into taking on the case.

"Excuse me. Have you seen my nurse in shining armor? I was told she wasn't going to let me out of her sight, yet her she is, abandoning her post." I turned to find Patrick. He was wearing a wicked grin, but no raincoat, dripping water onto my studio's white-washed brick floor.

Charlie stood next to him and decided that this was the right time to shake the water off her fur. Luckily for Patrick, she had short hair. The only thing that got sprinkled was a tray of herbs I'd started from seeds that were sitting on a delft-tiled table by the door.

I tried to remain stern but couldn't help but smile. "You're crazy, coming out in this weather after what you just went through."

"I had to take her out for a walk, matron," Patrick said.

"You were just in the hospital. You're incorrigible."

"Am I? You've seen nothing yet."

I swiftly grabbed his arm and led him to the corner of the studio, then made him stand in front of the gas heater. I turned the dial to high, then reached over and snatched a soft, chunky throw off an ornate cast iron garden bench piled with down cushions. I wrapped the throw around his wide shoulders.

It had taken two years of lessons at Karen's Kreative Knitting in Montauk to finish the throw. The reason it wasn't draped designer-like across my bed, or on the back of my sofa, was obvious if you held it up to the light and saw all the uneven stitches. Where purl stitches belonged, there were knit stitches, or vice versa. Regardless, it was still cozy and warm, and many times when working in my studio, I used it as a makeshift shawl.

"It's barely raining," he said, shivering.

"Is that so?" I said, pointing up at the studio's glass roof and the now steady rain.

"What are you working on?" he asked, sitting on the bench and clutching the throw tighter around his hunched shoulders. He looked like Miss Marple, waiting for the *4:50 from Paddington*.

"You should get back inside," I scolded. "I'll stoke the fire, and you can camp out on the sofa."

"That sounds good, but first show me what you're working on."

I wheeled the corkboard side around to face him. In the center of the corkboard I'd pinned a photo of the completed tree house.

"Wow. That thing is huge. I want one," he said with a grin.

"Me too."

"Let's build one together," he said. "Escape from mankind, like Thoreau—'I went to the woods because I wished to live deliberately, to front only the essential facts of life, and see if I could not learn what it had to teach, and not, when I came to die, discover that I had not lived.'"

I laughed. "Isn't that what we've already been doing. Only instead of the woods, we went to the ocean. You in your workshop, and me here in my studio. Surrounded by nature."

"True. But I still like the idea of a tree house."

"Well, let's see how this one goes. I've been toying with keeping the interior very organic. Maybe you could make me a couple of tree trunk tables in your workshop? Only when you're truly recovered, that is."

As I watched Patrick scan the pictures and drawings that I'd posted to the corkboard, I realized that my design aesthetic was leaning toward the Japanese-inspired Wabi-sabi style of design that I'd lectured Sheryl about during our tour at the broker's open house. Which reminded me to tell Patrick of what Felicity said about the Whitneys selling Windy Willows.

After I told him, he said, "How about we make a pact? I'm still celebrating that Evan's alive—"

"And that you're alive," I interrupted.

"Let's forget about any talk about Brett's murder or Windy Willows. At least until tomorrow. I already got a call from Southampton PD. I have an appointment in the morning—"

"If you're well enough."

"If I'm well enough. Then we—" Patrick's phone rang.

He took it from his pocket, then pressed the button on the screen to answer. He held the phone to his ear, and the throw slipped off his shoulders. "Julie," he said into the phone, then he trembled. I didn't know if it was a shiver from the cold or she'd told him some bad news.

Wanting to give him some privacy, I walked to the other side of the studio to the vintage sea-green McCoy biscuit jar that I kept on the top of an old wood filing cabinet. Charlie followed me, her tail wagging so hard it reminded me of those fans on the back of airboats. I reached inside the jar and removed a dog biscuit. My biscuits were store-bought, but Charlie had no problem devouring two at a time.

Occasionally, when Patrick was working on a screenplay or one of his novels, I would babysit Charlie. "Here, girl. Last one," I said, glancing over at Patrick. His head was bent, and he was talking softly into the phone.

Not wanting to be a voyeur, I looked away so that I couldn't read Patrick's lips.

Even though it was killing me.

Chapter 26

I waited in the parking lot of the East End Yacht Club.

Patrick was inside talking to Julie. He'd insisted on going in alone, worried that the paparazzi might be lurking in the shadows. He had an alibi for Brett's murder. I had one also, just not as strong as Patrick's. The papers had gotten ahold of the story of Brett's death. The word *murder* wasn't mentioned, but *suspicious death* was.

Patrick hadn't shared why Julie David wanted to see him. And miracles of all miracles, I didn't press him about it. It appeared that his wish to put off talking about the murder until tomorrow wasn't going to happen. I didn't want to be his mother, so I'd kept my mouth shut, wanting to say that he should stay home and rest from his ordeal. I knew Patrick had a mother somewhere. Another thing we never talked about. He'd once shared that his father had died when he was in his early twenties. It was his father who'd taught him his woodworking skills.

The rain thumped on the roof of my woody. My Motor City father had called in a few favors and had my new black Grand Wagoneer custom-made with side paneling. The paneling wasn't made from real wood, but vinyl. However, it still gave off the same wonderful vintage vibe. Thinking about my car reminded me that I hadn't heard back from my father. It had been almost two weeks since we'd talked. Now would be the perfect time to call.

The call went to voicemail. His smooth, comforting voice came through loud and clear via my hearing aids. I waited for the beep. "Dad, I'm starting to get worried about you. Call me back." I couldn't remember a time when I'd left a message and he didn't return it. I was calling for two reasons, to give him a heads-up about the murder and to see if Sheila had returned home. It looked like if I wanted to know anything, I'd have to go to Georgia, who would get it secondhand from my father's best friend, Doc.

I spent the next fifteen minutes searching on my phone for examples of adult tree houses, amazed at how many there were. I went to stow my phone in my bag at the same time I got a call. Elle's name flashed on the car's display screen.

I tapped the Accept button and heard Elle's heavy breathing.

"Hey, bud. What's up?"

"What's up?" she shouted. "Are you kidding? I had to hear from Georgia about Patrick. Then you ignore my calls. Why does it sound like you're standing in a downpour? Shouldn't you be nursing Patrick?"

"I'm in my car. I'm waiting for Patrick."

"Waiting where? He's not back in the hospital, I hope?"

I explained as succinctly and as vaguely as possible why I was at the yacht club. Ending with, "Don't say a word to your hubby. At least until Patrick tells me what's going on."

"That could take forever," she said. "You're always complaining about how Patrick doesn't share things with you."

Am I? It's funny how I never thought of myself as a complainer. But there it was. I said, "I think things might be different after what happened to him. He really did save someone's life."

"I saw a short blurb about it online in *Dave's Hamptons.* Not much detail. But Patrick sure is a local hero."

"What about the murder?" I asked. "Anything new?"

"Arthur refuses to tell me anything," Elle said, adding a long sigh. "Doesn't want me upset. He should know that I'm more upset that he's *not* sharing. What did Patrick say when you told him?"

"Oops. Can't talk. I see Patrick. And someone's with him."

"Who?"

"Sorry, have to go. Do me a favor, though. There's something that's been bothering me. Can you send me the photos you took yesterday of Brett's body?"

"You're lucky that I still have them," she said. "After I forwarded them to my cop husband, he made me promise to delete them. I didn't. You must be rubbing off on me. Why do you want to see them? Keep me in the loop."

"I can't right now, but I promise I'll explain later. Love you." I pressed the End Call button on the steering wheel and glanced toward two approaching figures sharing an umbrella.

One was Patrick. The other one was Julie David.

Right before the pair reached my car, I got a text from Elle with the three photos. One was a close-up of Brett's chest. It was as I'd remembered.

Loud tapping at my car window made me startle, my phone flew into the air, then did a flip and landed on my lap.

"Open up!" Patrick mouthed through the glass. He looked like a ghost through the sheets of rain coursing down the window. He needed to be back home in bed, not standing in the chilly rain. I unlocked the doors, then turned up the heat.

Patrick opened the rear car door, then ushered Julie inside, gallantly shielding her with his umbrella. Instead of coming to sit in the front passenger seat, Patrick folded the umbrella and got into the backseat with Julie.

Instead of Carson, it looked like I was to be Julie David's chauffeur.

"Have you two met?" Patrick asked. "Meg?"

I twisted in my seat and made eye contact with Julie. "Not officially."

"Julie," he said, "this is Meg Barrett. Meg and I are in a relationship. She told me everything that happened yesterday at Windy Willows."

I thrilled at him telling her we were more than coworkers.

"Meg, you were very kind to me yesterday." Julie's bright violet eyes looked feverish in her pale face. She was wearing her wig but little makeup. "I appreciate how you treated me in front of the others."

Patrick looked surprised, then said, "Now tell me, Julie. What was it you couldn't say in front of your chauffeur?"

"Carson confessed to something that I wasn't ready to share with the police. Not yet, anyway. It isn't my story to tell. But if Carson gets arrested for Brett's murder, or for that matter, I do, I want someone to know about it. Do you both agree not to say anything?"

Patrick glanced over at me, then turned back to Julie. "I don't know if we can promise that. Meg and I aren't lawyers or clergy, but before you begin, Meg told me that this Carson guy was violent toward her. Why don't we just say we'll listen. With no promises. Take it or leave it."

Go, Patrick.

"That's fair," Julie said, her eyes pooling with unshed tears. "Patrick, it has been a while since we've seen each other or even talked, but I will never forget how you saved my life and my sanity by taking me to rehab. It's been four years. I haven't had a drink or a drug since. It's all because of you and Carson. Carson would take a bullet for me, and vice versa. I apologize for his behavior, Ms. Barrett—"

"Meg," I said.

"Carson was probably trying to protect me. You see, Carson and I met at rehab. He was there as part of his probation. He used to be a stunt double and once got into a fight with a lead actor. Carson had been roaring drunk and on illegal steroids. The actor pressed charges. Carson and I went through a lot together in that rehab. We supported each other. We cried together. You would never know it, but Carson's really a big softy. After rehab, he needed a job as part of his probation, so I gave it to him. There's no excuse for his behavior. I will make sure he apologizes to you in person."

"Not necessary," I said, thinking of the dead koi. "All's good."

"Because of his record, that's why I wanted to share things with you, Patrick," she said. She looked from me to Patrick, then rested her thin, veiny hand on top of Patrick's.

Patrick looked down at her hand, then into her eyes. "Then start from the beginning. Why the hell did you get engaged to Brett Golden?" This was the first time I'd seen any reaction in Patrick about Brett's death. I knew him better than to think he was happy that Brett had been murdered. I imagined it was more of a protective mechanism because of what I'd told him about Julie saying that Brett acted like he wanted to kill her after she told him the engagement was off. Still. She had the choice of getting engaged to Brett. Unfortunately, all of us working on the set hadn't any choice of working with him.

"I met Brett in LA," she continued. "He was auditioning to be the director of a small independent movie. The filmmaker asked me to be one of the producers. I agreed. Being a producer seemed to be the only thing I could do since my stint in rehab. Especially after all the bridges I'd burned in the industry. Hollywood was willing to take the Black Widow's money, but not give her an acting role with more than three lines. Brett didn't get the job, but he asked me out. This was about three months ago. It was before he was hired to direct *Mr. & Mrs. Winslow*." She paused and looked out the car window like she was looking into the past.

After a few minutes went by, Patrick said, "So, let me guess, Brett wined and dined you, pretending not to be a narcissistic creep?"

"Kind of," she said. "We got engaged the same day that Jeremy Prentice hired him."

"Only he wasn't hired for the series," Patrick said. "He was hired to do episode three on a trial basis. I doubt if he would have been asked back for episode four."

"I didn't know that until yesterday, after I talked to Mr. Prentice," she said.

"How long have you been in the Hamptons?" he asked.

"A couple weeks. I got to see the real Brett. He didn't seem the same man that I knew in California."

The car's dome light accentuated the bags under Patrick's eyes. "So, you haven't been on the set the entire time you've been here?"

"Not until yesterday."

"Why did you wait until Thursday to call me?" Patrick asked.

My neck was getting a crick in it, so I turned sideways in the driver's seat, and put my legs across the gearshift and my spine against the door's armrest. Now that I was in a comfortable sitting position, I wouldn't miss a word that Julie said.

"I didn't even know you were the screenwriter until Thursday. I swear," she pleaded. "Brett was going on and on about all the old stuff he dug up with his private investigator. You were one of the things he discovered. He warned me to stay away from you. That you would be a bad influence on me, because you would be a reminder of my checkered past, warning me that the tabloids might find out and ruin *his* reputation. He was always acting like he was worried about me relapsing. But now I know that it was all a ruse. All Brett wanted was my money. I wasn't so stupid that I didn't hire my own investigator, and my lawyer was in the process of drawing up an ironclad prenup."

"I never said you were stupid," Patrick said gently.

"Oh, I was," she answered. "Once Brett found out about our connection, which wasn't really much of a connection, more of a kindness from you that unfortunately made the entertainment headlines—a new chapter in the murdering Black Widow's playbook. Brett used it against me and planned to use it against you."

"You're no murderer. You were never charged with anything," Patrick said, then quickly closed his mouth and locked eyes with me. Reading his expression, I gleaned he was trying to convey that we didn't know for sure that Julie was innocent in Brett's murder.

I agreed. Even though I felt for her and knew what a jerk Brett was, I believed she had a motive to kill Brett, or should I say, perhaps she had given Carson a motive to kill Brett. As Agatha Christie's Hercule Poirot said, *"Death, Mademoiselle, unfortunately creates prejudice — a prejudice in favor of the deceased."* No matter the motive, justice had to go to defending the dead.

"How did he plan on using our history against me?" Patrick asked.

She said in a whisper that had me reading her lips, "He knew about the accident involving your wife and child, and how the driver in the other car was drunk. I'm so sorry, Patrick. I never knew about that. You probably hated me and my disease and regretted helping me. I can't blame you. So, yesterday, when we were in the trophy room or billiard room — whatever you call it — Brett said that I had to promise that I would tell you to stop harassing him about changing the script or he would open old wounds. Yours and mine. That's when I told him to shove it. I canceled the engagement and threw the ring at him. But I swear that was the only violent act I did toward him. Though I fantasized about others."

Wow. All I could think about was thank God that Patrick had an alibi. It also made me wonder where all this was going, and how it related to what Carson had told his boss.

"Regardless," she said, "I'm just as much to blame as Brett. He promised me a major role and I fell for it. Even if I had to play a part like Maggie Smith in *Downton Abbey*, I would do it. Prove to everyone that I deserved the awards I received when I was younger. Brett also deceived me that he was very wealthy. I'd had no clue he was broke. Just like all those production companies and executive producers, all Brett cared about was my money."

Patrick looked at me and said, "Meg told me that Oliva and Matt are staying here at the yacht club with you. She also mentioned you got in a physical fight with Olivia."

Julie looked at me. "I felt sorry for Matt because of the father he had. I knew he would only come here if Olivia did. So, I invited them both. They had nowhere else to go. Brett controlled all their money. What little he gave them. As for the fight, you have to look at things through Olivia's eyes. She explained that she and Matt overheard my argument with her father."

I knew Matt and Patrick had gotten along during filming. They both played the guitar and Matt would sometimes try out new lyrics on Patrick. If he wanted to get involved, Patrick could always pull Matt aside and get his spin on the murder of his father. Olivia had already told us hers. "Did you meet Matt and Olivia back in California?" I asked, feeling confident at this point to add my two cents.

"Yes," she said. "I can't say Olivia was happy about the engagement. I think she thought Brett had much more money than he did. And she thought that I was out to take it. Matt just did as he was told. Honestly, I think of Matt as a friend. He has such a sweet soul. Now that I reflect on it, I can't believe he was Brett's offspring."

"Oh, you don't know. Matt was adopted," I said.

Patrick gave me a questioning look. I hadn't told him about Matt being adopted. In the scheme of things, since Patrick had come home from the hospital, I'd only had a short time to talk to him. Like him, owing to how close Olivia and Matt seemed, I would have never guessed that one of them was adopted.

"That explains some things," Julie said. "I bought Matt a signed Bob Dylan acoustic guitar and even gave him the name of a record producer who worked with my last husband, Parker. Brett had a fit when he found out. Said Matt didn't need to be coddled. That he already had a career. But if you're asking me if I think one of them killed Brett, I don't know. I do know I didn't. But I'm sure the police will latch on to my nickname and it will be the end of me. And I would bet on my life Carson didn't kill him, either. That's why I wanted to talk to you, Patrick, without Carson around."

"Let's hear it," Patrick said wearily, leaning back against the seat like he was bracing himself for what she would say next. Either that or he was just exhausted, and rightly so.

Feeling Mama Bearish, I asked, "Ms. David, did Patrick tell you where he was yesterday and this morning?"

Julie shook her head. "No. He didn't."

"The hospital," I said.

"What?" She turned to Patrick. "Why didn't you say something? Why were you in the hospital?"

He gave her a quick recap, being humble as usual.

When he finished, she said, "So that's how you got that black eye and bump on your head. I didn't want to pry when you showed up. I'm not surprised you saved someone's life. But you should have told me. I'm sorry. I'm being selfish. When Brett told me that you were the screenwriter, I was so excited to work with you. To show you how far I've come. I also wanted to warn you that Brett knew about what happened in California."

I couldn't help but interject. "I overheard you tell Olivia that you had no idea about the walking stick having a blade at the end of it. You never saw the scene they filmed? Or were you lying?"

"Yesterday was my first time at Windy Willows. I came early because I'd found out Brett lied to me about a bunch of things. I wanted to confront him. I didn't need another scene that could be splashed across all the East Coast tabloids—I'd already had my share of bad press on the West Coast." She turned to Patrick. "As did you, just being associated with me."

He managed a weak smile.

"I swear," she said. "I know nothing about the weapon that killed Brett. And neither did Carson."

"How can you be sure?" Patrick asked.

"Oh, I'm sure," she replied.

Chapter 27

I glanced over to the yacht club's portico. By this time, the car's interior windows were fogged. For all we knew, Carson might be crouching next to the car, gun or knife in hand, listening to Julie's every word.

Julie swallowed hard before continuing. "I told Carson about something that had happened Wednesday night, when Brett and I were waiting to be seated at the restaurant Pondfare in Montauk to celebrate the end of episode three. Brett went over to the bar and ordered us drinks. He came back and handed me my club soda and lime. Only, when I took a sip, I could taste that there was vodka in it. Whenever we went out, Brett would drink the same nonalcoholic beverage as me. He knew about my sobriety and seemed very supportive. Even claiming since he'd met me he hadn't had a drop of alcohol. He blamed the bartender for the mix-up."

Liar, I thought. I knew Brett had been lying, because Olivia had told me earlier that her father had a fondness for drinking the brandy in Windy Willows' library.

"The only reason I told Carson about it," she said, "was because it was the third time since coming to the Hamptons that something like that had happened."

Not sounding surprised, Patrick asked, "So, are you saying that you think Brett was trying to get you to fall off the wagon?"

"Yes. But I didn't know it for sure. Not until I broke off the engagement. Brett tried to blackmail me, saying if I ended things, he'd contact all the social media platforms and tabloids and tell them I was drinking again. Once we were married, I envisioned him trying to get me into long-term rehab so he could control my estate. I laughed in his face and threw my engagement ring at him. It was probably a fake, anyway."

She was close. It wasn't fake, but I knew it wasn't real either. Brett's scheme to get Julie committed seemed a little too Machiavellian for my ears, but then again, we were dealing with Brett Golden. Maybe Julie wasn't being paranoid. I knew for sure that Olivia thought what her father was saying about Julie's drinking was true.

What if it wasn't? I was leaning heavily toward believing Julie's version. And I'd bet Patrick was too.

"Carson didn't get along with Brett," she said. "When I told Carson about the drinks, he went ballistic."

"Not many people got along with Brett," I added, looking over at Patrick.

"I swear, during our time in California, Brett was the consummate gentleman. I would say, though, the only red flag was when he was with his children. But then, they were his, and I didn't know any of their backstories enough to make a judgment. Carson's been wary of Brett from the beginning but wanted to see me happy. He knows how much I've struggled to stay sober over these past four years. We've both struggled."

"Why did you break off the engagement?" Patrick asked, although by this time we both had a pretty good idea why.

"It was a combination of things. Mostly all the lies. The lies about where he lived and his finances. The lies about getting me a part that he had no say in. The way he treated his children. The way he talked about you, Patrick, even though I told him you had been a friend when I needed one. And lastly, I realized it was he who'd kept pushing for us to get married. I fought it every step of the way. For his sake, I didn't want him labeled as another husband of the Black Widow. I realize now I selfishly relented and got engaged because of the major acting role he'd promised me. I wanted it so bad. I let it cloud my judgment. The possibility that he'd spiked my drink was the poison icing on the cake. I'm stronger now that I'm sober, but no matter how long it's been, it's still one day at a time."

"So how does this relate to Carson? Or for that matter, Brett's murder?" I asked, glancing at Patrick to see his reaction. His closed fists told me everything.

"Earlier, when Carson had walked me to the billiard room, he'd wanted to stand guard outside the door just in case anything went wrong. I'd insisted that I'd be fine and told him to wait in the car with the engine running, so we could make our escape. Our plan was to pack our bags and immediately leave the Hamptons. After I broke off my engagement with Brett, I went outside to the Rolls. Carson wasn't inside. I'd assumed that he'd gotten worried and went looking for me. I got into the backseat of the car and sent him a text that I was waiting for him. I was nervous that Brett might find me, so I ducked down in the seat and hid.

"Brett had been beyond furious after I ended things — another side I never saw in him. I honestly thought he was going to throw something at me as I ran out of the billiard room." Julie took in a deep breath, then continued, "About twenty minutes later, Carson finally answered my text. Told me to meet him in the summerhouse, just beyond the party tent. So I did. That's when he told me — "

"Told you what?" Patrick asked.

"Carson told me that when he went looking for me in the billiard room, he found Brett lying on his side on the carpet next to the pool table. Brett had a huge gash on the side of his head. Carson checked for a pulse and found one. Carson told me that Brett even moaned something and flailed his arms. That's when Carson noticed a large sterling silver loving cup with a raised figurine of a fox on the floor next to him. It had blood on it. Thinking the worst, that I was the one who hit Brett with the loving cup, Carson grabbed it and ran out of the room."

I knew all about the fox-hunting trophy. Elle had brought it in from Mabel and Elle's Curiosities in order to stage the billiard room for a scene in episode two of *Mr. & Mrs. Winslow* that starred Jack Winslow's great-uncle Henry, who was written into the script as an accomplished sportsman. I recalled Elle placing the loving cup on the fireplace mantel, next to a dozen other trophies. All the trophies in the billiard room related to hunting of some kind. "Let me get this straight," I interrupted, worried that my car was going to run out of gas, Carson would surprise attack us, or Patrick might have to be dropped back at the hospital. "Brett was in the billiard room, on the floor, alive. Then how did he end up in the library with the blade of the walking stick in his chest?"

Julie shook her head. "That, I can't answer. Nor can Carson. But I didn't kill him. I swear. And I know Carson didn't either. I didn't hit him with any loving cup. On top of that, Carson and I never set foot in the library. I didn't know anything about that walking stick thing until we were in the kitchen, and Olivia accused me of killing her father.

"There's more," Julie said, turning to Patrick. "After I told Carson I didn't hit Brett on the head with anything, we sat in the summerhouse for a good hour, trying to decide what to do, just staring at the bloody loving cup. Carson decided we should bury it. Then, after he did, he'd take a different path back to the Rolls and we'd leave. You have to understand," Julie pleaded, "at this point, we thought Brett was alive. We knew he wouldn't be coming after us when he regained consciousness. He'd go after whoever walloped him with the loving cup." She nodded her head in my direction. "I guess Carson's plans got thwarted after you chased after him."

"Did Carson leave a dead fish on the hood of Meg's car last night?" Patrick asked. "And how do you know that in those twenty minutes that you waited in the car, that this Carson didn't drag Brett from the billiard room, then stab him with the walking stick?"

"Because I know he wouldn't do that. Plus, how would he know about a walking stick with a blade. I've never heard of such a thing."

She had a point there. When I was in the library, I'd retracted the blade. Whoever stuck it in Brett must have known about it.

"As for a dead fish," she said, "Carson and I left Windy Willows together last night. I think I would have noticed if he'd done that."

I believed her about that one. But like Patrick, I didn't totally believe that Carson hadn't killed Brett to protect Julie. I asked, "How did you end up in the kitchen after meeting Carson in the summerhouse?"

"Olivia. I ran into Matt on the way to the Rolls. Olivia saw us and ran out of the kitchen door like she was possessed, grabbed me, and dragged me back inside. Meg, you showed up not long after."

We were silent. My head was spinning. The only sound was the rain on the roof of my car, which had intensified as soon as Julie finished talking.

"Even if you don't want to believe it, Carson could be lying," Patrick said softly, turning to Julie.

"I don't think so. I just don't know how to prove it."

I noticed that Patrick didn't say, *you both could be lying*.

I reached next to me, where I had my phone charging, took it off the charger, opened it, tapped the screen and passed it to Patrick. He shielded it from Julie, then enlarged the photo with his fingertips. "Notice anything missing?" I asked him.

He looked up at me and said, "No."

"Look closer."

He held the phone to the tip of his nose, then scrutinized the photo. I saw his eyes light up at the Aha moment. Patrick wrote a lot of death scenes in his thrillers, and even in *Mr. & Mrs. Winslow*. He also had connections to the NYPD when researching his novels. I was sure he'd noticed what I had—there wasn't any blood around Brett's wound from the walking stick's blade.

Sad to say, I'd witnessed the aftermath of a fatal stabbing before. There was one thing I knew for sure, there should be blood if Brett was stabbed while he was still alive. Where was the blood? Which might collaborate Carson's story that Brett had been wounded in the billiard room and possibly died there, then after he was dead, someone dragged him to the library, where they stuck him with the blade of the walking stick. It sounded far-fetched. But it would also explain why the three of us in the dining room didn't hear voices or hear him call out in pain.

Arthur was no dummy, and I was sure the Suffolk County coroner wasn't either. It would be easy for them to figure out the same thing I had. If Brett was alive when Carson saw him, as Julie said, and then died because Carson didn't call for help, was that a crime? I knew destroying evidence was—as in the loving cup. But Carson didn't really destroy it, he buried it. It could be *un*buried.

I looked at Julie. "Did Carson wipe the prints off the loving cup?"

"You know what, dear. I don't know. Why?"

"Just wondering. Because if what you said is true, that you or Carson didn't hit Brett with the loving cup, then maybe the prints of who did are still on the cup."

Without showing the photo on my phone to Julie, Patrick handed my phone back to me.

Why hadn't he showed Julie the photo? Then I realized, if Julie and her Carson had been involved in Brett's death, I'd just told her to wipe the prints off the murder weapon.

If Carson hadn't already.

I had a feeling when I looked over at Patrick that he was thinking the same thing as me. Now that we knew all this information, true or false, what were we supposed to do with it?

A couple minutes later, when there was nothing left to say, Patrick walked Julie back to the yacht club entrance. He didn't go inside but came back to the car and got into the front seat.

We sat for a moment in stunned silence.

"What did you tell her?"

Seeming drained of all emotion, he said, "What do you think?"

"I think Julie shouldn't have put you in this position. It's up to her and Carson to do what a wise cricket once said — *Let your conscience be your guide.*"

"I told her I'd give Carson the night to sleep on it. If he doesn't go to the police, I will."

"Good. I agree."

"I shouldn't have put *you* in this position," he said. "But you wouldn't allow me to drive here on my own."

"True, I wouldn't. Nor your doctor, per your hospital release papers. I should have chained you to the bed. Let Julie and Carson wrestle with their own demons, instead of involving us."

He gave me a weak attempt at an Elvis lip curl. "There you go again with those bed references."

"You're hopeless. When you think about it, Julie has done nothing wrong. It's Carson who has to go to Arthur or Chief Boyle." I glanced out the window as the last light of the day disappeared. "If Carson's smart, he'll go tonight."

"We'll see. Thanks for bringing me here. Sometimes sharing things with others helps you get a clearer picture of how to solve a situation."

I turned to him, realizing he wasn't just talking about Julie, he was talking about us. I bent over and gave him a kiss on his bruised cheekbone.

"Ouch, Nurse Barrett. Careful with those rough kisses."

"Just be a good patient," I scolded. "Sometimes the cure hurts more than the injury."

"What poet wrote that?" he asked, the sparkle back in his gorgeous eyes.

"I don't know if you've ever heard of her. Her first name rhymes with keg, her second with carrot."

"Keg Carrot. Interesting. This poet is pretty wise. I might have to take a little more of her cure. But not until I am relaxing in front of a fire and holding this Keg Carrot in my arms."

The rest of Saturday evening was spent with me playing nursemaid and Patrick milking things to the max. He'd consumed four more grilled cheeses, polished off three-quarters of the leftover coq au vin, and ate a whole quart of Ben and Jerry's Super Fudge Chunk ice cream. I'd showed him the photo of Jo and Charlie snuggled together, and we'd played a game of Scrabble, which I was thankful that he'd won.

Our conversation with Julie in my car wasn't brought up, and even though he'd gotten involved in the murder investigation because of her, it didn't change his new outlook on life.

I couldn't have been happier.

Throughout the evening, Elle continued to text me, until finally I'd texted her back: *Unless it's a life and death emergency, I'll call you later tonight. Patrick and I are cuddling.*

I watched the bouncing emoji dots, telling me that Elle was typing.

Ew-w-w. 2 much info. Fill me in tomorrow when I pick you up to go to the Halstead prop.

OK. Give Georgia the address. She knows Everett.

She told me. Now go snuggle.

I obeyed.

Chapter 28

Sunday morning, I'd slept later than usual. Last night, around ten, Patrick had insisted on going home to sleep in his own bed and in his own clothes. Apparently, my loaned Detroit Tigers sweats weren't as comfy on him as they were on me.

I showered, dressed, fed Jo, and took off for town. At Paddy's Pancake House, I picked up an order of ham and cheese crepes and two extra-large coffees. I'd promised Patrick breakfast in bed. But when I arrived, he was already up and dressed and ready to take Charlie out for a walk.

"No way in H-E-double-toothpicks are you going out into this wind," I said in a stern schoolteacher's voice.

"That's a new one," he said, laughing.

"Even though you look like you're back to your young wonderful self, I insist on taking Charlie for a walk on the beach."

"Have at it," he said, handing me her leash.

When we returned and went into the kitchen, I chastised Patrick for not going ahead and eating his crepes without me. Telling him that he needed his sustenance after such a harrowing, near-death experience.

Again, I was starting to sound like his mother.

Not the relationship I was going for.

He gave me a mischievous grin and placed our plates on the kitchen counter. "Have a seat. I have a surprise." He opened the warming drawer below his double oven and took out a small ceramic pitcher, then he poured a lemony yellow sauce over our crepes.

"Are you serious? In the short time that I was gone, you made hollandaise sauce from scratch? Not that I'm complaining," I said as I grabbed my knife and fork, then cut off a piece and shoved it into my pie hole. "Heavenly," I added, licking my lips.

Patrick laughed and sat on the bar stool next me. "You're easy to please."

"You're easy on the eye," I answered, "not to mention the best hollandaise maker this side of the Rio Grande. Don't tell my father that I said that. Michigan is also east of the Rio Grande."

During the meal, neither one of us mentioned Brett's murder.

Then my serene bubble popped with Patrick's next words. "I

talked to Arthur this morning. He said that there was no need to go to the Southampton Police Department until I was up to it. Elle must have told him that I was in the hospital at the time of the murder."

"I'm sure she did," I said, as I held my breath for the answer to my next question. "Did you tell him about what Julie told us?"

He met my gaze. "I considered it. Then I decided to give them a little more time. How about this? If they don't go today and confess, tomorrow you and I will talk to Arthur. I don't know about you, but I believe this Carson guy's story. If he was Brett's killer, and knowing he has a record, I would think he would be in Mexico by now. In the meantime, I'm going to try to get ahold of Matt. Feel him out."

"Good idea. But you better not overdo it, buster."

He raised a perfect arched eyebrow. "Or what?"

"You'll answer to me. Plus, our mild-mannered Matt could still be our killer."

"It's hard to think of Matt killing his father. I don't know if he has the spine for it."

"Maybe Oliva told Matt to do it," I said. "It would be nice to get a copy of Brett's will, even though we know from Julie and Felicity that Brett was broke. Maybe your publicist could get her attorney husband to look into it?"

"That won't be happening. Even if we do some discreet sleuthing, Jessica Fletcher, I'm not involving anyone other than Arthur."

I smiled. "A young Jessica Fletcher, I hope. Though I do have a few extra lines on my forehead from worrying about you. Please check in after you talk to Matt. Elle and I are going out to the Halstead property this afternoon. Alice from Sand and Sun is hopefully signing the papers with the owner. If all goes smoothly, Elle and I plan to go through the contents of the house to see what stays and what goes for our staging." I gave him a quick recap of what Georgia had told me about Everett Halstead.

"Sounds interesting. There've always been a lot of rumors about supernatural phenomena going on at Camp Hero. Mind control and aliens, et cetera. Maybe the old guy will debunk them."

"Or prove them," I said, thinking of the strange man I'd assumed was Delia's grandfather, who looked like a wizened troll doll.

Patrick took his napkin and swiped a spot of hollandaise sauce from the corner of his mouth. "Did you know that in the sixties, there was a horror sci-fi film shot in Montauk called *The Flesh Eaters*? Pretty sure it was filmed on the shore near Camp Hero. It had to do with a Nazi mad scientist who created a sea creature that lived off human flesh. Not dead flesh, mind you."

"Live flesh must be the best flesh," I said, laughing.

"The movie's quite campy, but fun to watch as a comedy. And it's so interesting to see how old horror films were produced before computer and blue screen technology. I think the flesh-eater was made from papier-mâché."

"It's a date," I said. "Tonight I'll make the popcorn and you can come over and we'll watch it together. Afterward, we could do s'mores on the beach. If you're up for it?"

He grinned. "I'm up for it. But I'll make the popcorn. You make the marshmallows—they're meant to be burnt."

"Hardy-har-har."

Patrick got up and put our empty dishes in the sink. Then he filled our mugs with more coffee and sat next to me. "Speaking of Montauk locations, Jeremy is thinking of renting out Camp Hero State Park to film an episode of *Mr. & Mrs. Winslow*. It's not a bad idea. When the park was a military base, they had it set up like a small town to trick possible enemy aircraft from knowing what was really going on."

"They'd have to edit out that huge radar tower. But you're right. It would make a cute little town, circa the late thirties for the miniseries. After what happened, I hope the series continues."

"The series will continue. No matter who killed Brett. But we all could be replaced in a heartbeat. That's showbiz," he said with a grin.

"Not the screenwriter," I said. "That's why the series was greenlighted. The network loved your spec screenplay."

He laughed. "And they loved Jeremy's money. We're all replaceable. Even the show's writer. I was considering quitting, anyway, before . . ."

We were both silent, thinking about the murder.

"Elle's been very sneaky lately," I said. "Spying on her hubby. Maybe she'll have something useful to say about the case. That's if we want to know anything about the case," I added with trepidation.

"Don't think we have much of a choice. I'm not sure about you, but I'm not thrilled working on set with a killer who gets away with murder. Plus, I don't like the possible meaning behind that fish someone put on your car. If Carson didn't do it, who did? Was there anyone besides Carson that you might have pissed off on Friday, Ms. Barrett?"

"I've been thinking about that. Olivia got a little testy with me when we were chatting in the kitchen."

"Testy?"

"But she was all over the place, and rightly so."

"Her father not going forward with the special effects company that he promised to buy her could have also made her testy," he said.

"I forgot about that. Well, I'm glad you'll be talking to Matt. We haven't had that many conversations. How about our assistant director? You've worked closely with Nikki. She's an enigma in the scheme of things." I told him about the conversation I overheard in the garden when Nikki was on the phone.

"Whoa! One suspect at a time," he said. "I thought you told me to take it easy."

"I'm not saying today. Just sometime down the line. So—are we doing this?"

"Doing what?" he asked with fake innocence.

I gave him a light punch to his upper arm.

"Ouch!"

"OMG, did I hurt you?"

He gave me an evil grin.

I shook my finger at him, which he kissed. "Don't tease me. Just answer the question."

"As I said, do we have a choice? Especially knowing you, Ms. Snoopy Pants."

I smiled, knowing he was right.

Chapter 29

Elle picked me up at one for our trip to the Halstead property. Alice and Georgia planned on meeting us there. I was wearing a sweatshirt, jeans, and work boots. Elle was dressed in a red-and-white-check blouse, navy overalls, and her dark shoulder-length hair was pulled back in a handkerchief tied in rabbit ears on top of her head. Between her aqua vintage pickup truck and her Rosie the Riveter outfit, I thought that Elle was meant to be born in a different decade.

On the way to the Halsteads', I filled Elle in on anything that Georgia might have left out about Patrick and the surfing accident. I ended with how he'd mumbled *Catherine*. Until now, I hadn't given it a second thought. I was feeling confident in our relationship, mostly due to our romantic evening last night. I'd mentioned Catherine to Elle more as a diversion, trying to avoid telling her about Carson's confession to Julie. I rarely kept things from Elle, but in this case, we were dealing with a very sticky wicket because of her homicide detective husband (Georgia had once told me that the term *sticky wicket* came from the game cricket—not from a children's nursery rhyme). I would let Elle latch on to my *former* insecurity about Patrick's past and do what she did best—become distracted by propping up my ego.

"I wouldn't take it personally," Elle said, taking a sharp left onto Hwy 27, then a sharp right onto Edgemere, passing the village green and Montauk Manor. She pointed to the manor. "Look! There's the twin black Scotties that play the Winslows' dog Whiskey. I can never remember their names, or which one is which."

"Murphy and Max," I said. "They have completely different personalities. I have no trouble telling them apart."

"Maybe after the Halsteads, we could stop by Montauk Manor, see the dogs and then maybe run into Nikki and talk to her. You and I haven't had much contact with our assistant director."

"Thought your hubby said to stay away?"

"Yeah, from Windy Willows. Not Montauk Manor."

"You're nit-picking. We need to stay out of it."

"Doesn't matter, anyway," Elle said with a mischievous grin. "I already put Felicity on the case, seeing that she's also staying at the manor."

Elle swerved to avoid a pothole. "Friday, while you were out looking for Olivia's phone and being manhandled by Julie David's chauffeur, I had an interesting conversation with Olivia regarding Nikki Meyers."

"Really? What did she say?"

"First of all, I think Olivia is very immature and insecure."

"Wouldn't you be, having Brett as your father?"

"I don't think she cares half as much about her father as she does about her brother."

"Matt's adopted."

"Really? Well, that doesn't seem to matter to Olivia. When you left me in Windy Willows' kitchen with Olivia, Nikki came in. She was looking for Matt. She'd found out about Brett's murder from Felicity and asked Olivia if Matt knew about it. Olivia went nuts on her. I know she just lost her father, but her reaction was strange. She told Nikki to 'Keep the hell away from my brother.' That it was a family issue and Nikki wasn't family, telling her that she'd be the only one speaking to Matt. This was about the same time that Arthur arrived."

"That is bizarre. Good sleuthing. Did you tell Arthur?"

"I did. I don't think he thought it was important. But you never know. I think he's made his mind up on who's guilty. So far, though, there's nothing to prove it."

"Let me guess, he thinks it's Julie David."

"Yes. I'm leaning that way also. Maybe it's as simple as that. Just because Brett was an obnoxious human being, it doesn't mean his death shouldn't be avenged. You said the same thing earlier when we were talking about the Black Widow."

I remained silent, looking out the window as she continued, "Except for Julie David and her Carson, it seems between the four of us, we have our bases covered."

I avoided looking at her. "True, Mrs. Detective Shoner. But please leave my name out of anything when talking to your hubby. I'm already in the doghouse for telling him about Brett putting the moves on you. Speaking of which, have you learned anything more about the case when you were eavesdropping on Arthur?"

"How'd you know I was eavesdropping?" she asked, turning her head sharply to look at me and nearly missing the turn leading to the Halstead property.

"Because I know you."

She laughed. "I wanted to save this information — 'cause it's gonna blow your socks off. The blade on the walking stick wasn't the murder weapon. Brett was stabbed postmortem." She pulled the pickup to the side of the road, put the truck in Park, and looked over at me with self-satisfaction. I turned away, not wanting to meet her luminous chocolate brown eyes.

"Hey. Don't tell me you already knew that? Why don't you seem surprised?"

I turned toward her and thought out my words before speaking. "The photos you sent. Remember? There was no blood around the wound."

"Do you mean dead guys don't bleed?"

"Exactly." That was a close one. It was the perfect time to tell Elle about our conversation last night in my car, but I didn't want to betray Julie's confidence until she had a chance to make it right. At the back of my mind, I was hoping the pair would go to the police together.

"Learn something new every day," Elle said, pulling back onto the gravel road. "I think Carson is Arthur's number-two suspect. That guy's scary. Did you see all his tattoos? No peace signs or hearts with *I love Mom* and a Cupid's arrow. But lots of gargoyles, fire-breathing dragons, and bloody daggers."

"You can't judge a man or a woman by their tattoos. Maybe when he was younger he played a lot of Dungeons and Dragons," I said.

"I beg to differ. Speaking of Carson, how are your knees?"

"Fine," I lied. Last night, I must have slept like the dead with my legs stretched out flat on the bed, because when I got up to feed Miss Impatience and bent my legs to stand, I broke open newly formed scabs. I screamed in pain, and all Jo did was nip at the back of my PJ top in irritation, telling me it was no time for a pity party and to get moving downstairs to the kitchen.

"Carson doesn't scare me," I said. It was funny, after I said it out loud, I realized I meant it. Which also meant that I believed Julie was a good judge of character. After all, she'd gone to Patrick twice for help, and he'd given it.

"What about the dead fish on your car? Aren't you scared he'll come after you?"

"For what reason? I put the wrong Empire chair in the front parlor room on the set of *Mr. & Mrs. Winslow*? I have no ties to Brett Golden. Neither one of us do. Why complicate things."

Elle smiled. "That doesn't sound like you. But I'm happy to follow your lead. All this cloak-and-dagger stuff is fun for a while, but it wears off quickly when it happens in real life. I don't know how Arthur can separate his emotions when it comes to murder. Maybe you get used to it. Like Arthur, you probably are a little more objective because you grew up with a homicide detective father. I'm sure Jeff's seen a thing or two. Especially living in Detroit."

"That's what's great about my dad. Even though he's worked more cases than they ever would in the Hamptons, he's treated each case individually, trying not to bring it home with him at night. Sometimes he'd discuss it with Mom. He said that she was the best listener. Later, after her death, he'd sometimes share a case or two with me. But only after it made the papers."

"So, maybe someday, I can be like your mother. And Arthur will share with me?"

"Maybe. Speaking about my father—" As she traveled down the rutted road at a snail's pace, I told her about the argument between my father and Sheila.

"I'm sure they will work it out." She glanced over at me. "Do you want them to work it out?"

"I want whatever makes him happy."

"Of course. Now, let's focus on the hope that Mr. Halstead signs the contract and we can get started clearing out the house for staging. It will be a great distraction. One we both could use," she added.

"Hey, weren't you supposed to take a right back there?"

"Drats." Elle did a U-ie, then she turned onto Sandpiper Lane, another rutted dirt road, barely wide enough for two cars to pass. In the near distance, I could see the Halstead cottage. As Elle accelerated, I glanced to my right and shouted. "Wait! Do you see what I see?"

She pressed her foot on the brake and I flew forward, then backward, my seat belt tightening around me.

Elle leaned over and looked out the passenger window. Behind rusty iron gates, straight out of a horror movie, was a weathered sign posted: *For Sale by wner.* The *O* in *Owner* was worn away by what appeared to be decades of inclement weather. I rolled down my window and stuck my head out of the pickup. Down a super-long, overgrown winding driveway, I spied a huge white house—okay, it was more gray than white. Three brick chimneys were visible through the dense thicket of trees.

"OMG!" Elle said, pounding the steering wheel in excitement. "Is this one of those serendipitous moments that you tell your grandchildren about while you're sitting around the fire, knitting them an afghan?"

"I gave up knitting—now trying to crochet."

"I'm serious," she said, her eyes all aglow.

Then Elle went on about a dream she'd had last night, where she and Arthur found a cache of loot belonging to the local pirate Captain Kidd. "It has to be a sign. Aren't we near where Kidd buried his treasure?"

"Not really, but as you said, it was a dream. Did you look it up in one of your books?"

"No need to now. Just look over there at that house."

"You mean mini-mansion. Won't it be too big for you and Arthur to ramble around in? And if it's been for sale for so long, something must be wrong with it. Probably the price. The yard is overgrown, and the house looks uninhabited. Unless it's filled with ghosts. That would explain things."

I realized I better stop talking Elle out of loving the place, because, like her, I was dying to see what was inside. I took out my phone and went to my map app. I enlarged the map of our current location and almost choked on my excitement, saying, "The water! The Block Island Sound is behind that big house. Can you imagine the views?"

"That's what I've been trying to tell you," Elle said. "The treasure in my dream, it has to be that house beyond the trees. And there's no way I'm going to imagine the view. Let's go see it! We're already dressed for scavenging. Remember what your place looked like before you worked on it. You couldn't even see the folly. And what about your walled garden? I know it was a labor of love to restore them both. Because I was there to help you."

She was right. Best friends usually were. "Slow down, partner. We can't leave Alice waiting for us. You do realize that this property borders the Halsteads'. Let's go make sure the paper's get signed. We'll go through the contents of the house and tag what stays and what goes for the staging. Then, on the way back, we can do some exploring. Maybe Delia's grandfather knows something about the house that might just turn out to be a twin to the one in *The Amityville Horror*."

"Stop," Elle said. "Did you know that Amityville is about eighty miles from here? Plus, have you seen a recent picture of the house? It's a Dutch colonial that's been beautifully renovated. After I saw the most recent movie about it, I looked it up on a real estate app."

"I didn't think you liked horror films."

"I don't. Arthur does. He made me watch it. We take turns picking movies. I was happy to see a photo of the house in *Long Island Newsday*. It's a far cry from the one in the movie that was based on the real-life story of a depraved son who wiped out his entire family."

"So, even though they've updated the Amityville house on the outside, how do you know the inside doesn't still have a poltergeist or two? Or three?"

"I'm sure if there were any hanging around, we'd read about it."

"After a slaying or two, maybe," I said.

"You're not going to scare me away from this house, Megan Barrett. My point is, if that house can get a face-lift—so can this one," she said, pointing. "Don't you dare jinx what might be our next fixer-upper and my humble abode."

"Worse comes to worst," I said, glancing between the rails of the ornate rusty gates, "we could track down the owner and use the house for filming a scene in *Mr. & Mrs. Winslow*."

"No. I feel it in my bones. This is Arthur's and my new home. It doesn't belong to any ghosts or our production company."

I could have sworn she had tears in her eyes. I wondered what had happened to the unemotional Elle who was so calm, cool, and collected after the discovery of Brett's body.

"Okay. Whatever you say. But remember that you're newly married. Arthur might nix the idea of renovating something on such a large scale. Especially if it's haunted." I started to sing the theme song from the old *Addams Family* television show, just as a silver Mercedes convertible traveling at least fifty miles per hour flew by us. It left behind a cloud of dust that settled on the pickup's windshield.

"Oh, my!" Elle said. "I know that car."

"You do?"

"I've seen it multiple times on *Hamptons Premier Listings*. And I recognize the license plate. That was Finn Larsen's car."

I was sure we were thinking the same thing. Elle doused the windshield with washer fluid and we took off.

Finn was here to poach Alice's listing.

Chapter 30

As we pulled in behind Georgia's and Alice's cars, I said to Elle, "If Finn Larsen made a trip out here for such a small listing, things must be getting pretty competitive in the Hamptons."

Finn's convertible was parked on the front lawn, not the gravel driveway. He seemed to be in a hurry. I wouldn't be surprised if he'd left the engine running.

As soon as Elle put the pickup in Park, I jumped out, then sprinted to the Halsteads' front porch.

Finn, dressed in a suit, fuchsia tie, and matching pocket square, was talking to Delia through the screen door.

Out of breath, I bent over to regain my composure. After I stood, that same composure vanished when I heard Delia say, "Come inside, Mr. Larsen."

Darn. She'd recognized him from the television series.

Delia ushered him inside, then closed the screen door in my face.

"That was rude," Elle said from behind.

"We better get inside. We need to protect Alice," I whispered. I tugged on the handle to the door, then held it open for Elle to pass through. I walked inside, making sure to slam the screen door to get everyone's attention, alerting them that the cavalry had arrived.

But it appeared that Georgia, who was standing next to a threadbare armchair with her hand on Everett Halstead's shoulder, had control of the situation. Everett Halstead was indeed the same figure I'd seen peering out from the metal outbuilding. At the top of his head was a thinning section of white hair that sprouted like a kewpie doll's. His complexion was almost as pale as his hair, as if it'd been years since he'd seen a drop of sunlight. His back was hunched, his thin frame almost skeletal, and his eyes, most likely once a bright blue, were covered with milky cataracts.

Finn handed Delia his business card. Delia took it but didn't look at it. It was obvious that she already knew who he was. Georgia, on the other hand, had no clue. "I'm sorry, whoever you are, the contract has already been written up and we were about to ask Mr. Halstead if selling his home is something he wants to do." Georgia looked over at Delia, waiting for her conformation. Delia didn't give one.

"That's true. It hasn't been signed," Delia said. "Mr. Larsen, I'd love to get your input."

"Call me Finn," he said, smiling at her with a white-toothed smile that resembled a cartoon shark's. "And you are—"

Before Delia could answer, I yelled out, "She's the granddaughter. The homeowner is sitting in the chair over there, and he's already picked what company he's going with. Sand and Sun."

Finn turned toward Elle and me. "You two look familiar. Oh, yes, you were at the broker's open house. The one where I won the multimillion-dollar listing. Wasn't there some kind of embarrassing incident?" He swept his gaze around the room and settled on Alice, who, if she'd been confident when she'd walked in, clearly wasn't now. Her spine was pressed against the grimy, peeling wallpaper like she was about to get executed by a firing squad. Her eyes resembled a deer's caught in headlights of Finn's Mercedes. Alice opened her mouth a few times, then closed it.

"Multimillion," Delia repeated. "Congratulations. I'm Delia Halstead." She extended her hand, and Finn took it, then bowed to kiss it.

"Mr. Larsen, how did you find out about this?" I asked. "This will be a pocket listing. And it won't be on MLS." I'd learned the real estate lingo from watching the show, but I wouldn't let him know that.

"I'm the Hamptons' number-one broker. I have connections everywhere. And as this beautiful young woman just said,"—he nodded his head in Delia's direction—"nothing has been signed." Then Finn shouted, "Shazam!" and did his signature fisted air pump.

Delia was the only one who reacted by clapping her hands. She said, "Grandfather, did you hear that? Mr. Larsen is the best broker in the Hamptons. He will get us, I mean you, the best price for this place."

Georgia leaned down until she was eye to eye with Everett, then asked in a soothing voice, "What do you want to do, dear? Do you want to sell your house and property?" She took his thin, veiny hand in her strong one.

Everett looked confused. I had a feeling that he'd been blindsided by the whole idea of selling his home. He shook his head in the negative. Then he grabbed an old *Popular Mechanics* from the coffee table, opened it, and flipped through while humming Frank Sinatra's "I've Got You Under My Skin."

"We talked about this, Grandfather," Delia said with an edge to her voice. "Daddy wants you to sell. We'll find you a nice place to live. Where someone can look after you."

Everett looked up from the magazine, then blinked a few times. He said, "Oh, you're Freddie's kid. Not selling. Go away. I have Madison to take care of me."

I think everyone in the room was surprised by the clarity with which he spoke.

"Grandfather, you don't know what you're saying. I'm calling a doctor. Daddy said if you don't agree, we'll have to have you seen by a professional."

"No doctor. I want Madison. The doctors will take what's left," he said cryptically, pointing to his head. Then he covered his mouth with his hand and whispered something into Georgia's ear.

"My cousin's out of the country," Delia said, looking over at Finn, her cheeks pink in embarrassment. "I think in some god-awful country in Africa. You don't need her, Grandfather. You've got me." Then, like an afterthought, she said, "Madison told me to take care of you."

"Pshaw." His long earlobes wiggled as he continued to shake his head no. With a little help from Georgia, Everett got up from his chair. Still holding the magazine, he walked across the living room with a slight limp and went out the screen door. Through the screen, I saw him open the magazine and place it on his head like it was a hat. It wasn't raining, and there were only a few clouds in the sky.

Delia stepped closer to Finn. Grinning nervously, she said in a chirpy voice, "He gets a little confused sometimes. He's agreed to the sale, Mr. Larsen. I swear. Do you want to have a tour?"

"Call me Finn," he said, glancing around the room at the shabby furniture and dusty knickknacks. "I've seen enough. This will be a teardown. How many acres?"

"Two," Delia answered.

"I'd like to take a look at the grounds," he said. Then, not waiting for Delia's approval, he started toward the door.

Delia followed him outside, leaving us not knowing if we should stay or go.

After they were out of hearing distance, Elle asked, "Georgia, what did Mr. Halstead whisper to you?"

"He wants me to meet him in the building outside."

"You go," I said. "We'll wait here for Delia and the Hamptons Wolf of Main Street."

After Georgia left, Alice came and sat on the sofa next to Elle, sending up a cloud of dust. "I don't feel good about trying to sell this house from under Mr. Halstead. Where will he go? What would Aunt Barb do?"

Elle turned to her and said, "Exactly what you're doing. She'd have empathy for the homeowner. That's why Sand and Sun Realty has lasted so long in Montauk. Maybe after Georgia talks to Mr. Halstead, we'll find out more about his mental state, and his true feelings about selling."

"I think we have time to figure things out," I said. "Alice, trust me, Finn Larsen would never do a four-percent commission like you told Delia you would do. And even if she decides to go with another company, she would still have to get her grandfather to agree."

"Maybe we should just walk away," Alice said in a beaten voice. "But if we do that, what will become of Mr. Halstead? He might need our help."

"Let's wait to see what Georgia reports back," Elle said. "It's a good sign that Mr. Halstead remembers her and wants to talk to her."

The spark returned to Alice's eyes. "I did get a new listing from a family that's been coming to Montauk for generations. They're good friends of Aunt Barb and Uncle Jack. I met them in the office. Because of the two of you, I think I was more confident when talking to them, especially compared to how I handled this deal. Do you want to come along when we sign the papers tomorrow?"

"Alice, that's great," I said. "You don't need us. I think you'll be fine on your own."

"I agree," Elle said.

"But, of course, we'll be there to help if you need any staging," I said.

"Oh, Meg, that's the good part. This cottage belongs to the Kittingers. Your company, Cottages by the Sea, already did the interior. It doesn't need a thing."

"Oh. Wow. Why are they moving?" The Kittinger property was

one of the first cottages that my then fledgling business had been hired to decorate. It was located in Montauk, just east of my cottage, on the ocean. I could only imagine the price it would sell for in the current market.

"They want a bigger summer cottage for their growing family."

"Let me know if they need any help once they find their dream cottage. Which I'm sure you'll be able to find them. Such a nice couple to work with."

"Oh, I'm sure they'll call you for the interior design of their new cottage. Anyone that comes into Sand and Sun gets one of your business cards. Aunt Barb insists on it."

"I miss her," I said, taking a seat in the chair Everett had vacated.

"So do I." Alice was dressed differently than when I'd first seen her at the broker's open house. If I wasn't mistaken, it appeared that Elle or her assistant, Maurice, had given Alice a few fashion and makeup tips. At the thought of makeup, I was reminded of the murder at Windy Willows and *Mr. & Mrs. Winslow*'s head makeup artist, Olivia. Before I had time to ruminate on it, Georgia walked inside.

"Hurry. Everyone outside while that granddaughter and showboater are walking the grounds on the west side of the property. I need to show you something."

Chapter 31

We gathered our things, then filed out the cottage door and down the steps, following Georgia to a huge metal outbuilding that was large enough to house my cottage.

One by one, we snuck inside the dark cavernous space. In the center of the building was a large open trap door. Georgia held her fingers to her lips, and we followed behind her like she was Mother Duck and we her ducklings. She motioned that we should get down on our knees and look down.

When it was my turn, I saw what might have been a large bomb shelter that had been converted into Everett Halstead's home and workshop. I opened my mouth wide, then covered it with my hand in order to muffle my squeak of surprise.

Below me, on the south side of the large space, was a queen bed, a kitchen with modern-looking appliances, including an espresso maker. Above the espresso maker were glass kitchen cupboards packed with canned and boxed food. Adjacent to the kitchen was a small living area with a newer-looking sectional sofa that faced a huge widescreen television. On top of a coffee table was an open laptop, and under the table, a fluffy tan rug. Metal bookcases were packed with books.

Wow!

Everett was standing beyond the living area with a blowtorch in his hands, working on some kind of steel object that was the size of a lawn mower.

He wore safety glasses. On top of his head was a stainless-steel mixing bowl.

After everyone had enough time to take in the scene, Georgia motioned toward the building's exit.

Once outside, she explained what had happened when she'd been alone with Everett. "He definitely doesn't want to sell. As you saw, Everett, through his granddaughter Madison, has access to multiple delivery companies via his laptop. He brought me down the staircase. In the kitchen, I saw a note on the counter that Madison had written him, saying that she would be home next week and that until she returned, there was a neighbor coming to check up on him—a Mrs. Willis. Madison left her cell number at the bottom of the note. I added it to my contacts on my phone. I plan to call her when I get home. I think Everett has some mental issues, but he's still creating and inventing things and at times seems quite lucid."

"He'd have to be in order to buy things on a laptop," I said.

"Why doesn't he live in the cottage?" Alice asked.

"I think it has something to do with his deceased wife and his time at Camp Hero," Georgia answered. "I remember his wife. A lovely woman. I don't think he ever leaves that building. We'll know more when I talk to his granddaughter Madison."

"Do you think Delia knows about him living down there?" I asked.

Georgia clenched her fists before saying, "Not a clue. Everett said that the first time he ever met Delia was a week ago. I believe him. He told me she came with his least favorite son, Freddie, who he's been estranged from for decades."

"I'll put the listing on hold, Georgia," Alice said, "until you contact the other granddaughter. After seeing how Mr. Halstead has everything he needs in the outbuilding—"

"And more," Elle added.

Alice turned to Georgia. "I have an idea. What if we split his property in half? He could sell the house and the land it sits on, but continue living as he has in the outbuilding?"

"That's a fabulous idea, Alice," Georgia said. "I'll bring it up to Madison."

I agreed. But in the back of my mind, I didn't think Delia was beyond forging Everett's signature if she did decide to go with Finn Larsen. "We can talk about this later. We should get out of here before Delia and Finn come back. Huddle up, gals," I said. "Whose all-in?"

The four of us formed a circle and put our hands on top of each other's, like in a football pregame huddle. Then we made a sisterhood pact of protection for Everett Halstead and scattered to our vehicles, wanting to get out of Dodge before Finn and Delia returned from their stroll around the grounds.

Elle and I hopped inside her pickup.

As soon as we put on our seat belts, Elle peeled out of the Halsteads' driveway. "We have to hurry and hide the *For Sale* sign on the property next door," she said breathlessly. "I don't want Fin Larsen anywhere near the place."

I murmured, "Okay," my mind still back at the scene we'd just witnessed.

She punched me on the arm. "Are you listening? I'm going to stop at the gates. You get out and open them. Then, I'll pull in and hide the pickup where it can't be seen from the road."

I turned to her. "You sure you want to do this, now?"

"Oh, I'm sure," she said, her hands wrapped so tight around the steering wheel I was afraid it might crack.

Chapter 32

It took me five minutes and every ounce of strength I had to open the right side of the iron gates. It was clear that they hadn't been used in a long time. I was barely out of the way when Elle pulled the pickup through the opening, then veered to the right, trampling her way through overgrown weeds straight out of the film *Little Shop of Horrors*. She finally came to a stop behind a border of fifteen-foot-tall yews. Like a madwoman possessed, Elle charged out of the pickup, ran to the sign, ripped it out of the ground, then threw it into the weeds.

"You might want to retrieve that," I called over to her.

"What are you talkin' about? I'm hiding it from Finn."

"Well, you might want to jot down the faded phone number at the bottom of the sign."

She glanced toward the road, then dove into the weeds. "Get out your phone and put in this number," she shouted.

I did as she ordered, then she joined me on the overgrown trail leading to the main house. I called it the main house because in the distance I saw another structure. A large horse stable in need of a good makeover. At the thought of a makeover, my thoughts once again centered on Olivia. Before pocketing my phone, I glanced down to see if Patrick had texted.

"There's no time for love messaging, we're on a mission," Elle said. "Lover boy can wait." She grabbed my hand and pulled me along what was once a long circular drive. I had no choice but to stow my phone back in my pocket.

When we got closer to the front of the house, we looked on in awe. The two-and-a-half story house was a melding of the Queen Anne and Shingle styles of architecture, with gables, dormers and verandas. I guessed it was built in the late 1800s or early 1900s.

"Do you think someone lives here?" I whispered to Elle.

"Let's find out." We stepped under a porte cochere, a covered structure over the driveway that allowed passengers to get out of their cars and onto the porch without getting rained or snowed on.

"This looks better than I thought," Elle said, grabbing on to the baluster. She hopped over a missing step, then landed on the wood-planked porch. I followed behind her, amazed that the porch was completely intact, not one section of floorboards was missing. All it needed was paint.

We stood in front of a large door with robin's-egg blue peeling paint, At the top of the door was a fan-shaped leaded glass window.

"You know what this house reminds me of?" Elle asked excitedly.

"What?"

"Teddy Roosevelt's Oyster Bay, Long Island, summer White House, Sagamore Hill."

"Wow. You're right. Wonder if there'll be tons of taxidermy inside," I teased, knowing Elle had a fear of stuffed dead animals. I wasn't a huge fan, either.

Elle reached for the door knocker. Not just any door knocker, but something that in all my years of antiquing, thrifting, and junking I'd never seen before—a brass Victorian life-size lady's hand, holding an apple.

Elle lifted the hand, then let it fall so that the apple hit the strike plate. We waited for someone to answer, hoping it wouldn't be the ghost of a deceased homeowner.

"Try again," I said. "Only harder."

Elle whispered, "Look at all the details on the hand. She's wearing a ring and there's lace around her wrist. After I buy this house, I'll leave this doorknocker just as it is. No polishing."

I grinned. "You will, will you."

Elle tried once more, this time using more force. Then she put her ear to the door. "I think it's uninhabited." She grabbed the large brass door handle and twisted it. "Locked. Oh, well. Let's go around to the back of the house. You might want to tuck your jeans into your boots, I can only imagine the deer ticks."

We exited the porch through a connecting side veranda. The sky had turned cloudy, without a hint of sun. The weeds and bushes were so overgrown that I wished we had a machete. Which in turn made me think of the walking stick that *didn't* kill Brett Golden. I took out my phone and hit the compass icon so I could figure out which direction was west, hoping for a glimpse of the Block Island Sound.

Elle stopped to give me a dirty look.

"I'm not texting Patrick," I said. "I'm using my compass app to find where the water is. Follow me." I grabbed her elbow and guided her to the right. At a crumbling brick archway, we stepped into what was once a walled garden.

"Oh, Meg. Look, I'll have my own walled garden, just like yours! That's one of the things I miss living in Sag Harbor. I don't have enough land for a proper garden.

In her excitement she tripped over the decapitated body of a toppled Aphrodite-like statue.

"Good thing I had ahold of you," I said. "You might have fallen face-first onto the base of that broken sundial. Maybe you shouldn't get your hopes up. I know sometimes the reason these estates stand empty is because the heirs don't agree on selling. Or the property is in probate for decades."

"Don't be a wet blanket."

I turned to her. "I'm not. I'm as excited as you are about this place. I just want you to be realistic about all the hurdles you might have to go over."

"Hurdles smurdles," she said. "Remember, money talks. I'm willing to sink my every last dime into this place."

"You are. But remember you have your better half to consider."

Not deterred, Elle forged ahead, pulling me with her.

We passed the stables, which upon closer inspection someone had turned into a six-stall garage. We kept walking west. To our left, beyond a spikey iron gate, was a small overgrown cemetery. I thought for sure that the tilted headstones might be the one thing to dissuade Elle from purchasing the estate. It would be a true test to gauge my usually superstitious friend's commitment to the property.

I soon got my answer. "Wouldn't it be fun," she said, peering over the wrought iron spiky spires, "to bring tracing paper and a pencil out here to etch the epithets on the headstones. Some date from over a hundred years ago."

Seemed Elle was all-in. Her glass wasn't just half full, it was over-flowing.

As her bosom buddy, I decided that I would dive in after her. My eyes rested on the largest monument in the center of the cemetery. "Hey, look," I said, pointing. "There's the name Willis. That's the name of Everett's neighbor who's supposedly checking in on him while his granddaughter Madison is away. Maybe someone does live here?"

"Could be. But I don't think anyone is living in the big house."

We looked back at the house. Its rear façade was as majestic as its front. There was a second-floor veranda and a small crow's nest balcony on the third-floor attic room. I put my phone with the compass app away, feeling in my bones that the house was built to face the Block Island Sound.

Elle must have realized the same thing. She broke away and charged ahead, following a surprisingly cleared path through the trees. I followed her, hoping we wouldn't end up at a gingerbread house with a broom-holding witch with a preheated oven.

A few minutes later, at the same exact moment, we saw a jaw-dropping panoramic view of the Block Island Sound.

A minute after that, I got a *jaw-dropping* text from Patrick.

They've turned themselves in. I sent Justin to Southampton to be Julie's lawyer. Call when you can. XO P.

"Oh my God!" I shouted.

"What? What's wrong?" Elle asked.

"Uh, nothing. Just get a load of that view."

Elle grinned. "I know. Soon it will be my view."

"Cheers to that," I said as we watched a great white heron land on the rocky shore below.

"Could it get any better?" Elle asked, making prayer hands. "Native American fishermen believed that when they came upon a heron, it forecasted that patience and good luck would be with them."

"The key word is *patience*," I said.

A happy tear slid down Elle's flushed freckled cheek.

I was thrilled for her, but I couldn't help thinking about Patrick's text. "Come on, let's go call the number on the sign. If that doesn't work, we'll call Barb. Sand and Sun has been in Montauk for forty years. I bet she'll know what the deal is." I put my arm around her shoulders, and we walked toward the pickup.

When we reached the pickup, Elle called out, "You get inside, I'm going to sneak down the road to make sure Finn Larsen's car is gone."

"Okey dokey." I thought Elle was going a little overboard, but I knew it would give me time to call Patrick without her overhearing our conversation.

Unfortunately, he didn't pick up the phone.

Not again, I thought.

Chapter 33

Patrick and I were in his Range Rover on our way to Windy Willows.

It was Friday, exactly a week since Brett Golden had been murdered. Jeremy had gotten permission from Chief Boyle to return to Windy Willows. Felicity, Elle, and I were meeting to discuss what was needed, décor- and furniture-wise, for the opening scene in episode four, and Patrick planned to go over the new *un*plagiarized ending with Jeremy and Nikki that he'd written for the final scene in episode three. A final scene that wouldn't use Dashiell Hammett's words from *The Thin Man*.

Tomorrow, if the thunderstorms predicted materialized, the reshoot would take place in the evening at the Montauk Point Lighthouse. I just hoped that except for the weather theatrics, the shoot would go without a hitch.

As Julie had prophesied, the death of her former fiancé had made all the local and national papers, and her nickname, the Black Widow, was resurrected from the Page Six ashes. So far, Patrick and Julie's past or present connection hadn't been exposed. The police hadn't given out any details about the murder, and *Mr. & Mrs. Winslow*'s producer hadn't been upset about the notoriety, mainly because the miniseries was still a good year away from its streaming premiere. If he had to, Jeremy had said, all he'd have to do was change the title. No one would be the wiser.

A lot had transpired in the past four days. With Patrick's publicist's attorney husband by her side, Julie had been questioned, then let go. Carson, on the other hand, wasn't as lucky. He was charged with obstruction of a murder investigation and tampering with evidence. Assuming that Julie had been the one who'd walloped Brett on the side of the head, Carson had admitted to wiping the prints off the loving cup. A hefty bail was posted. Which Julie paid.

The coroner had determined that a brain bleed, caused by the blow to the head, was the cause of Brett's death.

As for brother and sister, Olivia and Matt, Patrick told me that after Julie had bailed Carson out of jail, she'd kicked the pair out of her suite, knowing it was possible one or the other, or both, had committed patricide and was worried that she might be next on the killer's hit list. Julie and Carson had vacated the yacht club and were holed up in a rented cottage somewhere in the Hamptons that only the police knew about.

Of course, it was still possible that Julie or Carson were the guilty culprits. I just didn't think so. And neither did Patrick.

Felicity hadn't learned much from her meeting with Nikki at Montauk Manor, nor had Patrick when he and Matt had met at the Montauk Beer and Coffee Brewery. All Patrick discovered was that Matt seemed to have more confidence and direction than when his father had been alive. It didn't make Matt a killer, then again, it sure didn't rule him out.

On Wednesday, Elle had met with *Mr. & Mrs. Winslow*'s costume designer at Mabel and Elle's Curiosities to go over what production might want to rent from her room-sized closet of vintage clothing and jewelry — many pieces of which she'd inherited from her great-aunt Mabel. Elle had called the number on the *For Sale* sign from the property next to the Halsteads' and left a voicemail — so far, she hadn't gotten a return call.

Georgia, on the other hand, had contacted the woman meant to check in on Everett Halstead and told her what was going on with Delia and the selling of Everett's home. Georgia had told me that Mrs. Willis assured her that nothing would happen to the house or Everett until Everett's granddaughter Madison returned, and when that happened, she would give Georgia a heads-up.

So it looked like things were moving along — I just hoped they stayed moving in a positive direction. I had mixed feelings about returning to the scene of the crime. Things in the investigation had progressed without either Patrick's or my input. Elle had tried to get intel from her husband, but because of my big mouth about Brett accosting her, Arthur's lips were sealed tighter than if he'd used Gorilla glue.

Carson had said that Brett was alive when he saw him. Whoever whacked Brett with the loving cup might have thought they'd just knocked him out? Did that make it less of a crime? During the past few days that question kept repeating in my head, like a song I couldn't get rid of. Were we dealing with a cold-blooded murderer or was it accidental manslaughter? And how about the person who stuck

Brett with the blade from the walking stick *after* he was dead? What if they weren't the person who hit him with the loving cup? Would that still be a crime?

In my book, it was.

Patrick and I agreed not to discuss the murder unless one of us came up with any news that the police weren't privy to. But now that we would soon be reunited with a few of those present at last Friday's murder. I thought it was the perfect time to bring it up.

As we passed though Windy Willows' open gates, I turned to Patrick and said, "It looks like Brett's killer, whoever whacked him with the loving cup, might be in the forty percent of getting away with it. The stabbing with the walking stick was just a bit of theatrical staging. If we eliminate Julie and Carson from the killing pool, that leaves Olivia, Matt, and Nikki."

He turned to me. His black eye was now a pale shade of yellow. It gave him a sexy, roughish, tough-guy look. "Sadly, so far, there's been no forensic evidence linking any one of them."

"What about that paper Elle pulled out of the fireplace grate?"

"It's not like you see on TV or in books," he said. "I know from my novel research—"

"Murder research."

"Murder research," he said with a grin. "That it takes a lot longer than a week to analyze forensic evidence."

"Still—"

"Maybe you should ask your friend who's married to a homicide detective about the paper," he said.

"Oh, Elle's been so distracted about finding out who owns the property next to Mr. Halstead that she doesn't even discuss the investigation."

Patrick raised an eyebrow. "So, you have been hounding her?"

"Just a teensy little bit. A girl's gotta sleep at night."

"Teensy?"

Patrick pulled up to the white Georgian mansion's front steps and idled the Range Rover.

"I don't see any police presence," I said. "You'd never know what happened here." I glanced over at Patrick's perfect profile and realized that last Friday was also the day that I'd almost lost him. Yesterday, we'd attended a happy-tears event at the home of Evan, the man Patrick had saved from drowning. Patrick had been given a hero's welcome, not only by Evan but also by Evan's wife and two small children. As I'd watched Patrick playing catch with Evan's kids, I realized what a wonderful father he must have been to Lucy, which had me projecting that perhaps one day in the future . . .

"You get out. I'll go park," he said.

I glanced toward the parking area that fronted Windy Willows. "Looks like Elle's here. Her truck's parked next to Brett's rental car. It's packed with boxes. Must mean Olivia or Matt got the go-ahead to remove whatever they hadn't taken to Julie's from the third floor. Elle said that the engagement ring will be held in escrow until Brett's estate is settled. I'm sure Julie doesn't want it. Wonder where Matt and Olivia are staying?"

"Take a breath, Ms. Barrett," Patrick said. "I don't have a paper bag handy."

"Ha, ha. It's just strange being back here, knowing that we'll be stuck with a few of the *un*usual suspects. One thing that's been bothering me about our assistant director, possibly new director, is the explanation for her signing up to be an *assistant* director in the first place. I recently read that Nikki's last rom-com on the big screen had netted her millions."

"I don't have the answer," he said, looking in the rearview mirror, "but there's Jeremy, why don't you go ask him. Actually, I'm just as curious as you."

"Good idea," I said, reaching for the door handle.

"Wait! Aren't you forgetting something?"

I looked down at my feet and grabbed the large vintage tapestry carpetbag that Elle had given me for my last birthday. It held everything I needed, including Reese's Peanut Butter Cups.

"Ahem—" he said, pointing to his cheek.

I leaned in for a smooch. When I sat back up, I saw Jeremy peering through the passenger side window. In a knee-jerk reaction, I said, "Oh, no. Now he'll know about us."

Patrick laughed, waved at Jeremy, then pulled me in for another kiss.

Chapter 34

It was while we were in the middle of discussing what would be needed for tomorrow's reshoot at the lighthouse that Olivia burst into the kitchen.

"How come I wasn't invited to this meeting," she shrieked through gritted teeth. A vein at her temple looked ready to burst. Today, her hair was dyed the same pale blonde color as her brother's, as if she wanted everyone to think they were blood-related siblings. "Why is Matt here and not me?" Olivia asked, looking at Matt, then resting her blistering gaze on Nikki.

I'd been wondering the same thing.

Elle, Felicity, Patrick and I were seated at Windy Willows' kitchen table. Nikki, Matt, and Jeremy sat across from us. It had been a natural choice not to convene in the dining room—too gruesomely reminiscent of what had happened the week before.

I took Patrick's hand under the table as Olivia continued her tirade. She stomped over to Nikki and Matt. Then, looking at Jeremy, she said, "You fire me from the set, but you're keeping on my brother and *her*!" Olivia pointed a fuchsia-painted nail at Nikki. "She probably killed my father. Matt, are you crazy? Have you been drinking her poisoned Kool-Aid? Just because she's paying for our rooms at Montauk Manor doesn't mean we owe her. As soon as the will is read, we'll pay her back. Not that she needs the money."

"Th-that's unkind," Matt stammered.

Olivia kept going. "We talked about this, brother. We're a team. We'll soon be starting our own business with Daddy's money."

What money?

"You know that I don't want to do that," Matt said softly, looking over at Nikki.

"Why are you looking at her?" Olivia wailed, her eyes filling with unshed tears.

"Hey, kiddo. Relax," Jeremy said, holding up his hand. "Ms. Meyers has pulled some strings. She found another gig for you."

"Gig? What kind of gig?" Olivia asked. "The only gig I want is this one with my brother. So we can continue honoring our father's legacy."

Jeremy clicked his tongue in annoyance. "Calm down, Olivia. Ms. Meyers just told me that she got you a job as the head makeup artist for a new Hallmark Mystery series."

"No way!" she said, making a fist. "One of those silly shows about an amateur sleuth who can bake a cake and take on a killer without breaking a sweat. How about, instead, we find out who killed my father in *real* life. I can guarantee you that it wasn't our awful craft services cook that murdered him."

I couldn't help myself. "I love those mysteries. They have a huge following. You could do a lot worse."

Olivia puffed out her cheeks. Then, looking at me, she said, "Quiet from the peanut gallery, Nosy Nelly, or I'll drop another present on your car."

Patrick, who hadn't said a peep since Olivia charged in, said, "You put a dead fish on Meg's car?"

"She stole my phone. I only got it back because of her big mouth. She asks too many questions. How do we know that she didn't kill—"

"Because she has an alibi," Patrick said. "How about you?"

"What-t-t are you talking about?" Olivia stammered. "Matt, tell them."

After a couple beats, he answered, "Yeah. She was with me."

Ignoring Patrick, Olivia turned back to Jeremy. "Where is this stupid series being shot, anyway? There's no need for someone with my caliber of makeup artistry and experience to work on a modern-day Hallmark series. I'm an expert on period makeup. Hell, those actors on those Hallmark shows could put on their makeup at home, then come to the set. No one would notice the difference. Where's it shooting, anyway?"

"Canada," Matt answered in a whisper.

"You knew all about this before talking it over with me?" Olivia said, clenching her jaw. "You agreed for us to be shipped off to Timbuktu?"

Matt bent his head. "I'm not going," he mumbled.

"What does that mean?" Olivia asked, putting her hand on his shoulder. Then she squeezed so tightly that Matt winced. "We work together. It's always been you and me against—"

"Don't get angry with your brother," Nikki interjected in a soft controlled voice. "I found something for him too."

"I'm sure you did," Olivia said.

"He's going to work with me on my next romantic comedy." Nikki looked fondly at Matt. "His music and lyrics are amazing. Matt has inspired me to cast a well-known male lead for my next movie. He'll play a singer-songwriter like your brother. One who finds love—"

Olivia cut her off. "And where will this be? You better say Canada."

The hope in Olivia's eyes quickly dissolved with Nikki's next words. "We'll be filming on the West Coast. Matt will be an understudy of sorts. I plan to use his original songs. You should be happy for him. And happy for yourself." Nikki glanced at Matt with a huge smile.

Without his oversized black-rimmed glasses, Matt really did resemble a young Paul Newman. I recalled Elle saying last Friday that if he got rid of his Clark Kent glasses, he'd be drop-dead gorgeous. She was right. Maybe, like his sister, with her over made-up face, Matt had been hiding behind his glasses. Now, with his bully father out of the picture, he didn't need to hide anymore.

Wait. Matt had definitely worn his glasses *pre-murder*. But when I'd looked out the kitchen window at him and Nikki sitting on the bench after the murder, he hadn't been wearing them.

At this point, did it matter? Arthur would definitely laugh at me if I brought it up. But I could tell Elle.

"Are you kidding?" Olivia said with obvious hurt in her voice. "Matt, why would you want to be involved in one of her silly romantic comedies? Those went out in the nineties. They're even dumber than this supposed amateur mystery series she wants to ship me off to. I'll never go to Canada without you. I've always been here for you," she croaked, tears rivering down her overly blushed cheeks.

"Nikki," Jeremy said, "are you sure you won't reconsider? Is it the money?"

"No, Jeremy," Nikki answered. "It has nothing to do with the money. And this production will do just fine without me. You have a hit here. I guarantee it. I'll even invest in it and help you find a new director. And I promise that I'll be on set tomorrow at the lighthouse to reshoot the last scene in episode three."

Jeremy bent his head, chin to chest, finally looking beat.

"I'm sorry," Nikki said, sounding sincere.

I squeezed Patrick's hand. He gave me a blank stare, then I nodded my head in Nikki's direction. I didn't want to chance whispering my suspicions to him that she'd turned down the job of being director because she'd finished what she'd signed up for. Murdering Brett Golden. *Cut. That's a wrap.*

Earlier, while Patrick had been parking his car, I'd corralled our producer into a quick conversation about Nikki Meyers. The only thing I'd learned, besides Jeremy's hero worship of her, had been that Nikki had been the one to approach Jeremy about the job of assistant director. I'd asked Jeremy if he didn't think it was strange for Nikki to sign on for such a lowly position, especially seeing that she was a famed producer and director in her own right.

All Jeremy had done was shrug his shoulders and say, "She probably wanted to work with me. Now, I just need to convince her to stay. At least for the first season. I don't know why she's having misgivings. I've offered her more money than we have in our budget, along with a percentage of the take." Just as I was about to mention to Jeremy that Nikki was still a suspect, Nikki, Matt, and Patrick had approached us from the parking area. I'd had no choice but to save my questions for another time and follow them inside.

Then I recalled an earlier conversation with Nikki. She'd said that she'd had her share of bad relationships. Had Brett been one of those? Suddenly, it was clear that it was a blessing that after tomorrow's shoot, the three of them would be out of our hair. It seemed Elle had the same thoughts. She was busily writing down something on her pad of paper. I couldn't read her handwriting, but I was sure it had something to do with the murder. Something she planned on telling her hubby? Or maybe she was just jotting down decorating plans for when she bought the estate next to the Halsteads—either way, Elle was a woman possessed.

Maybe I would take a note from Elle's playbook and just let the next couple days pass so I could move on with my relationship with Patrick while decorating adult tree houses. With that thought, I leaned back in my chair and looked on like I was watching act three in the play *The Mousetrap*, hoping that the curtain closed far, far away. Maybe in Canada or California.

Suddenly, a loud voice coming from the direction of the hallway off the kitchen broke into my tranquil thoughts.

"Shazam!" I heard a familiar male voice shout. "This place is what you Americans call the bee's knee socks, or is it the cat's nightgown? Huzzah!"

What the heck was Finn Larsen doing at Windy Willows?

Chapter 35

Finn stepped into kitchen. We looked at him with our mouths open. He was followed inside by Paige, Michael's wife twice over and the daughter of the owners of Windy Willows. Trailing behind Paige was my ex-fiancé Michael. When Paige glanced over at me—if looks could kill, I'd be as dead as Brett Golden. Michael cowered behind his wife, his face as red as Finn's artfully arranged suit jacket pocket square.

Michael and I had made our peace long ago. As for Paige, that would never happen. At least on my end.

"Sorry to break up your little party," Paige said, "but Daddy plans on selling. Mr. Larsen—who I'm sure you recognize from TV—needs to look at all the new appliances. If you don't mind, please go into another room. Or better yet," she said, looking out the window over the sink to the dark sky and the rain pelting the windowsill, "move outside."

Jeremy jumped up. His chair hit the floor with a bang that matched an epically loud boom of thunder. "We'll do no such thing. We have a two-year rental contract with your *daddy*. And I am the one who added all the modern appliances. If you want, you can show this clown the third floor, the only floor your family has access to while we are filming."

Paige didn't seem worried. "Oh, I don't know about that. I'm sure after we hire a lawyer and tell them about the death that happened at my family's summer home, all under your watch, Mr. Prentice, justice will prevail. I assume you are Mr. Prentice. You've done a great job of ruining the Whitney name. Now we must find ourselves another estate, to replace this one. Though it will be hard. All the memories—" A large crocodile tear slid down her perfect high cheekbones, and I saw a hand come from behind her that was holding a white handkerchief. One of Michael's monogrammed ones. What was that about? I'd always wondered why you needed a monogram on something that you use to blow your nose. But that summed up Michael in a nutshell. Outward appearances were way more important than inner integrity.

That's why Paige and Michael made such a great Barbie and Ken couple—they were both hollow inside.

173

"I'm calling the police," Jeremy said. "I'll show them our contract. Elle, why don't you call your husband, Detective Shoner."

"No need for that," Finn said. "We'll just do a quick tour. Then we'll be out of your face—hair, I think it is."

Jeremy stomped toward them, then followed them into the hallway.

Olivia wore a smug look on her face. "What goes around comes around. Matt, come with me. I need help with something that I can't carry. I think we need to have a chat without *her* around." She didn't bother looking at Nikki. We all knew who she was talking about. "I want to remind you of something," she added with a wink.

I thought I saw Matt flinch. Was Olivia holding something over his head? He got up, took a quick glance at Nikki, then followed Olivia out of the room, acting as if he was going to his own execution.

I watched Nikki, wanting to gauge her reaction. She just smiled and said, "I think it's a good time for me to leave. Patrick, I'll see you tomorrow night at the lighthouse." Acting as if she didn't just turn Jeremy and Olivia's world upside down, she calmly got up from the table, collected her notes, and said her goodbyes.

After she'd left the kitchen, Felicity said, "I can't imagine if we have to leave here to find another location. But Patrick, I'm sure you could write something in the script. Maybe a fire?"

"If there's a fire," Elle said, "then we would have to completely find a whole new houseful of vintage to furnish the next location. I'm gonna call Arthur. We need to stop the Whitneys."

"And stop Finn Larsen," I added.

Patrick, the voice of reason, said, "Let's table this for a while. I'm sure Jeremy can take care of things."

"You're damn straight I can," Jeremy said from the open doorway to the kitchen. "Ms. Whitney, her husband, and that over-the-top real estate dude are gone. I watched them go out the gates." His face was flushed with anger as he came inside and addressed the table. "I'm going to stay until everyone leaves, then lock up. I'm also going to change the alarm code. I think you kids should head out. I'll see you tomorrow. Don't lose any sleep. I've got this."

"You want me to stay with you?" Patrick asked, just as Matt stepped back into the kitchen.

"I'll be fine," Jeremy answered.

Matt looked over at the table. "Where's Nikki?"

"She just left," I said.

Matt looked surprised. "I came in her car."

"After we lock up, I can give you a lift to the hotel," Jeremy said. "Then maybe you can clear the way so that I can have a chat with Nikki about staying on as director. And I'll even sweeten the deal to include you, kiddo. Maybe even make you assistant director. What do you think?" He slapped Matt on the back like they were old buddies.

"I don't think she'll change her mind," Matt said. "But I would appreciate the ride. What about Olivia? Would she stay on as head makeup artist?"

"Sure, son," Jeremy answered. "Whatever Nikki wants."

Suddenly, there was a huge flash of lightning out the kitchen windows, followed by a rumble of thunder so loud that I felt the table vibrate.

Then the lights went out.

I grabbed Patrick's arm and whispered, "What next?"

It was then that we heard the screams. Even with my hearing loss, I recognized Olivia's high-pitched howls. That meant that the other scream must be coming from Nikki.

She was the only female missing.

Chapter 36

The generator kicked in. The lights came on. And we all ran toward the front foyer.

Olivia was standing over Nikki's crumpled body.

Nikki lay prone on the black and white marble floor. Her hands covered her head like she'd been warding off Olivia's blows. Her eyes remained closed, but thank God, she opened her mouth and moaned, "Leave me alone. I'm not stealing him away from you. If you loved him, you would know that."

Matt ran to Nikki and got down on the floor next to her. He turned his head and looked up at his sister. "Olivia, how could you?"

"I didn't do anything!" Olivia started to cry. "I didn't touch her. She must have fallen when the lights went out. She's the one who attacked me."

Matt looked up at his sister. "This time, you've gone too far."

"How can you say that! After everything I've done for you. You owe her nothing."

Matt ignored her and helped Nikki to a sitting position.

"Should I call an ambulance?" Elle asked.

Nikki slowly shook her head. The whole scene reminded me of when Julie and Olivia had been brawling in the kitchen "No. I'm fine," she said. "Just keep her away from me."

Matt put both hands on her shoulders and looked into Nikki's eyes. "Oh, I will. Are you sure you're okay?"

Nikki nodded her head yes.

Then Elle, morphing into a version of her cop husband, gave Olivia a scathing look and glanced down at Nikki. "Ms. Meyers, do you want to press charges?"

"No. I'm fine. But until I leave the Hamptons, Olivia, I would appreciate it if you'd stay as far away from me as possible." She took her right hand, rubbed it against the right side of her head, and flinched.

"Olivia, stay away from me, too," Matt said, helping Nikki up from the floor.

"You don't mean that!" Olivia sobbed.

Patrick went to Olivia's side and took her elbow. "Let me take you out to your car."

Olivia wouldn't have it. She shook his hand off, looked over at her brother, and said, "I think you should reconsider shutting me out of your life. You know exactly what I mean by that."

This time it was Jeremy who grabbed her arm. "Let's go."

"Don't touch me," Olivia screeched. "Unless you want a lawsuit. These are my witnesses."

He let go of her arm. "We're also a witness to what you just did to Nikki," Jeremy said.

Patrick opened the front door, and Jeremy followed Olivia outside. Matt and Nikki followed without saying a word.

"I think it's time for us to go," Felicity said. "Before something else happens."

"I second that," Elle said.

"I third that," I said. "Patrick?"

"We're outta here."

• • •

Ten minutes later, Elle, Patrick, Felicity and I stood next to Elle's pickup.

"Maybe there's a curse on Windy Willows and we'd be better off at a new location," Elle said, adding a sigh.

Patrick gave Elle a sideways glance, then said, "'Out flew the web and floated wide. The mirror crack'd from side to side. The curse is come upon me, cried —'"

"The Lady of Shalott," I finished for him. "Tennyson."

"You two and your poetry," Elle said, laughing. She gave the three of us a kiss on the cheek. "Drive safely. And Patrick, let me know how tomorrow night goes. Because, believe me, after what just happened inside, you might want to hire extra security."

"Not a bad idea," I said, turning to Patrick.

He shrugged his shoulders. "I'm not worried. But Meg, maybe this time you shouldn't come along."

"Oh, no, buster. I'm coming. I'm determined to see a happy ending to this episode."

"Okay, don't say I didn't warn you," he said with a smile.

"I'm warned," I said as lightning split the sky and hit something nearby.

"Yikes," Felicity said.

Double yikes, I thought.

Chapter 37

Saturday evening, things seemed to be going smoothly for the reshoot in the Montauk Point Lighthouse's tower room.

Maybe too smoothly, I thought, looking over at Matt Golden's silhouette on the step above me.

Nature had been more than accommodating — thunder, lightning, and torrential rain provided the perfect storm for the final scene in episode three of *Mr. & Mrs. Winslow*. Like the last time we'd filmed at the lighthouse, the actors had used the gift shop for makeup and wardrobe. But unlike the previous shoot, Jeremy had called in a favor and hired a replacement for Olivia. He'd given the substitute makeup artist the stills of Zoe/aka Lara from last the shoot. A few minutes ago, when Zoe had passed me on the stairway, I thought she looked just as drop-dead gorgeous as she had on the night Brett Golden had been directing.

Patrick and I had pulled up to the lighthouse in his Range Rover at the same time Nikki and Matt did. Nikki seemed bright and chipper, and when Patrick asked how she was feeling, she'd said she felt fine and ready to finish the episode. Matt, on the other hand, had dark bags under his eyes. I was sure the fight between Nikki and Olivia had something to do with his ashen complexion and possible lack of sleep. I wasn't sure why Matt had come along. Bodyguard?

Nikki was playing director, but I had to wonder what part Matt was playing.

Before leaving my cottage last night, Patrick and I discussed what went down at Windy Willows. Not the Finn Larsen, Michael, and Paige part of it. Patrick knew all about my past with Michael and the Whitneys. We'd rehashed Olivia's attack on Nikki, and her threat that Matt better not shut her out of his life. But when it came down to it, we were still missing the whodunnit part of the Brett Golden Murder Mystery. Not to mention the *why*dunnit.

Had Nikki murdered Brett? Or had Matt murdered his father, and Olivia covered it up by dragging her father into the library after he'd succumbed to head trauma from the loving cup? Or was it the other way around, and Olivia had killed her father and Matt had moved his body to the library? Matt and Nikki? Nikki and Olivia seemed the only pairing that didn't make sense. Which could be a red flag in itself. We were back to square one, remembering that even Julie David and Carson hadn't been proven innocent.

Last night, I'd also tried to get my father on the phone. This time, when I reached his voicemail, he'd left a recording that he was out of town. Not the smartest thing for a retired cop to do, and something he'd taught me never to do—alert criminals that I was out of town. I'd then called Georgia, but she'd told me that Doc hadn't heard from him either.

What the heck was going on?

Last night before kissing each other good bye, Patrick and I had agreed on one thing—when Julie, Carson, Matt, Nikki, and Olivia left the Hamptons, the case would be closed as far as we were concerned.

"Bang!" The sound of a gun vibrated down the dark stairwell.

Only this time, I didn't startle.

But I did startle when I felt a hand on my shoulder, and heard a "Shush!" in my right hearing aid.

I turned and looked behind me.

Lightning flashed and filtered down onto Olivia's damp face. In the eerie light, I almost didn't recognize her. She had on a fuchsia pink raincoat that glowed fluorescent in the darkness. She wasn't wearing any makeup, and her round face looked ghostly and at the same time ethereal. Her blonde, almost white hair was flattened against her head from the rain. She put a finger to her pale lips and pointed to her brother, then motioned that I should get his attention.

Not wanting to disturb the scene in the tower room, I tapped Matt gently on the arm. He jerked toward me, then noticed Olivia.

Matt glanced up the stairwell, then down at his sister. After a beat or two, he turned and silently followed her down.

It was then that two things happened almost simultaneously. My pocket vibrated, telling me that I'd received a text, then a call came through to my hearing aids.

I took out my phone and glanced down at the screen. *Elle.* I hit the Accept button. "Meg, you there? Hello-o-o? Well, if you're listening, you won't believe what I just found out. Call me back."

Then I read my text. It was from Patrick: *Hang in there. Should be the last take. I should be done in ten. XO, P.*

I was torn on what to do next. Then I realized I could kill two birds with one stone—hopefully eavesdrop on Olivia and Matt. And two, call Elle back.

I pocketed my phone and crept down the lighthouse stairs.

Halfway to the gift shop, I hit a wet patch left by Olivia's dripping raincoat.

My left foot shot out from under me, and I grabbed on to the railing for dear life.

A warning to slow down? I thought, my heart pounding against my rib cage.

I righted myself and continued down to the gift shop.

Mistake number one.

With more to follow.

Chapter 38

Olivia and Matt weren't in the gift shop. Shondra from wardrobe was in the middle of mopping up the wet wood floor with paper towels.

"Shon, you see where the Goldens went?" I asked.

Still looking down, she clicked her tongue in annoyance. "Follow the wet footprints to the door."

I glanced out the glass door at the driving rain. "You wouldn't happen to have overheard where they're going?"

"If they didn't go to their cars, there's only one other place they could go. The snack bar. It's where they're housing all the cameras, dollies and electrical equipment. There's coffee on over there, too."

"Thanks, Shondra. Should I bring you back one?"

She stood, went to a hanging rack by the counter and handed me my navy hooded rain slicker. "You might need this," she said with a grin. "I'd love a coffee. No milk. Just sugar."

"You got it," I said as she helped me on with my coat.

"Is it all good up there?" she asked, pointing toward the stairwell. "With everything that went on with Mr. Golden, we all need to be careful."

It was the first time I'd considered the anxiety the cast and crew must be going through following Brett's murder. So far, not one person had resigned. Which said a lot for our producer.

"Everything's going fine," I said, reaching for the door handle. "It's what's going on outside the lighthouse that I'm worried about."

"Anything you want me to tell easy-on-the-eyes lover boy if he comes looking for you."

"Shondra!"

She grinned. The cat was not only out of the bag about our relationship. The bag was ripped wide open.

"Just tell him I'll be at the snack bar. I also could use a coffee," I lied. I never drank caffeine after noon.

"Will do," she answered.

I pushed against the door and stepped into the storm.

Under the streetlights in the parking lot, I saw Brett's rental car. The one that Olivia had been using. The backseat was still piled with boxes from yesterday. But no one was in the front seat. Nikki's yellow Tesla was parked next to it, and I was shocked that Olivia hadn't smashed Nikki's windshield, or at least thrown some dead thing on top of Nikki's hood.

On the way to the snack bar, I passed the trail leading down to the shore, where many times I'd gone on guided seal walks. I picked up my pace, thinking that as soon as our five possible suspects left the Hamptons, my copesetic life in Montauk could resume.

When I reached the overhang to the vestibule outside the snack bar, I pulled off my hood and called Elle.

She told me something that was a game changer.

Why hadn't I noticed it earlier?

Chapter 39

I snuck inside the glass-enclosed vestibule to the snack bar. Luckily, the vestibule's overhead light wasn't on. Dripping buckets of water, I went to the glass section to the left of the snack bar entrance and peered in.

There they were. Olivia faced me. Matt had his back to the glass. Olivia was on her knees. She'd grabbed on to Matt's shirttails as if begging for food in a scene from *Oliver Twist*—Olivia Twist. Even through the glass, I could hear her sobs. I pressed my left ear against the plate glass window and the feedback from my hearing aid made me jump back as if I'd been tasered.

I wished I could get a visual on Matt's face so I could read his lips, but I'd have to be satisfied with reading Olivia's.

Olivia pulled herself up to a standing position. She pushed Matt and he stumbled back a step. Then she took her fists and beat them against his chest, pushing him even farther back to where I was leaning against the glass, spying. I tried to meld into the corner, happy I was wearing a dark raincoat.

I read Olivia's lips when she said, "You aren't leaving with her. I have your glasses. I found them under Father's body in the library. I didn't tell anyone because I'm your sister. I also covered for you by saying you were with me under the tent. I'll always protect you. But if you go with her and leave me, I'll tell the—" I couldn't make out her last word, but I assumed it was *police*.

Matt must have said something that brought her once again to her knees. Then he turned toward me. Oliva grasped on to his ankles. He tried to shake her off, but she held tight.

Not wanting to be discovered, like Cato in a Pink Panther movie, I quickly sidled against the vestibule glass walls, then slipped out the door and into the rain. I scurried behind a bush and peered through the glass. Olivia came into the dark vestibule, then pushed against the outside door. The door pushed back, she stumbled, then tried again. Finally, she beat the swirling tempest wind and made it out the door and onto the sidewalk. Taking slow measured steps like her feet were encased in cement, Olivia walked zombielike in the direction of the lighthouse—oblivious to the torrential rain, lightning, and thunder.

I waited a couple of minutes for Matt to come outside. But he remained in the snack bar. Soon, I saw why. Headlights approached from the direction of the lighthouse.

Nikki's yellow Tesla stopped under the streetlight in front of the snack bar.

The headlights went out. Nikki emerged from the car. She wasn't wearing a raincoat, but she hesitated before going inside, looking both ways to make sure no one else was around. Then she hurried inside. Matt must have phoned her.

Let me rephrase that.

Matt must have called his *mother*.

The paper that had been thrown in the library's fireplace, the half-burnt smoldering one that Elle had rescued, turned out to be the top-half remains of a lab report. A DNA lab. Chief Boyle contacted them and had given them the names and DNA results of everyone who'd been at the scene of Brett's murder. Nikki Meyers's DNA was a familial match to Matt's. He was her biological son.

I should have seen it earlier. They had the same eyes and fair looks.

At this point, I knew I should walk away and call for backup. But I also knew Patrick would soon come looking for me. After my success at reading Olivia's lips, there was a chance this might be the only time I'd be able to overhear mother and son confess to killing Brett.

Waiting only a few seconds, not wanting to miss anything, I slunk inside the vestibule and returned to my previous viewing position. Only, much to my dismay, both Matt and Nikki were nowhere in sight. I had an instant to decide what to do. I crouched down, slithered over to the snack bar door, opened it, and slipped inside.

Hiding behind a tall candy display, I listened for voices.

Chapter 40

I discerned, though it took a while because of my hearing loss, that Matt and Nikki were in the snack bar's kitchen. To get closer to the voices, I got down on my hands and knees, crawling past the lighting and sound equipment, and found refuge behind a huge drum spotlight used for filming *Mr. & Mrs. Winslow*'s nighttime scenes.

"She didn't take the trophy," I heard Matt say. "She found my glasses. I must have dropped them when I—"

"That's good," Nikki said. "You didn't tell her about our connection, I hope. There was a time I wanted to shout it from the roof. But we need to wait until we are back in—"

I wasn't sure, but it sounded like Matt was crying. Then I heard him say, "No. I didn't tell her."

"Then what happened to the trophy?" Nikki asked in an angry voice. "Are you sure Olivia didn't take it? I don't trust her. She probably plans to blackmail you later and take you away from me."

"If she doesn't have it, then who does? Father was still alive when I left. When we went back to pick—"

In a raised voice, one I wished Nikki would keep talking in because of my hearing loss, I heard, "Olivia threatened you with the gla—. She must have the loving cup. What kind of sister is—?"

I was dying to peek around the corner to read their lips for missing words. Nikki and Matt had no clue that Carson had taken the loving cup. I was grateful that the police had been hush-hush about that detail. Reaching into my pants pocket, I removed my cell phone, went to the recording app and tapped the red Record button. Lying flat on my belly, I extended my hand so that my phone was at the edge of the kitchen's open doorway.

If my hearing aids couldn't pick up what they were saying, possibly my phone could. Plus, the recording might come in handy as evidence in a murder trial.

Suddenly, a huge mouse or small rat came cruising by my nose. "Holy Moses!" I yelped. I fell back against a spotlight, and my phone went flying out of my hand. It skidded across the tile floor and disappeared into the snack bar's kitchen.

Before I could crawl away, Matt and Nikki came into view from the kitchen. They squeezed together under the threshold and looked down at me in surprise.

Matt narrowed his eyes into a squint and said, "Meg! What are you doing? Were you spying on us?"

"Spying? Why would I do that? I just slipped on the wet floor. Shondra wants me to bring her back a cup of coffee."

Matt looked at his mother. Pointing, Nikki said, "Coffee's right there on the counter."

She didn't ask if I was hurt, but she seemed to believe my story. I got up, went to the counter, grabbed a cup, opened the spout on a large silver coffee urn, filled the cup, then added a top. My hands shook like I'd already had too much caffeine. For effect, I grabbed a packet of sugar just in case they knew how Shondra liked her coffee.

When I turned back, they were smiling at me. Mother and son had the same exact smile. I sniffed the air and said, "Ahh, smells like road tar. That should keep Shondra awake. Okay, you guys take care. Glad the filming went well."

I really didn't know that the filming went well, but I assumed, since Nikki was here, that they'd wrapped the episode.

I walked toward the exit, feeling their eyes burning two identical holes into my back.

Chapter 41

Outside the snack bar, I once again hid behind the bushes adjacent to the glass vestibule. The heavy rain had turned to a drizzle. Through the mist, in the direction of the lighthouse's parking lot, I saw Patrick step under the streetlight. *Hallelujah.*

I shot out from the bushes, ran to him, and dragged him into the shrubbery, where I gave him a spine-cracking embrace. Keeping my eyes peeled on the exit from the vestibule, I presented him with a quick summary of what had just happened inside.

Before Patrick could respond to what I'd told him, Matt and Nikki stepped into the vestibule. We crouched low to the ground and watched them exit and scurry to Nikki's Tesla. As soon as they got inside, Nikki started the engine and they took off.

"Nikki didn't even turn on her headlights. Shouldn't we follow them?" I asked Patrick, not really wanting to.

"No," he said, his lips blue from the cold. "Let's go get your phone and pray that it's still recording. I'll send Arthur a text."

It took a few minutes to locate my phone under the sink in the snack bar's kitchen. Miracle of miracles—it was still recording. I pressed Stop, and we went back into the snack bar. Patrick pulled out a chair for me at one of the bistro tables, and I sat. He sat across from me. Then with shaking hands I took my index finger and pressed Play on my phone's recording app.

It was too easy.

Everything we needed to close the case was on the recording.

Just as I was about to pat myself on the back about the fortuitous fall that had caused my phone to go sliding into the snack bar's kitchen, I felt excruciating pain at the back of my head.

Goodnight, Irene.

My last thought before everything went black was — *I'll have to ask Georgia where that saying came from.*

Chapter 42

I opened my eyes and blinked away tears from the pain splitting the back of my head in two. Slowly, I lifted my head from the table. When my vision cleared, I saw that once again Olivia was wrestling with someone—only this time, her opponent was Patrick.

She didn't have a chance.

"Give me that phone!" Olivia screeched.

Patrick ignored her, managing to secure Olivia's arms behind her back. Then he marched her over to our table.

My hero.

Patrick glanced over at me, his eyes filled with worry. "You okay?"

It was a struggle to sit up straight, but after I did, I said, "I'm fine. What the hell did you hit me with, Olivia? A brick?"

Olivia glowered at me. "Don't be such a baby. It was just a sugar shaker."

It seemed that Olivia had been hiding in the snack bar, listening to the entire phone recording. The recording that revealed that her brother had been the one to hit Brett with the loving cup. Any gaps in Nikki's and Matt's confessions were now easily explained. Or, should I say, mother's and son's confessions.

Patrick gave Olivia a death stare. He was angrier than when he'd had his fight with Olivia's father in the lighthouse—times a zillion. "You hit Meg hard enough to make her pass out. You can tell it to the police. Have a seat," he said, pulling out a chair, then forcing her to sit. He handed me my phone, took out his phone, then called 911.

Olivia started sobbing. "He's my brother. I need to save him. Please give me the phone." Then, like she was a spoiled toddler wanting sweets, she reached out her arms and gestured toward me with *give-me, give-me* hands.

"Not a chance," I said.

Olivia attempted to get up from her chair. Patrick pushed her back down.

"Why would you want to protect Matt?" Patrick asked. "He was the one who hit your father with the loving cup."

"You heard the tape," she said. "After Matt handed Father the DNA report and told him that he was leaving with his so-called mother, Father went ballistic. I've seen Father that way before. I

189

would have done the same thing. It was self-defense. Plus, Matt didn't kill him, just knocked him out. It was Nikki that stabbed my father with the walking stick thingy. You heard her admit it. I bet she was lying that she did it to cover for Matt. You can tell by her voice how much she hated my father for the way he treated her supposed son. She probably hid that trophy that Matt used. And it was her idea to move the body then stab him. Who does that? Why don't we just erase half of the tape? Let the great Nikki Meyers plan her next romantic comedy from a prison cell. Leave my brother out of it. Matt's birth mother is a monster. You heard Matt sobbing. What do you think? Ple-e-ea-se, just erase half the tape," she pleaded. Olivia avoided looking at me but kept her eyes on Patrick. "I could go for that arrangement."

Patrick ignored her and turned to me. "You sure you're okay?

I shook my head yes, which was a mistake. "Yowie!"

"Shouldn't that be owie?" Patrick said. "Or is that another Michigan expression? After we turn her over to the police, I'll play nurse, like you did for me."

"Yuk. Get a room," Olivia said, sticking out her tongue. "This isn't funny. You will be ruining a man's life. It was an accident, for God's sake. I thought you liked Matt?"

"How about the fact that Matt hit your father and left him without getting medical attention," I said. "He thought you took the loving cup so that you could blackmail him. Then Matt dragged him to the library. What were you holding over his head? That doesn't sound like a *loving* sibling dynamic in my book — or anyone's book."

"In your book," she spat. "Who cares about your book! My brother loves me. No matter what demon spawned him. I gave him an alibi, that's what I did."

"Too bad this recording refutes that." I kept going. "On the flip side, you aren't any better. You planned to blackmail Matt about his glasses that you found under your father's body. And you just whacked me on the head to get ahold of my phone."

"How do you know about the glasses?" she asked. "You snoop. Matt said you read lips. I should have known. I only wanted to get him as far away as possible from *her*. I demand to see a lawyer *and* my brother. If I must, in order to save him, I'll confess to hitting my father in self-defense. That's what family does — they stick up for one another."

"Dysfunctional families," I said under my breath, as I rubbed the huge egg forming on the back of my head. "You're willing to go to prison, just so that your brother can be with his birth mother? You are a good sister."

Patrick leaned back in his chair, looking on in amusement at our tête-à-tête.

Ignoring me, and turning to Patrick, Olivia said, "I'll only take the rap if Nikki Meyers confesses to dragging my father unconscious to the library and stabbing him to death."

"This isn't a game of Clue," Patrick said. "We can't move the pieces to fit our version of the crime. I want to warn you. If you say you hit your father, you might be brought up on first- or second-degree murder charges. Does that change things at all?"

"Yes, Ms. Golden," Arthur said, coming into view from the direction of the kitchen. "I would like to know that myself."

I handed Arthur my phone. He took it, then removed his raincoat and took a seat next to Olivia at the table.

Finally, Olivia looked beaten.

"Anything else you want to confess to?" Arthur asked. "Besides taking your brother's glasses," he asked, narrowing his steely black eyes on her shrinking form.

Olivia squirmed, then stuck out her lower lip. "Well, one thing. Not that it matters now. I also threw the lab report with the DNA results in the fire. It was in Father's pocket when I found him. Maybe you can find out what lab Nikki used and charge her with murder. She abandoned Matt as an infant, then comes and kills the only father Matt's ever known. Hope she rots in hell. That woman is psychotic. She needs to be far, far away from Matt."

Arthur didn't respond. He hadn't heard the tape. But he knew that the coroner ruled that Brett Golden had died from his head wounds—not from the blade of the walking stick.

I had to say, I somewhat agreed with Olivia. Even though Olivia didn't know that Brett was already dead when Nikki stabbed him, as Olivia said—*Who does that?*

Chapter 43

Sunday morning dawned warm and sunny. The ocean was calm. Too bad my thoughts weren't. I'd woken with a headache that reminded me of last night's head-bashing. Everything was wrapped up in neat packages and tied with perfect little bows. I should be happy.

Why wasn't I?

Something was still bothering me.

Last night there'd been nothing for Patrick and me to do but wait until we heard from Arthur saying that Chief Boyle had rounded up Nikki and Matt. I would think that would happen sooner than later because of Nikki's banana yellow Tesla.

Plus, the pair had no clue that my phone had recorded their confessions, so why would they run?

Wisely, Olivia had decided not to take the blame for hitting her father with the loving cup. Her tears of contrition hadn't moved me. Even though she'd only used a little ole sugar shaker, Arthur had arrested her for hitting me on the back of the head. Patrick had followed me home from the lighthouse, and despite the fact that I would have loved to have fallen asleep in his arms in front of a crackling fire, we'd chosen to go to our respective cottages, feed our pets, and circle the wagons in the morning.

After feeding Jo and finishing my second cup of morning coffee, I decided that before touching base with Patrick, I needed to clear the cobwebs. The only way I knew how was to go have a chat with the ocean.

I threw on my fleece robe and slipped my feet into flip-flops. Then I went out onto the deck and down the steps to the beach.

As I walked the shoreline toward the lighthouse, I tried to make sense of everything by rehashing the chronological series of events — before and after Brett's death.

When Matt showed his father the lab report that Nikki was his birth mother, Brett had gone ballistic and attempted to leave the room and confront her. Matt hit him with the loving cup, then ran to warn Nikki that Brett was on the warpath. Carson had taken the loving cup, thinking Julie had hit Brett. At that point, Brett was still alive. When

Matt confessed to Nikki what he'd done, he brought her back to the billiard room so they could address Brett together. That was when they found Brett dead and the loving cup missing. Mother and son assumed that Olivia had taken it. Matt and Nikki then dragged Brett's dead body to the library, where Nikki stabbed Brett's corpse with the blade of the walking stick, *postmortem*. Had Matt witnessed that? The recording on my phone hadn't been clear.

Later, after Olivia found her father's body in the library, she discovered the lab report proving Nikki was Matt's birth mother and Matt's eyeglasses. Olivia threw the DNA lab report into the library fireplace (which Elle later saved) and pocketed the glasses. I wasn't sure why Olivia wanted to burn the lab report. Maybe as some kind of leverage? Or to protect her brother, who she thought was the one who killed Brett?

It all made sense—so why was I still feeling that I was missing something. I turned back and walked toward my cottage. Freezing water lapped over my flip-flopped feet and I nearly jumped in the air from the shock. My thoughts went to what might have happened to Patrick when he'd tried to save Evan from the riptide.

Buck up, Meg. Everything is good. Patrick is alive. Justice will be served. The storm is over.

In front of my cottage, I found a fortuitous piece of driftwood. Then I penned in the wet sand one of my favorite William Cullen Bryant passages:

> *Lo, the clouds roll away – they break – they fly,*
> *And like the glorious light of summer, cast*
> *O'er the wide landscape from the embracing sky,*
> *On all the peaceful world the smile of heaven shall lie.*

Chapter 44

Tuesday afternoon, Patrick and I walked hand in hand down the steps of the Southampton Police Station. "Isn't it funny," I said, "how sometimes in a murder investigation, things just fall into place. No missing or broken pieces. A rhyme and reason for every unanswered question."

Patrick glanced down at me, then raised a perfectly arched eyebrow. "Why do I feel that you aren't as convinced as Chief Boyle and Arthur that now that Nikki Meyers and Matt Golden are in custody, the case is closed."

"I am. I am," I stuttered. "Well, almost—"

"Out with it," he said, as we headed toward his car. "What's niggling at that beautiful brain of yours?"

"Nothing."

"Nothing, my—"

"Olivia!"

"Olivia. What about her?"

I pointed to Olivia, who'd just stepped out of her father's rental car. She was almost unrecognizable. Her hair looked to be a natural shade of brown that matched her roots, and she wore little face makeup. She locked eyes with me. Then looked left, then right, as if weighing her options of retreating or continuing toward us. She chose the latter. I also weighed my options and decided to stand my ground.

The woman unnerved me.

I pulled Patrick to a stop, then watched Olivia literally skip toward us with a strange smile on her face.

"Well, well. Hope you're proud of yourself," she said, glancing only at me.

"Why is your brother's arrest my fault?" I asked.

"The stupid recording on your phone. That's why. But I'm not too worried. A murder charge won't stick. Matt acted in self-defense. A jury will see that. As for Matt's Mommie Dearest, it will be fun to see her talk herself out of stabbing a dead man. Toodle-oo. I'm going to see about collecting my father's things."

"You mean the engagement ring that belongs to Ms. David? The one you hid in your room."

"Yes. You snoop. It belongs to me now. See you guys — uh — the twelfth of never!"

She started walking toward the station. I let go of Patrick's hand and said, "Wait here. There's something I need to ask Olivia."

I took off after her. Right before she reached the steps to the station, I grabbed her wrist and spun her around.

"What the hell! Get your hands off me."

I held up my hands in surrender. "I'm just curious. Earlier you said that you thought Nikki killed your father with the blade of the walking stick. A few minutes ago, you said Nikki stabbed a dead man?" How had Olivia known something that only the police and a handful of other people did, that Brett had been dead when he'd been stabbed?"

She laughed. "Don't you have a hearing problem or something? Matt said you can read lips."

"What about it," I said, not letting her get to me.

But she did get to me. It wasn't what she said — nothing that I could record. She got inches from my face. "Read my lips," she said. Then she mouthed, *"How do you or anyone else know that maybe I took one of those needlepoint hunting pillows from a chair in the billiard room, then gently placed it over Father's face as he squirmed a few times. It only took seconds. Did I? Or didn't I? No one will ever know."* Then she turned and walked up the steps to the station and disappeared inside.

It was the first time that reading lips *hadn't* been to my advantage.

Chapter 45

"Hey, Meg. Patrick just told me that you made the dough for that fabulous brick oven pizza of his," Claire said, squeezing my elbow. "If I knew there was a chance you could learn to cook, I would have postponed my trip to California for a little while."

"Yeah, right. You're dying to help your daughter and see your little granddaughter enter this crazy world. Bet you've already written a dozen journals of poetry for her."

"You do know me, Megan Elizabeth Barrett!" she said, beaming.

"Plus, we're a week away from Memorial Day, and soon the crowds will be arriving. You're getting out just in time."

"Meg! I love Montauk! No matter what the season."

"And, for the record," I said. "Earlier, Patrick was telling you a white lie. I didn't help with this batch of pizza dough—only the first and second batches, which you might or might not find in the trash can under my kitchen sink. By the way, he used my father's recipe for Detroit-style pizza."

"I've heard of Chicago-style pizza—not Detroit."

"If my father was here, he'd tell you all about it," I said with a grin. "And you'll be happy to know that Patrick and I made a pact. From now on, he'll do the cooking, and I'll provide the fresh herbs and do the cleanup."

"Sounds like a good deal for everyone involved," she said, laughing.

"Oh, Claire, I'm going to miss you so much. You're my spiritual guru."

Claire swept her right arm in the air and cupped her fingers ballerina style to encompass my walled garden. You'll just have to make do until I come back. Look at all our wonderful friends. Plus, If I stayed, where would Arthur and Elle go now that they'll be staying in Little Grey while they renovate the old Willis estate? You and your bestie will be neighbors. I wish I could be here to see their progress."

"I promise they will be moved into Montaukett Manor by the time you get back," I said.

"Montaukett Manor?"

"Yes, Elle's already renamed it."

"Well, no need to kick them out if they go over the six-month rental period. Little Grey is big enough for us all. Between you and Elle and your construction team, I know it will turn out perfectly. Thanks for throwing this going-away party."

I took Claire's elegant long-fingered hand in mine and looked into her kind eyes. "I really will miss you," I said again, feeling a tickle at the back of my throat, telling me that I might start blubbering any second.

"We will video chat. And I still plan to virtually attend our Dead Poets Society meetings."

"True," I said. "And when it's my turn to host, you won't be able to smell the —"

"Charred aroma of another one of your Hamburger Helper casseroles."

I put my hands on my hips. "I want you to know, I now use ground chicken. Patrick says it's better for you. Though with our new deal, he'll be doing all the cooking."

"Lucky you," she said with a grin.

I glanced over at Patrick, who was talking to Elle and Ashley, his nine-month-pregnant publicist. "Lucky me is right."

"Meg, Meg," Elle called out. "You and Claire, come join us. You must feel the baby kick. I'm saying it's a boy. Patrick says it's a girl."

I tried to read Patrick's face. Looking for any signs that the thought of Ashley's pregnancy might remind him of the loss of his daughter. But his smile seemed sincere.

As Claire and I walked across the flagstones toward them, the scent of peonies and lilacs floated on the salty air. Being surrounded by all our loving friends, I wished I could bottle this moment forever.

When I was steps away from Patrick, his eyes lasered in on mine. It was clear our spark hadn't fizzled — it was still there, its pilot light burning deep in my soul. Even with Olivia getting away with murder, I still believed in happy endings.

When I'd told Arthur and Chief Boyle about Olivia's lip-read confession, I knew they believed me. But without verbal proof, Olivia walked away scot-free. (Georgia later told me that *scot-free* was a Scandinavian term referring to tax-free.) We would never know if she'd been lying. Well, I knew she wasn't lying, based on her specifically mentioning the needlepoint pillow in the billiard room that had come from Elle's shop. Arthur had made sure to tell me that Olivia was back in California, and he'd even taken the liberty of setting up an order of protection against her, in case she came anywhere near me.

"Meg, your turn to feel the baby kick," Elle said excitedly.

After I did, and by the strength of the baby's kick, my money was on a boy. Then I thought of all the strong women athletes like Serena Williams, and I changed my mind. Girls could be as strong as boys.

After Ashley was led away by her husband so she could rest her swollen feet, Elle nudged me. "Can I talk to you for a minute, there's something I've been meaning to tell you."

"Nothing bad, I hope?"

"No. No. Something really good."

I followed her to the garden's small covered alcove, where I'd set up two wrought iron chairs and a bistro table. I sat and motioned for Elle to take a seat.

"I'd rather tell you this standing up," she said, nervously moving from one foot to the other, her cheeks the color of strawberries, her freckles the strawberry's seeds.

"Yes?"

"Arthur and I are going to try to get pregnant."

"Wow! That's amazing. You know that I'll be the best aunt."

"Of course you will."

"Isn't it a lot to put on your plate while you're renovating Montaukett Manor?" I asked.

"It would be, if I didn't have you. We aren't in a big hurry. I just feel that if it happens, it happens," she said, plopping down beside me.

We were both silent for a moment as we looked at our eclectic crowd of friends and loved ones.

"Isn't it amazing how everything just works out when you least expect it," I said.

"I know," she said dreamily. "Arthur and I will be your neighbors for six months. We both have our dream homes on the water. Alice sold the Halstead house, leaving the outbuilding for Everett to live out his last years, and Brett Golden's death has been avenged."

I hadn't told her about Olivia's fake or real confession because Arthur had told me not to. After I'd told Patrick, he'd called kindhearted Julie in California and told her to cut Olivia out of her life. He didn't explain why, just told her she would have to trust him. And she had. Implicitly.

"Time for a toast," Patrick called out. "Gather around, everyone."

Elle and I got up, grabbed our glasses, and moved to the center of the garden. Claire stood next to Patrick. He raised his glass and said, "'Think where man's—'"

"And woman's," I added.

He laughed and said, "'Think where man's and woman's glory most begins and ends, and say my glory was I had such friends.' To Claire!"

"To Yeats," Claire said, laughing, her face flushed with happiness.

Hear, hears rang out.

I raised my glass to my lips, just as I felt a gentle tap on my shoulder. Someone with a very familiar voice chanted, "To Claire! Chin-chin."

All eyes, including mine, turned to see Jeff Barrett. "Dad! What the heck are you doing here? Everything okay?"

"Why, daughter. I'm here for a long visit and to wish Claire bon voyage." He nodded his head, and I followed his blue eyes, which were the same shade as mine, to four huge suitcases standing sentry by the garden gate.

"Daddy, how long are you staying?" I asked.

"I'm moving in with Doc. If that's okay with you?"

"What about Sh—"

He kissed me on the cheek. "We'll talk about that later."

Doc ran over and gave his best friend a hearty slap on the back. "That was quite an entrance, Jeff."

I glanced at Georgia, who was beaming. Seemed everyone was in on the surprise but me.

As I'd thought, earlier—

I wished I could bottle this moment forever . . .

Recipes

Jeff Barrett's Detroit-Style Pizza

Detroit-style pizza is actually a real thing.

It's been around since the mid-1940s, when it was first introduced in Detroit at Buddy's Rendezvous (Six Mile & Conant), and was, over time, copied by other local restaurants (and former employees), like Shield's, Louis', and Cloverleaf (Cloverleaf was opened by the original inventor of the pizza recipe, Gus Guerra, after he sold Buddy's). While extremely popular in the Detroit metro area, it never expanded much beyond it.

That all changed for good when, in 2012, local restaurant cook Shawn Randazzo entered a Detroit-style pizza into the Las Vegas International Pizza Expo—and won. Its popularity has grown nationally ever since. In 2019, *Esquire* called the style "one of the hottest food trends across America," and both the *Detroit Free Press* and *Eater* said Detroit-style pizza was "having its moment."

I have personally been making—and perfecting—my version of Detroit-style pizza all my adult life, and this is how I do it.

There are basically three things that differentiate Detroit-style pizza from others.

The first is the pan. Its roots go back to the early days, when a deep-sided, heavy-gauge metal pan was needed to hold up to the thick nature of the pizza. It is characterized by deep sides, rectangular shape (13x9), and heavily seasoned finish. Second is the cheese, which is traditionally made with brick cheese. However, unless you live in Michigan or Wisconsin, brick cheese is hard to find, so I offer a couple of very viable substitutes below. Third is how the pizza is assembled. It's sort of upside down, with dough on the bottom, followed by meat, then cheese, then sauce, and last, any veggie toppings.

This recipe is for the most classic version of Detroit-style pizza there is: Pepperoni and Mushrooms.

201

Dough

2½ cups (300g) unbleached bread flour
1½ teaspoons active dry yeast
1 teaspoon (6g) salt
1 cup (227g) lukewarm water
olive oil, for greasing the pan

Sauce

2 tablespoons (25g) olive oil
2 garlic cloves, finely chopped
28-ounce can crushed tomatoes
1 tablespoon granulated sugar, optional

Toppings

8–12 ounces (227g–340g) pepperoni, thinly sliced
1 pound brick cheese, grated; Havarti is the closest substitute. The next best alternative is equal parts whole-milk mozzarella and sharp white cheddar.
8 ounces white mushrooms, thinly sliced

To make the dough:

Measure the flour by gently spooning it into a cup, then sweeping off any excess. Mix and knead all the dough ingredients — by hand, mixer, or bread machine set to the dough cycle — until a shaggy dough forms. Cover the dough, allow it to rest for 10 minutes, then knead it again until it becomes smooth and elastic. (If you're using a bread machine, skip the previous step and allow the machine to complete its kneading cycle.)

Form the dough into a ball, place it into a lightly greased bowl, cover, and allow to rest until doubled, about 2 hours.

Drizzle 1–2 tablespoons of olive oil into a Detroit-style pizza pan or a 9x13-inch baking pan.

Gently stretch the dough into the edges and corners of the pan until it starts to shrink back and won't stretch any farther.

Cover the pan and allow the dough to rest and relax for 15–20 minutes before stretching it again. Repeat one more time, if necessary, until the dough fills the bottom of the pan.

Cover the dough in the pan and allow it to rest for 30–45 minutes while you prepare the sauce.

In the meantime, position a rack at the second-lowest position of the oven and preheat the oven to 500 degrees F.

To make the sauce:

Heat the olive oil in a saucepan set over medium heat until shimmering. Stir in the garlic, cooking until fragrant, about 30 seconds. Add the tomatoes and sugar, bring to a simmer, and cook until the sauce has thickened and you have about 3 cups of sauce, about 20 minutes. Remove the sauce from the heat and set aside.

Assemble the pizza:

Gently press the dough down with your fingers to release some larger air bubbles. Make sure the dough reaches evenly all the way to each edge. Avoid making too much of a ridge at the edges.

Top the dough with a complete, even layer of pepperoni, followed by the cheese, making sure to spread to the edges of the pan.

Next, ladle or spoon the sauce over the cheese in three lengthwise rows. Then add your sliced fresh mushrooms.

Transfer the pizza to the second-from-the-bottom rack of the preheated 500-degree oven and bake until the cheese is bubbly and gold and the edges have turned nearly black, about 15–20 minutes.

Remove the pizza from the oven, run a spatula around the edges to loosen it from the pan, and let it rest for 10 minutes, or until you can handle it. Using two spatulas on one long side of the pizza, carefully transfer the pizza to a cutting board, cut into 8 equal-sized pieces, and serve.

Meg & Patrick's Apple Crisp Pizza

9-inch homemade or store-bought pie crust (Of course Patrick made this one from scratch!)
3 tablespoons all-purpose flour
⅔ cup white sugar
1 teaspoon ground cinnamon
4 cups peeled and diced apples diced in ¼-inch pieces (we used Gala)

Topping

½ cup all-purpose flour
⅓ cup packed brown sugar
½ cup old-fashioned rolled oats
1 teaspoon ground cinnamon
¼ cup salted butter, softened (Patrick says that the salt cuts the sweetness of the pizza.)

Drizzle

½ cup caramel topping (Luckily, we had a jar on hand of Sanders Candy Co. caramel. Sanders had been in business, in Detroit, since 1875. My father had included it in my last Michigan care package— yum!)

Preheat oven to 350 degrees F.

Roll pie crust to fit a 12-inch round pizza pan. Mix together flour, sugar, and cinnamon in a bowl. Add the apples and toss together. Layer the mixture so that it covers the entire pie crust.

Combine the flour, brown sugar, oats, cinnamon, and butter in a bowl. Mix it together using your hands or a fork. Sprinkle the topping over the apple mixture.

Bake at 350 degrees for 35–45 minutes until apples are tender. After you remove pizza from the oven, immediately drizzle with the caramel topping on top of the pizza. If you're really adventurous, you can drizzle caramel *and* chocolate fudge on top of your pizza. (Sanders also makes a fudge topping—but alas, I'd emptied that jar ages ago.)

Cut it into pizza slices while still warm.

Makes 12 servings.

Meg and Elle's Think-Outside-the-Box Guide to Decorating Your Own Creative Space

Calling all artists, writers, scholars, crafters, dancers, jewelry makers, sewers, home workers, creators and dreamers! Here are a few ideas for decorating your own studio or creative haven.

Make it a place that gives you confidence to believe in yourself and your talents.

A space that is *all your own!*

Meg: If you don't have a glass folly like I have, or a carriage house like Elle, or a poetry studio like Claire, a tree house, guest cottage, greenhouse, pottery or he/she shed — you can still apply these tips to an unused room in your home, or an attic, a basement, a corner of your kitchen, bedroom or great room — even a large closet. You can also set up your space on a porch, a sectioned-off area in your garage, or turn a small outdoor space into a cozy retreat and create en plain air.

Elle: The first thing to do is to carve out your space. Remove everything but the furniture you plan to use in your studio. You can even remove *all* the furniture and start from scratch. Pack away your items in labeled containers. This is also a good time to donate or throw away — do you need all those paper clips and twenty years of taxes? What parts of the space do you rarely use? You get the idea. If you have a window in your space, take down the curtains or blinds and let the light flow in. If you are going for a cave-like ambiance, buy darkening draperies or shutters.

Meg: Reimagine the furniture placement in your space. Does your furniture serve a purpose and at the same time spark joy? Maybe all your old furniture needs is a little fixer-uppering? You can combine what furniture you do have with new or secondhand finds. Donate or sell furniture that clashes with your vision, or simply transfer pieces that don't work to another space in your home. Now stand in the middle of your empty room or space and look around. Take a few photos and measurements. Then walk out and close the door. Let the ideas percolate.

Elle: You could also take a trip to a paint store and bring home swatches of colors or wallpaper that makes your heart sing. But don't buy anything. You're just trying to capture a feeling. If you do want to purchase something at this stage, make it a journal, scrapbook, or corkboard to display your ideas. Jot down five or six descriptive words that sum up the space you are going for. Don't rush the process.

Meg: Before filling your space, take time to create a plan that fits your needs. Your space needs to be functional. Create an inspirational corkboard. I love looking at art and home décor magazines, Instagram, YouTube home tours, and Pinterest for visual inspiration. Perhaps tack on a few of your favorite mottos to your corkboard. Two of my favorites are: George Eliot's — *It's never too late to be what you might have been*, and Sylvia Plath's — *The worst enemy of creativity is self-doubt.*

Elle: After your vision is clear, pull up the photo you took of your bare-bones studio space and glance at it and remember your five inspiration words as you stroll through your favorite home décor, thrift, and vintage shops. Look for art, posters, furniture, and decor that fits the ambiance you're going for. Your future studio doesn't have to be designed in a style similar to the rest of your home. This is your chance to create a room that is for your eyes only.

Meg: Now walk around your home. Is there any furniture, like an unused chaise in the living room, that would go perfectly in your studio? How about your favorite soft chunky yarn throw or slippers? Look for a few small sentimental items in your home that make you happy when you see or touch them. For storage in my design studio, I like to use vintage wall baskets, handmade pottery to store pens, rulers, and paintbrushes, a rolling cart — or anything on wheels — vintage crates, baker's racks, old printer's typeset drawers hung on the wall, stylish file folders, portable caddies, old dressers, even wicker laundry baskets, and of course in my studio my antique armoire is my favorite storage solution.

Elle: Make sure you incorporate things that activate your five senses. You can use soy-based candles or essential oil diffusers to activate you sense of smell. Jump-start your creative brain by adding a small coffee maker to your space. Inhale the rich aroma as you pour coffee into your favorite mug. Or, if you're a tea lover, plug in an electric tea kettle, then plunk in your favorite herbal tea and let its scent permeate the air. Maybe add a small refrigerator in you space, so that you don't have to leave your studio while you're creating. A jar of your favorite candy or nuts for a pick-me-up stored in a vintage Ball jar or bowl that your child made at summer camp is always nice. Oh, and if you plan on sharing your space with your furry friends don't forget pet treats.

Meg: Incorporate a few family photos, posters or old maps for visual appeal. Bring nature indoors—flowers from your garden, a houseplant, branches from a tree, or even a rock or seashell. You don't want a cluttered workspace. You can always switch out items and replace them with others to fit the season. Now you can feel cozy and cocooned, surrounded by a few objects that you hold dear. Don't be afraid to start over if your vision gets muddied. No one will know but you.

Elle: Once you're happy with all you've accomplished in your space, you can begin your time in your studio by meditating or reading devotional daily passages from your favorite inspirational gurus. Hang a *Do Not Disturb* sign on your door. And when you've lost your muse and you need a break, put on some headphones and listen to your favorite music or podcasts.

Meg: And remember, you can always mix vintage design elements with modern—or vice versa.

Wishing you many happy finds and cozy creating! XO, Meg

About the Author

Kathleen Bridge is the national bestselling author of the Hamptons Home & Garden Mystery series and the By the Sea Mystery series. She started her writing career working at *The Michigan State University News* in East Lansing, Michigan. A member of Sisters in Crime and Mystery Writers of America, she is also the author and photographer of an antiques reference guide, *Lithographed Paper Toys, Books, and Games*. She teaches creative writing in addition to working as an antiques and vintage dealer. Kathleen blissfully lives on a barrier island in Florida. Readers can visit her on the web at www.kathleenbridge.com, on Facebook at www.facebook.com/kathleen.m.bridge, and on Instagram @authorkathleenbridge.

Made in United States
North Haven, CT
03 August 2023

39909875R00131